BAD SEED

THE MIDNIGHT CRIES *of an* ISLAND GIRL

A Novel

CHERRY D. FAGBEMI

2

TRIGGER WARNING:

This book contains scenes of violent sexual assault that may be

distressing to some readers.

"There is no greater agony than bearing an untold story inside you."

— **Maya Angelou**

Contents

Chapter 1

The Naked Chase

Vivienne

Montego Bay was where I should have died in the summer of 1985.

The moment I stepped onto the roadway, strolling through the fern and bamboo grove below my brother's house, echoes of a dark past of unspoken secrets and mysteries hung over me. My heart pumped with a rhythm of unease as I cautiously made my way through the deserted grove.

Rows of bamboo stretched as far as my eyes could see as the mysterious grove creaked against the force of the sea breeze.

The smell of Ganja wafting through the night air came from the man across the street, puffing on his joint.

I shouldn't have been out so late by myself since I wasn't yet familiar with the intricacies of Ironshore. But the distant throb of a reggae beat, a pulse slicing through the darkness, piqued my interest. With each step, the rhythm boomed louder. Its allure was irresistible, beckoning me to join the feat as shadows danced in the flickering disco light and laughter mingled with the music, a rhythm bound to get me.

The magnetic force pulled me toward the euphoric pulse. It was more tempting than my eighteen-year-old body could resist. But as my wandering feet drew close to the hypnotic sound, the silhouette of a man invaded my space, stopping me in my tracks.

I wanted to run but couldn't as if my feet were stuck. The man probably knew every crevice and corner of the dense grove, making it impossible to outrun him.

I cowered before him as my anxiety deepened and my knees weakened. Rumor had it that the Black Heart Man, a notorious mystery figure rumored to be dangerous, had been on a rampage.

The flash from a distant car light illuminated a shiny object in the man's right hand. "Oh, crap, this doesn't look good," I muttered under my breath as I caught a glimpse of his nakedness and a machete.

But before I could get my brain to focus on how much danger I was in, he advanced on me, gripping the machete above his head and trapping me in the dark, deserted grove.

All I could think of was that I would die before I got to put Greenspring on the map, as I had promised my best friend, Jasmine.

With the ocean to my left and the hill to my right, there was only one way to run.

I kicked off my shoes, pulled my skirt above my knees, and sprinted until I was out of breath, taking me farther away from my brother's house. As the naked man advanced on me, I tripped over a log, my heart racing. I shuffled farther away from him, but barely.

His scrawny frame and bony ribs showed signs of emaciation as if he hadn't eaten in a very long time. But stripping himself meant one of two things: either heat had overwhelmed him, or he was full-blown crazy. Since it was a windy night, I would say it was the latter.

I picked myself up and ran, bleeding and screaming as the man advanced on me. I clutched my chest to prevent my breath from leaving my body. But the faster I ran, the closer he seemed to get. I gasped as if every breath was my last, and every step, my final one, as a *pop, pop, pop* sound echoed in the distance.

The half-starved naked man lunged forward. I limped and crawled in the darkness through a ditch, covered in the muck and grime draining into the water below.

My eyes burned from the black substance running down my face, and I rubbed the mixture of tears and dirt from my eyes. If the stench from the gutter or the man chasing me didn't kill me, the pain in my chest might.

"Where are you?" The voice roared above me soon after I found refuge under a bridge. My left arm scraped against the rough concrete, and my bare feet were inches from the slimy water below while he paced above my head, raving like a lunatic.

It was difficult to avoid falling into the bug-infested water.

As creepie-crawlies slithered around, I forced my mind to reflect on the doves I fed out of my hands and the hummingbirds sucking nectars out of the flowers that bloomed and lined the roadway of the countryside where I traveled to school. My father's warnings that the city would swallow me rang in my brain like a Sunday morning church bell.

I shifted from where I crouched for ten minutes to ease the numbness in my legs and find relief from the bruises on my knee. If the maniac caught me, that would be the least of my worries. A girl hardly survives a full-on attack by a menacing, machete-wielding schizophrenic.

My brother should have warned me that the grove below his house, wrapped around the neighborhood with its lavish homes, could be deceptively alluring and should not be underestimated for its false sense of security. I wouldn't have listened anyway.

When I could no longer hear footsteps, I leaned forward and crawled on my hands and knees out of the gutter. There was no way my life would end one week after my move to the city. I would have gotten an earful if I had not been home before Sean returned from work. He might pack me up and march my inquisitive sightseeing ass back to Greenspring.

How do I get back home? It is dark, and I don't know where I am.

But suddenly, another bright light tore through the darkness, jolting me from my thoughts. I scrambled up the hill, my heart pounding as I desperately tried to escape the relentless madman. I frantically waved down the passing motorist and cried out for help.

"Get on!" the rider commanded. His voice pierced through the engine's roar. Without much thought, I trusted this shadowy figure, for the alternative was a gruesome fate at the hands of the madman. It was then that I realized the fire-cracking sound from earlier, I thought were gunshots, came from the bike's muffler, now blaring at my feet.

I jumped onto the sleek black leather seat, my heart racing. The rider, cloaked in black, revved up the engine and accelerated to a heart-stopping speed, leaving the madman in the distance.

The wind whipped through my hair, stinging my face as I clung to this stranger. I blew the strands out of my eyes and leaned against him.

"What are you doing here alone?" he asked as if scolding me. "It's not safe here at night."

I leaned in closer so he could hear me over the engine's roar. "Who are you?" I asked, clinging to him.

"Tonight, your knight," he shouted.

Relief surged through me as I narrowly evaded my pursuer, the tension of the chase finally dissipating. The weight of fear and uncertainty lifted from my shoulders, my breaths coming in ragged gasps of relief, albeit temporarily.

"Stop!" I cried out. It had suddenly dawned on me that the Black Heart Man might have picked me up.

Could it be that I escaped one raving lunatic only to be snatched up by Jamaica's most infamous kidnapper?

I leaped off the motorbike as soon as it stopped. I sprinted up the steps and didn't stop running until I was inside my brother's house.

I collapsed onto my bedroom floor.

My hands shook uncontrollably. I could not make them stop. Sensations shot through me as if I were drawing my last breath.

Fifteen minutes after the knight rider dropped me off, I still could not get off the floor. I dragged my body closer to my bed and braced against it while my heart pounded in my ears.

I sat in the dark, afraid to turn on the lights. A tiny face flashed before me, scrunched up against a filthy palm. Moments later, the face morphed into mine when the hand shifted from my eyes and covered my mouth as the man shoved me up against a wall.

At first, I didn't recognize the weeping brown eyes as mine. It couldn't be me. If something so horrific had happened, I would have remembered. But the terrifying memories seeped in faster than I could control them, leaving me dizzy as if my spirit had left my body.

I eased off the ground, feeling light like a feather. I wanted the memories to stop pouring in, but what was happening was beyond my control. I screamed, but there was no sound, only tears pouring down my cheeks as a sickening feeling engulfed me while I scrambled toward the bathroom.

The last time I asked Sean about Dallas, he shut me down faster than I could utter the words: *"Why did we leave Dallas?"*

Chapter 2

Cupid

Jonathan

My heart skipped a beat whenever I thought about the girl at the grove. It was as if I could still feel her arms wrapped around me like they had left little throbbing puncture wounds.

It had been a week since she moved into my friend's house, and my life had been a whirlwind of emotions. Whenever I thought about her, I couldn't control the grin on my lips.

Full disclosure: I was a complicated young man. To some, a tortured soul, and to others, their *Romeo*. If I were running for public office, I'd have no right to be anywhere near power, not with the string of broken hearts I had left in my path.

People called me anything from Heartbreaker to Casanova. One ex-girlfriend had the nerve to call me a user because I wouldn't introduce her to my mother. Another claimed I was a spoiled, entitled brat. But at the risk of sounding egotistical, these women were not always blameless. It was difficult for them to let go, even long after the relationship had ended.

As one newspaper put it after my last girlfriend tried to mow me down with her car, "Jonathan Hastings' Chickens Have Come Home to Roost." But now, this enchanting girl humbled me with her presence and became the focus of my thoughts. She was my new pursuit, and I had all the trappings to get lucky.

I parked the car my parents gave me for my twenty-first birthday in my assigned space next to my dad's. Sunday was my least favorite day of the week. It was the day the city stopped moving. There was no work, no school, only the bells ringing down the street at the church my parents attended.

I jogged up the steps without breaking a sweat. My mother often complained that I was too hyper and could not sit still long enough for her to have a meaningful conversation with me.

I inserted my key into the front door, but it swung open before I could turn it. My mother eagerly waited for me. She flung her arms wide, then pulled me in for her usual embrace.

"See, I made it, and you didn't even have to ask me to come this time," I said, looking over her shoulder at my dad as he got off the couch. "Hi, Dad," I greeted my father from across the room.

"Hello, Son." He nudged his chin and smiled. He was not as hard on me as my mother, who always made it seem like she had not seen me in years, even if I had seen her the day before.

Mom slid her arm through mine and led me through the large living room. "We gave you the car for a reason, Jonathan, and it's not to attract or parade around with the poor, half-naked, flat-chested girls running behind you."

"Mom, be nice," I laughed, following her into the dining room. It was unusual to hear my mother describe the girls I dated, although they were not flat-chested, as she put it.

"I shouldn't have to beg you to visit your parents. Would it kill you to drop in without me begging?" she asked, running her hand over my arm.

"I showed up, Mom, how is this begging?" I replied.

"I always have to be pleading to see you," she mumbled. Her soft voice was full of disappointment.

A familiar aroma smacked me as we entered the spacious dining room. "Mmm, something smells delish," I declared, hoping my mother would stop with the guilt trip long enough for me to savor her mouthwatering cooking.

But I was hit with a dose of reality when I saw the newspaper my dad was holding. It had a picture of me on the front page.

This Sunday dinner for three was designed with one goal. I realized it was a subtle interrogation disguised as just another family dinner.

I pulled out my mother's chair and took my place in the middle, an equal distance from her and my father.

"It's a good thing I brought my appetite. You wouldn't want me to be a picky eater today," I said. "Not when you've gone all out to prepare this meal, Mom."

I opened the container closest to me. The steam swirled up to my nostrils. I closed my eyes and inhaled deeply, my stomach rumbling with anticipation.

The colorful bowl of salad and the juicy chunks of oxtail opened my appetite, and I moved in and placed the most succulent piece of meat on my plate. I hugged it with two grabs of salad and then topped it off with a couple of slices of fried plantains and a scoop of rice and peas.

I took a deep breath, anticipating my mother's grilling about the latest trash-talk about me splashed across the local newspapers, like a world event breaking news.

I didn't mind my mother's questioning so much since my parents' relationship gave me hope that there was someone, somewhere out there, to love me as much as my parents loved each other. Still, it was my mother, and I would rather not talk to her about who I may or may not be dating or whose heart I was breaking. The accusations were endless.

I never understood how people thought I could date so many women simultaneously.

I braced for the time-to-settle-down talk that was coming.

My mother cleared her throat and fixed her eyes on me. "Jonathan, with all the girls you date, why haven't we met any of them?" she asked, her hands folded under her chin. Her gaze penetrated me, leaving no doubt I was in for another grilling.

Whichever girl I'd introduce to my mother, she couldn't be wishy-washy. She would have to be damn near perfect.

"Mom, when I find the right girl, you will be the first to meet her. I promise. You cannot believe what you see on TV or read in the papers. I am not sowing my wild oats as much as they say," I replied, my eyes had not left my plate.

"So, you're telling me that everyone, including the newspaper, is lying about you?" I hated the disappointment in her voice, but there was no way I'd confirm such unfounded rumors.

"Mom, I'm only twenty-two, I'm nowhere near ready to be anyone's husband, let alone father," I said.

"Then why are you going around, messing with the heads of these girls?"

"You and half of the mothers in Montego Bay seem to be in a hurry to marry me off. You, I don't understand, and I'm not so sure why the other mothers think I am the perfect catch for their daughters, since there are so many rumors flying around about me. You'd think I'd be a cautionary tale. And yes, Mom, they are just rumors. I didn't think you'd be so quick to believe such gossip about your own son."

My lips were saying one thing, but inside, I was bursting with glee, itching to tell her I had met the perfect girl, the one I was sure would be the mother of her grandchildren. It was hard not to fall for her. But getting her to reciprocate my affections was not a done deal—not even the start of one.

Two obstacles stood in the way of my heart's desire. One was my friend, Sean, and the other was the girl who had left an indelible mark on my heart.

"Do any of those girls mean anything to you? You can't be toying with their emotions then toss them aside like yesterday's trash," my mother said, eyeing me intently.

I savored the mouthwatering flavor and sighed warily. "You have truly outdone yourself, Mom. This meal is delicious." I pointed to my plate, smiled at her, and gave her the three-finger approval.

"Jonathan!" she snapped, not biting the bait to change the subject.

"Mom, neither can I marry the first girl who thinks I'm the love of her life. What happens to mutual love? Don't I have a right to be in love too?" I replied, aware of how often we have had this same conversation.

"What's the story of you and that Jennifer girl everyone said tried to run you over with her car? Why are you dating girls with whom you have no future?"

It was true that Jennifer tried to mow me down, but I didn't have to confirm it with my mother. It would only make her worry more. "Dad, say something, help me out here. Tell her not everything she reads is gospel," I begged.

My dad shook his head. "I learned not to come between you and your mother, Son," he said, smiling as he spread the napkin across his lap.

"Mom, I finally accept your dinner invitation, and this is what I get? It is like the Spanish Inquisition and the third degree rolled into one. I thought you missed having me over for dinner. Do you do the same to Damien? Because you know that boy needs this talk more than me. He needs more than just a talk. He's the one budging thirty with more than a woman problem. I am still in my prime. His reputation is becoming irreparable."

"Well, Damien is not in front of me. I prefer to do this with one son at a time."

I gestured to my father, chewing fast as if I could outrun my mother's barrage of questions. "Dad, we both know Damien's reputation needs Mom's intervention." I swallowed the last morsel of rice and peas and leaned back into my chair.

"Like your mother said, Damien is not here now, Son. It's your time in the hot seat. Your brother has had his time, and no doubt will have more."

I loved making my parents happy, but either my happiness was elusive, or I would let my standards get in the way.

"When we gave you the house two years ago, it wasn't for you to turn it into a brothel. It was for you to settle down. We hardly get to see you, and when we do, it's one of your pitiful, half-hour visits. You are a grown man, Jonathan; find someone and settle down before you have babies with every girl in town."

"I miss your home-cooked meal, but not the allegations and barrage of questions," I told her.

Two hours after I had eaten my mother's delicious meal and had received a proper scolding, I kissed her goodbye, swung my glasses on, and was ready to hit the road.

"Make sure you're on time tomorrow, Jonathan. You cannot be late," Dad said. "Don't disappoint us again. You skipped out on the last staff meeting, and your mother had to fill in for you."

"I will be there bright and early. I promise."

With Maxi Priest blaring on my stereo, I sped through the gate, heading home to Ironshore. The usually vibrant and bustling city was now tranquil. People were either chilling at home or sunbathing on the beaches across the city, bringing the usual hustle and bustle to a serene halt.

As I drove onto Valence Avenue, the girl who had consumed my thoughts for the past week stepped out onto her veranda, and my heart skipped a beat.

Chapter 3

The Creep

Vivienne

Pain shot across my forehead, a warning for what was to come. I woke to the Monday morning sunlight peering through my bedroom window, but the beacon of light only intensified my splitting headache.

I was still battling emotions, stirred up by my encounter with the madman at the grove, which sent my mind into a tailspin.

It had been ten years since my parents moved with us to one of the most remote villages in Jamaica and one week since I moved to Montego Bay to live with my brother and his family.

The cryptic puzzle of my past held unspoken secrets. But, with the first day of my summer job at the souvenir store downtown moments away, I decided to set those aside and focus on the day ahead.

I boarded a black station wagon taxicab heading into the city at eight o'clock, not wanting to ride the Jolly Bus, which was usually overcrowded and habitually late. Whether it was my mind gone awry from the splitting headache or because of the man who came in after me, I had a strange feeling my ride was about to get bumpy.

A foul stench rushed in. I could hardly catch my breath from the smell of ganja that came in with the man who sat beside me.

He leaned against me like he was inebriated, slowly pushing me up against the man to my right. He rested his hand on my knee, and it didn't take long before it started crawling and slithering under my dress. He eyed me slyly, slightly lifting his chin as if to let me know to be a good girl about his callous hand sliding up my thigh.

This man must be what my father meant when he warned me the city would swallow me.

Things were becoming real.

If I were to survive the creep to the left of me, I would have to remember everything my father had drilled into me since we arrived in Jamaica. I was damn sure not about to become a victim of this grown-ass man a week after I convinced my father I was old enough to survive the city on my own.

But the man to my right jammed a metal object against my ribs, which scared me more than the hand crawling under my dress, slowly making its way up my thigh. I could think of nothing except how to get out of the frightening situation I was in so that my death would not end up killing my father.

Fear paralyzed me as they trapped me in the back of the packed Taxicab. As the only female in a car with four other passengers and the driver, my chance of survival was next to nothing. To survive a blatant assault this early, I would have to use more than the face that attracted this horny creep so early in the morning while I tried not to think of the object sticking into my ribs. There was no way I could have survived being shot at close range since the pepper spray in my bag was no match for a trigger-happy hooligan and a man with slippery fingers, especially since I had no idea how I would escape from the speeding car.

The driver swerved to avoid a collision with an oncoming vehicle, flinging me closer to the creep trying to fondle me, and pinning him against the door. I inhaled the stench from the ganja leaking out of his pores as my body pressed up against him. I regained my balance soon after and shuffled away, relieved his hand was no longer touching my skin but still terrified I was closer to the hard object pressing onto my side.

He moved closer minutes later, and his hand started creeping again. I gasped each time his hand touched my skin, and my blood ran cold.

There is no way I will let this place be a memorial where my parents come to grieve on the anniversary of my death. When I wake up from this nightmare, it will be a rainy Monday morning. Sean will play music like always, and I'll be wrapped up in bed.

Except, that was just wishful thinking. When I forced my eyes open, we were still in the Taxicab, heading downtown from Ironshore.

The man to my left nudged his head toward me and grinned. "What's up, Beautiful?"

His mouth full of gold or metal that looked like gold he thought was attractive scared me even more.

Before I left Greenspring, my dad had warned me I would see the good, mostly the bad, and the ugly. This man, trying to fondle me, was a combination of the bad and the very ugly. Under no other circumstance would we be riding together, but I had to share a taxicab with the gold-teeth-grinning, bug-eyed creep trying to finger me.

The passenger to my right had not said a word, and the object he jammed against my side felt as if it was stuck there. From the corner of my eye, I realized he was visually impaired, and the bulge rubbing up against me was his cane. I did not take the time to look at him. I immediately assumed he was holding me up at gunpoint.

"Beware of pickpockets, Viv," Jasmine had warned the day I left Greenspring. *"I'd hate for anything to happen to you. After all, you are a country girl, although with the way you look, they might not be able to tell."*

But she said nothing about encountering this creep and would be horrified to know that it was just my first week in the city, and there were already two instances that exposed me to grave harm.

Realizing the man to my right was no longer a threat, I exhaled, turned my attention back to the hand inching up my thigh, and focused all my attention and rage on him.

"I hope you're prepared to kill me this morning because that hand will not get any farther." I had my fist inches from his face, waiting for the next time he moved his hand. "You better get your hand off me, now!"

"Damn, girl, you are beautiful," he said, holding his stupid grin while ignoring my fist and warning. "I have never seen eyes this big, brown, and beautiful." From the look of his mouth, he desperately needed to see a dentist. None of his teeth were spared the weight of the metal plastered across his gums.

I clenched my jaw, closed the eyes he was so enthralled by, and growled. "Get your hand off me!" At that moment, I realized what a grave predicament I was in because he did not seem fazed by me, and I was sitting between a deviant predator who thought I was just another pretty face he could grab between my legs and a blind man who could not help me.

"Driver, stop the car!"

Chapter 4

Lucky Monday

Jonathan

The HR manager handed me the morning newspaper. The smirk on her face let me know the story was about me again. Sure enough, my picture was plastered across the front page.

The publication proclaimed me as *The Wild One*. I read a few lines from the article aloud and then tossed it aside.

"You're getting too much amusement out of this trash, Melanie. I'm beginning to think someone is out to ruin my reputation."

She crossed her legs, leaned forward as she sat on the chair next to my desk, and folded her hands over her knee.

"At least it's not as unflattering as last week's issue when they claimed your chickens have come home to roost," she laughed.

"It's not a laughing matter. You wouldn't know who is doing it, would you?" I asked, wafting my hands over my forehead.

"Would you like me to question the staff to find the culprit?"

I shook my head. "I'm not that insecure," I said. "But why do people always assume that I'm a playboy?"

"I don't know, Jonathan. Could it be because you behave like a playboy?" she replied, peering over her glasses at me sneakily.

"Not you, too. I might be an overly charismatic guy, but I'm not wild."

"I know you believe that. At least you're nothing like your brother." She stood, picked up her clipboard from my desk, and turned to leave. "Can I be honest with you?" she asked.

"Always," I replied. I valued Melanie's advice and relied on her honest opinions. After all, she ran her department very well and could have easily held my position.

"Forget about what people think. Look at where you're standing. You have more to worry about than what a trashy magazine article says about you. You're Jonathan Hastings, for God's sake. Never forget that. Now that Jennifer is no longer a part of your life, take it as an opportunity to show your critics that you are much more than a pretty face. Take it easy with the ladies, and you'll be fine."

I laughed, thinking about the conversation I had the day before. "You sound like my mother," I said.

"I'll take that as a compliment. After all, your mother is a saint."

I shoved my hands into my pockets and walked to the large window to my left.

"Are my parents here yet?"

"They arrived fifteen minutes ago. Remember we have a new staff member today. The concierge is out this week on vacation. His replacement has arrived, and I need to show him the ropes. Everyone is waiting for you in the conference room. Don't let them wait too long," she said, walking towards the door. "By the way, your mother assigned Blaise to you today. He's waiting in his office."

Blaise had been my unofficial bodyguard and best friend since high school. "Tell him we'll be going to Negril as soon as I wrap up the meeting." I glanced at my watch to ensure I was on schedule.

My parents breathed a little easier whenever Blaise traveled with me out of town. Not that I couldn't take care of myself, but he had a specific skill set they knew would be helpful if needed.

Melanie closed the door behind her. I folded my arms over my chest, leaned against the large glass window, and peered ten stories down at the vacant seashore, contemplating. I had heard the same advice from the people closest to me, each in different ways.

The white sand beneath the clear water looked like you could grab the seashells off the ocean floor. It was the perfect day for a glass-bottom boat ride or scuba diving. Tourists loved those kinds of adventures.

The lone swimmer seemed relaxed, floating about a hundred feet out into the deep. The shore would be lined with umbrellas and half-naked tourists in another forty-five minutes. But the real influx wasn't expected until the tour buses arrived in the next two hours, and I was responsible for making their vacation memorable. I needed to finalize the list of priorities I had been working on to meet expectations, and my dad was expecting me to bring my A-game.

But I couldn't stop thinking about the girl from the grove.

I was anxious to tell Blaise about this girl who had consumed my thoughts, although I already knew what his reaction would be.

Something extraordinary had happened. I wished I knew how to deal with what made me feel so discombobulated over a girl I knew in my gut was off-limits. For the very first time in my life, I wasn't sure I could measure up. She was not just an ordinary girl. She was the most beautiful girl I had ever seen, and she was related to my friend and colleague.

The strange feeling brewing in me was threatening my relationship with one of the most valuable employees of this establishment.

I hustled into Blaise's car and headed to Negril two hours later. The minute I hit the seat, I gushed about my attraction to the girl my heart had latched on to and wouldn't let go.

"You want to make a move on someone related to Sean?" Blaise looked at me as if I had lost my mind. "You and I both know there's no chance in Hell he will let you anywhere near anyone related to him. He knows your track record and it's not a good one. Hell, your last girlfriend tried to kill you."

I laughed at how spot-on Blaise was.

It was both funny and deadly, the day my life flashed before my eyes.

"Am I that bad?" I asked.

Blaise took a long breath, shook his head, turned the key in the ignition, and drove off. "Take it from me, forget about this girl. Don't expect me to take your side over Sean's. Nor will I stop him from kicking your ass."

"I can't just forget about her, man. Sean is someone you don't mess with, but I can't help how I feel about this girl. If you saw her, you'd act just as crazy as me."

"You must forget about her. You don't mess with Sean. Don't wreck your friendship because you can't control your feelings. Sean is not just your friend; we work together."

"I'm tired of girls who see me as a cash register. This girl would be a welcome change in my life. I need her. How many times have you told me to settle down? Plus, I'm tired of my mother getting on my case for things I'm not even guilty of."

"What makes you so sure about this girl? Why her?" Blaise looked at me with worry.

"I can't explain it, except to say my heart beats differently whenever I see her. You know me, I never make a fool of myself for anyone. Yet here I am, feeling like a fish out of water."

"I don't doubt you have it bad for her. But it's Sean we're talking about." Blaise fixed his eyes on the road, and I knew he was right to warn me.

***

"The group of eight that came in today will need a bus to take them to Ocho Rios on Wednesday. Can you ask Tony to arrange a tour?" I asked Blaise.

"Isn't this something up Sean's alley? He's in charge of excursions. Why are you asking Tony?" Blaise looked at me with one of his intense stares; I could almost see the wheels churning in his brain with concern. "You didn't hear a word I said. You still intend to go after that girl. That is why you don't want to face Sean."

"Sean has his hands full. Plus, Tony knows what to do."

"Well, if you say so. I'll swing by the hotel after I drop you off," Blaise said as we cruised through the Monday evening traffic and returned to Montego Bay.

"If he has questions, tell him to talk with Melanie, she'll give him details about the tour."

When Blaise pulled onto the street to my house on Valence Avenue an hour later, I had the same reaction as the day before. My heart skipped a beat.

"There she is, Blaise!" I declared excitedly, pointing at the girl on Sean's veranda looking out at the ocean. "Look at her. How do you expect me to stay away?"

"Good God!" Blaise remarked as he slowed to a crawl, then drove to the top of the hill and circled back.

She seemed mesmerized by the luxury cruise ship as it sailed towards the harbor downtown. I couldn't stop staring at her. She had a perfect body, a beautiful face, big brown eyes, and curly hair that bounced gracefully off her shoulders when she turned her head as if in slow motion. Her presence was spellbinding, suspending my thoughts midair as if the world had stopped spinning. She was flawless and needed no makeup. A girl with such a perfect face and body was bound to put my life at risk.

It was good that she could not see me behind the tinted windshield, though I doubt she'd recognize me from two nights ago. She gazed at the boatload of vacationers sailing towards the city. Occasionally, a wave broke through the calm sea.

She turned to her left, where I sat. Her smile illuminated her eyes, and emotion coursed through me, igniting unfamiliar feelings and awakening every nerve in my body.

She closed her eyes, took a deep breath, stretched out her arms, inhaling the cool evening sea breeze, and I was riveted.

"She is Sean's sister, all right," Blaise remarked, bringing me back to earth. His eyes fixed on her like he had the same out-of-body experience. "They have the same complexion, cheekbones, and eyes," he said.

"If you believe in love at first sight, count me in as a new convert. Since the first day I saw her, I have had weird feelings about her. It's as if we were meant for each other."

"I hate to be the bearer of bad news," Blaise said. "There is no way Sean will let you anywhere near her. So, please find a way to get her out of your system. Nothing good will come from you dating this girl." He leaned back in his seat, gripping the steering wheel. "I'm being serious, Jonathan. If you go after her, you will start a war with Sean."

I let out a long breath, glanced over at Blaise, and then turned my head back to the beauty. Sean knew my reputation with women wasn't exactly squeaky clean. Dating someone related to him would be out of the question. But I was never one to accept things as they seemed. When I decided to remove myself from the dating scene after the incident with Jennifer, no one knew what to make of it. But it was not up to my mind or body to ignore this girl in front of me. Not when my heart had a mind of its own.

That was how I knew Sean and I would go to battle.

Chapter 5

Something about Dallas

Vivienne

Not even the picture-perfect ocean view could clear my head of the traumatic memories that had resurfaced.

My father had reluctantly loosened his grip and released me into Sean's care in a city filled with men of all ages who looked at me like I was a piece of meat and a tall glass of ice-cold lemonade to wash it down. Reality hit me and brought me down two notches from the lofty ideas in my head that I could blend in and no one would notice me. That was how I convinced my father I could survive Montego Bay.

But after my narrow escape from the madman and the creep in the taxi, I was no longer sure I would last long enough to begin college.

Ironshore bore no resemblance to the noise and congestion of downtown, although littered with hypersexual men on the hunt, constantly catcalling me.

The cool evening sea breeze was a welcomed relief from my long day at work and the encounter with the ganja-smoking pervert earlier in the morning.

"Hello, Viv?" Sean walked into my bedroom, carrying a hammer and a small bag of nails. "Are you ready for me to hang the picture frame we discussed earlier this morning?" he asked. His eyes wandered to the bare wall across from my bed as if that was the perfect spot to hang it.

"Yes, but before you do that, can we talk?" The image of the little girl pushed against the bathroom wall had been plaguing me at work all day, no matter how I tried to block out the memories.

"What is it? You don't like it here?" Sean asked, his eyes wide with concern.

"I love it here," I said, shuffling onto my bed.

"Then what is it?" He placed the hammer and nails on the table beside my bed and sat across the room on the gray two-seater sofa.

"Tell me about Dallas," I said, rubbing my hand across the soft pink comforter to ease the discomfort building up in me.

"Did something happen to me there? Why don't Mom and Dad, or you, ever talk about Dallas?"

"Not again, Viv." His face carried a discomfort that I had only recognized whenever I asked him about my life before we came to Jamaica.

He got up and turned to walk back out the door.

"Sean!" I yelled, my frustrations escaping. "Don't ignore me. What was it like living there? I don't remember anything about the place where I was born. How did I lose seven years of my life? Please do not tell me nothing happened because I'm beginning to remember little things. Why did we come to Jamaica?"

Sean leaned against the door frame, crossed his legs at the ankles, and exhaled, fidgeting with his fingers. "I don't want to talk about Dallas. It was a long time ago," he said, shaking his head. He had always had a peculiar need to bubble-wrap me as if he could protect me from everything.

"Someone will have to tell me why we ran away. You, Dad, or Mom can't keep me bubble-wrapped forever. You make me feel as though I'm crazy or that I did something wrong each time I ask," I said in a tone matching his discomfort.

"Why the sudden interest? It's been ten years."

"Sudden interest?" I pulled myself off the bed and narrowed my eyes to him. "For years, I have been begging you to tell me about our time there. Anything would have been better than the total blackout you've given me as if I had no right to know."

"That's not true," he said, shifting his eyes from my stare to the bandage wrapped around my knee.

"Then tell me this. What did Mom mean when she said Daddy couldn't survive another Dallas? Memories are slowly coming back, Sean. Eventually, I'll remember everything. I'd rather you tell me now so I won't think I'm going crazy when they return."

"Your imagination is running away from you. I don't know what you're talking about," Sean chuckled nervously.

"It's not my imagination!" I screamed at him, my voice breaking from the weight of his denial bearing down on me like cinder blocks. Tears rolled down my cheeks while my brother seemed unaffected by them.

"Are you done yelling at me?" he asked. "I'm going to let that little temper tantrum go this time because you seem like you're hurting, and I don't like to see you this way. It's not you. "You don't scream at me because you don't get your way."

"You don't get to ignore me because you're scared to answer my question."

"I'm not afraid of anything. I can't help with what you're asking."

"Daddy couldn't let go of me when I said goodbye. I have never seen him so terrified. It was as if he would never see me again. You were there. You saw how I had to wrestle out of his grasp."

Sean uncrossed his legs and drew close to where I sat. He gripped my chin with his right hand. "What happened to your knee, Viv?"

I pressed my lips together and quickly brushed away the tears rolling down my cheeks. "I had to run from a madman down at the grove Saturday night," I said.

"Why didn't you tell me? You need to stay away from the grove. It's not safe at night."

"Please don't change the subject. I need you to tell me why we left Dallas," I insisted. "My knee will improve, but if you refuse to talk to me about why we came to Jamaica, I'm not sure my mind will." His eyes glossed over as he bit into his lower lip. The look in his eyes scared me.

"Oh, my God!" I cried, feeling a deep sense of betrayal. There it was, the guilt for something terrible that had happened, which never manifested until now. "All this time, and you knew. I was beginning to think I was going crazy, Sean. All this time, you know they left Dallas because of me. What are you hiding from me?"

"Viv, let it go," he said, then took a picture frame out of my suitcase, the hammer and nails he picked up off the nightstand, and walked to the other side of the room.

"What is it you want me to let go of?" I asked, my voice straining. "What is so embarrassing you think I need to forget? Is it the hand wrapping around my throat, squeezing the life out of me? Or that my parents and brother conspire to hide it from me?"

"Girl, don't even go there. Whatever you are thinking about Mom and Dad, don't." His eyes pierced me as if they were burrowing a hole in my forehead. I could tell I had hit a nerve.

"In case you haven't noticed, I'm not a girl. Stop treating me like one!" I shot back forcefully. It was the only time I was this furious with my brother.

I took a deep breath to regroup, not wanting my first week at his house to be awkward. However long it would take, he would have to find the courage and come up with a better answer than his evasive non-answer about why I was the only one with a memory problem. My mother's cryptic warning lodged in my brain since I left Greenspring, and all I could think of was that I had another life everyone in my family was trying to keep me from remembering.

Something must have erased the years before I arrived in Jamaica. I did not lose my accent, so I needed to know what had caused my selective amnesia. But I would have to pretend for a bit longer that what was eating at me had nothing to do with why we ended up in my father's homeland.

"I had no idea you were living so large." I wiped my eyes, trying to mask my anxiety and pain. I wasn't sure how well I could. "Your house overlooks the beach. How do you afford this life on your modest income? Are you into something shady? Scandalous? Do Mom and Dad know you're such a big shot?" It was my poor attempt to move on from the unwelcome topic of my early life.

I eyed him suspiciously, rolled onto my elbows, and flipped my legs behind me. "I can't get over how mesmerizing the ocean is, Sean. You have a private beach and don't need binoculars to see the cruise ships sailing toward the harbor. I could spend every day just looking out and listening to the waves."

"Modest income, ah," he chuckled, then drove the nail into my bedroom wall to hang the large picture frame.

"Do you remember when we took that?" I asked, admiring the eighteen-inch photograph of me dressed in my green, yellow, and black mini dress and Sean in his black polo shirt and blue jeans.

"Of course. It's not that long ago."

"It was my first year in high school, at the Christmas concert you attended with me. I was thirteen, and you were nineteen. Mom and Dad would only let me go if you accompanied me. I didn't think there was anything strange about it then. But now that you are all acting suspicious, and Mom dropping hints about a life I don't remember, it makes me rethink everything I know about myself."

"I don't know what's gotten into you, Viv. It's like you've changed into a completely different person overnight."

"So, you're just going to pretend my concerns are invalid? You can't keep treating me like one of your underage daughters just because you don't want to answer my questions. You can't ignore me forever." I furrowed my brows, surprised by his determination to keep me in the dark.

"Someday, you'll realize that not everything is worth remembering," he said as he walked toward me. "I must pick up the kids from the babysitter before Danielle returns. I'll be back in fifteen minutes. Please don't go back down to the grove. You're just lucky you got away with just a scratch," he said, then tapped me on my shoulder and left me alone with my thoughts.

Chapter 6

Sleeping Dogs

Vivienne

I exhaled wearily, whimpering like an injured puppy, angry at my brother's unwillingness to treat me as his adult sister instead of a child our parents left in his care. Albeit I was barely an adult.

It had been twenty-four hours since I asked him to tell me about my childhood.

I lay in the middle of my bed. I locked my fingers behind my head, staring at the ceiling and listening to the ocean waves as cars zipped by on the roadway below the house. My memories fought to break free as I surveyed the 500-square-foot turquoise green bedroom my brother spent days renovating for me. The smell of paint filled my nostrils even now.

Something in my mother's remarks kept pulling at me, forcing me to think about a life I couldn't remember. *What does Mom expect me to do with the information about Dad? I'm the reason they left Dallas.*

Sean wouldn't be much help. That much was clear.

A memory suddenly forced its way to the surface of my mind, then disappeared as quickly as it entered. Over the next hour, flashes of my time in second grade came and went until I lost the battle to stay awake.

A light flashed through my bedroom when a switch flickered on.

"Vivienne!" the voice came from the doorway, and I jumped, shaken and confused.

I propped my head out of my blanket to find a shadow clutching a pillow. As the silhouette came into focus, eyes filled with utter fear, I pulled myself into a sitting position and wiped the fog of sleep from my eyes.

"Danielle? How long have you been standing there?" I asked, terrified as to what she might have witnessed or heard.

"Not long," she said.

"What time is it?" I pulled the curtains aside, surprised by the darkness outside my window.

"That was some nightmare you had," she said.

The long hand on the clock beside my bed slowly ticked toward ten o'clock. "Have I been sleeping all this time? Why didn't you wake me?"

"You've had a very long day. I figured you must be tired." She fluffed the white pillow she held against her chest, furrowed her brows, and leaned forward. "I am worried about you, Viv. Someday, you must tell me what that nightmare was about," she said, gently sliding the pillow under my head.

"Was I talking in my sleep?" I asked.

"Screaming is more like it," she said as if she had just realized her and my brother's colossal mistake, allowing me to live with them.

The thing about remembering what had happened in Dallas was that it did not come to me lying on a couch as a shrink dragged the memories out of my drug-infused body. It was much more dramatic than that. I had awakened the horror that had been lying dormant, which everyone did their best to keep me from remembering.

I had hoped the flood of memories were figments of my imagination. But who in their right mind would imagine such terror upon themselves? I was face to face with my seven-year-old self, and my sister-in-law might have just witnessed me reliving every gruesome moment of my childhood trauma.

"Did the girls hear me? I don't want to scare them. Please don't tell Sean," I pleaded. "He'll just get worked up for nothing. The waves must have triggered it," I said, not wanting to get my overprotective, secret-keeping brother involved.

"The girls didn't, but your brother did. He sent me to check on you. Go back to sleep. I'll let him know it's nothing, and we'll talk about it in the morning or whenever." Danielle shrugged, then backed away from me. Perhaps she sensed my story might be too dark for her to handle.

But it was not *nothing*, as she suggested. It was not just any old nightmare or flashback I conjured up when she walked in. It was the whole enchilada of trauma.

I am tired of everyone pretending I had no right to know my life had a monster-sized past.

"I'll see you in the morning," Danielle said, turning towards the door.

I grabbed her hand. "Please don't leave," I begged. "If I don't talk to someone about what just happened, I'll go crazy." Chills sprung up all over my arm. "Did Sean ever tell you why we left Dallas?" I asked.

"No," she replied, shuffling onto my bed, her eyes filled with concern and sympathy as if she sensed the weight of my words. "I didn't think there was a particular reason."

"I didn't know there was one until moments ago," I said, my desperation evident in every word. "I couldn't remember living in Dallas, and no matter how I begged Sean to tell me about our time there, he refused to talk about it."

Danielle's eyes grew wild with dread. "Viv, what's going on? You're scaring me." She rubbed my arm.

"Something horrible happened to me when I was little. That's what the nightmare was about," I said, looking at my clenched fists. "I was about seven," I grumbled, almost incoherently, hoping Danielle would not judge me. It would not be easy reliving the minute-by-minute torture I endured.

"Talk to me, Viv." Her voice was calm but eager, and my heart overflowed when her eyes met mine. I unearthed secrets that should never have been resurrected. But if my brother had eased me in, I would not have been so desperate to seek comfort in his wife.

"He must have been scouting me out for the perfect time to pounce on me. I ran, but he yanked me off the ground, lifting me from behind. I screamed for help, but the long corridor was empty. He body-slammed me against the bathroom wall, then forced me inside one of the tiny stalls."

"When did that happen?" Danielle's eyes widened in disbelief.

"In second grade," I said, wiping my eyes. I leaned against her shoulder and snuggled up to her. Exhuming my life before Jamaica caused my voice to break under the weight of the tension in my throat.

Sean was right—not everything was worth remembering.

"He dragged me into the bathroom, his breathing erratic, and his commands echoed and shook the screams out of me. When I wouldn't keep quiet, it infuriated him. He squeezed my jaws to shut me up. I tasted blood when my teeth pierced the inside of my mouth. It was just me up against this giant.

"I froze when he pulled down my underwear and pressed his body up against me. Beads of sweat formed on his forehead, and my body tightened while tears dropped from my eyes.

"His jeans fell around his ankles as he pushed me backward. He clutched me tighter, then pushed into me harder the more my tears poured out. I tried to wiggle out of his stranglehold, but his large body covered mine and held me in place," I said through tears.

Tears poured out of Danielle's eyes as if they were coming from a faucet. "Oh, Viv," she cried openly, grabbing onto me, her body vibrating. It was hard to tell if she was afraid of me, scared for me, or terrified I was bringing that much trauma into her children's lives.

Considering all that had transpired in Dallas, I was surprised my mother didn't put a chastity belt on me to keep me safe from predators. I should have paid more attention to why after we had arrived in Jamaica. Every night, I'd wake up screaming, and my mother would rush to comfort me. It must have been the reason I had no interest in boys in high school when girls my age were bragging about their boyfriends. In some cases, sugar daddies.

When Sean agreed to let me move in with his family, our father grabbed his shoulders and made him promise he would guard me with his life. Which was not necessary since he already knew how fiercely protective Sean was of me.

I should have known my fierce reaction to the passes from guys in Greenspring was not normal when they whispered about my face and "Coco-Cola bottle shape." Neither was my brother's reaction to anyone who dared look at me for more than two seconds. The boys would run and hide whenever they saw Sean coming. And after I told him about Greg Simpson's fixation with me, I hardly went anywhere without him.

Danielle switched off the lights and closed the door behind her after I relayed the details of my assault. I laid my head against the soft pillow, listening to the waves beating against the rocks as they calmed me, making their way back out to sea while I dredged up old memories that were supposed to be dead and buried.

I pulled the covers back over my head, clutched my knees up to my chin, and rocked back and forth, wrestling with the memories seeping into my consciousness and drowning out the tranquility created by the ocean waves. I finally understood why my father feared the city would swallow me and why my brother guarded me like a pit bull. I could almost hear Sean's ferocious snarls at the boys who dared to make passes at me. He was determined to prevent another Dallas from ever happening.

But whatever my mind had summoned, it would surely test my ability to survive Montego Bay.

As I closed my eyes, my mind took me back to the day I crawled to my desk, dragging my feet along the hard surface, hoping no one would see the blood trickling down my legs as they left faint streaks and my lingering footsteps made their way forward. It was not my period. I wasn't supposed to get a period at seven.

I limped toward my classroom. It took fifteen minutes to get to my seat from the bathroom. I sat quietly and stared at the chalkboard as Miss Thompson wrote her first math problem since recess, expecting the class to solve it in less than a minute. Her face twisted out of shape as she locked eyes with mine, peering over her pear-shaped lenses, and my body twitched, terrified she would call me to the board to solve the problem. She did not have to call out my name. Everyone knew the dreaded stare we all feared. She moved toward me, gripping the white chalk between her thumb and index finger. My body vibrated harder, shaking faster and faster against my desk as she approached me.

She knelt before me, slowly removed her glasses, then pushed up my chin with her left hand and used her thumb to wipe the tears pouring out of my eyes.

She could not see the bloodstains on my dress, but she knew something was wrong.

"Vivienne, come with me," she said softly, offering me her hand. But before I could stand, my head hit the desk, sending the unstable one-piece furniture and me tumbling to the concrete floor. She yelled for help, snatched me up, and dashed to the nurse's office.

It had been eleven years since, and I had never once heard my parents talk about that day, buried in the deepest part of my mind and hidden from my consciousness. It took the calm ocean waves and the whistling of the night to resurrect when Denton Reese cornered me in the bathroom hallway of my elementary school, raped and beat the crap out of me.

It was the inconvenient truth my family refused to talk about, hoping I could erase it from memory.

Looking back at the certainty that my past would come crashing down on my head like a meteoroid, I would have been better prepared to handle the nightmare that presented itself if my family wasn't so hellbent on hiding my past from me. Somedays, I wished I were a typical teenager, with everyday teenage problems like acne, a first crush, or even getting my heart broken, instead of being saddled with a tragic past not to be spoken of by my family. And even after so many years, I wept for the loss of my innocence, in part because it almost killed my father.

Chapter 7

The Mystery Man

Vivienne

According to Jasmine, I was either too beautiful to be single, too opinionated to hold on to a man, or too ambitious to need a husband. She must have known me better than I knew myself. Apparently, my beauty, opinions, and ambitions got me to Montego Bay.

My childhood trauma didn't leave lasting damage, especially since Jasmine thought I had more confidence than the typical teenager. The early morning sea breeze gently caressed my face as it wafted through my bedroom window. The sun rose over the hills, gliding across the sky, leaving an orange glow as it glistened against the turquoise-blue pristine waters of the

Caribbean Sea. I inhaled the clean air one last time before rushing into the early sunrise to make it on time for work at the souvenir store downtown. I stumbled against the living room chair as I hurried to catch a cab. My mother stared back at me from the picture hanging on Sean's living room wall as if warning me of danger. An airy feeling swept over me as if my past and future were about to collide.

"Welcome to Montego Bay, Beautiful."

If I hear the word beautiful one more time, I will holler. Why are these men so obsessed with the way I look?

I couldn't go anywhere without men telling me how pretty or curvy I was. The way I looked became a burden more than anything else.

The baritone voice over my shoulders jerked me away from the tour buses, filled with vacationers, streaming through the narrow Gloucester Avenue roadway, and I spun around to see to whom it belonged. The voice sounded vaguely familiar. It was deep, soulful, and intriguing, like the bass in a male quartet.

I stared at him longer than I should have. He was the most breathtakingly handsome man I had ever seen.

His half-open shirt underneath his suit held my eyes captive as I stared at the six-footer before me. I was being hypocritical, but in my defense, I didn't tell him he was gorgeous. I just thought about it. He looked like he had a celebrity stylist who catered to him, not like the rest of us who dressed ourselves.

I couldn't look away. It was as if I had forgotten how to blink.

His right foot rested on the bumper of his brand-new sports car. He hung his left hand from his knee as if posing for a photo shoot. There was no sense of urgency about himself as if he was out on an early morning prowl, while I was eager for Mr. Khan to open the store to begin my morning shift.

"Excuse me? Do I know you?" I asked, finally recovering from the momentary daze.

His smile enhanced the toned structure of his cheekbones. My heart didn't stand a chance against him.

But I was determined to push back at his advances as hard as he was spellbinding.

"Hopefully soon, but I know you," he said with a broad smile that took my breath away.

Suddenly, there was an uneasiness growing in me. How could he have known me? I've never laid eyes on him before.

I stepped back, trying to make sense of what he had said.

What does this serpent want from me now? Is this how my life will be from now on? God, I will need your help to fight off these horny-ass men. Now, this man claims he knows me.

I had only seen guys like him in fashion magazines. I didn't think I would encounter one in person. Usually, I'd flash my signature eye roll and move on whenever anyone commented on my looks. But I saw the perfect specimen of a man before me, and at that moment, my eyes betrayed me.

I was under no illusion that men wouldn't target me. When we turned seventeen, Jasmine told me it was time to find our soulmates, as if seventeen was the magic number to start looking for a husband. Or when our biological clock started the countdown. But the eye rolls I'd give her were enough to let her know to back off her constant need for me to find a boyfriend. I wouldn't be pressured into hooking up with the first guy who said he saw me in his dreams. She knew I wasn't in a rush to be anyone's girlfriend, wife, or soulmate. I had bigger ambitions than allowing anyone to claim me as their own.

My long, curly brown hair cascaded down my back and glistened under the morning sunlight as I stood outside the souvenir shop. I added ruby lipstick to highlight my lips.

My spaghetti-strapped yellow dress hugged my hips with a flare at the hem, slightly lifting each time there was an occasional breeze from the ocean, revealing the legs my next-door neighbor, Greg Simpson, once said he'd give me his father's entire farm if I'd let him rub them.

I folded my arms to calm the unexpected flutters in my chest while I waited for the stranger to tell me how he knew me since I had no clue who he was. Then again, it could be one of his cheesy pickup lines. From his overwhelming self-confidence, he seemed to think he was God's gift to women.

"Let me stop you right there," I said, wagging my finger at him. "Whatever you think you'll get from me will not happen, so you might want to keep your ego in check. I barely survived an assault on Saturday, chased by a damn madman, and fondled by a creep. I am in no mood for whatever it is you're selling. So, please don't embarrass yourself," I hissed.

Usually, I'd just cut my eyes and walk away, but his presence made me incapable of shutting him down completely. I wished he wasn't so damn good-looking.

He eased out of his GQ posture, stood upright, drew closer, and my heart raced. This phenomenon completely caught me off guard. My body had never reacted to anyone like that.

"Someone what?" he asked, sounding concerned.

"Like you care," I replied, looking out at the street in front of me, lined with stalls of red, green, and gold trinkets with the world's most famous Rasta man's photo printed on almost every T-shirt.

"You must be new in town," he said. His eyes were hidden behind his fancy sunglasses to block the rays from the morning sun penetrating the sky.

"Do they only assault strangers here? What makes you think I am new in town? Is it the sign on my back that says *just come?*" I scoffed, aware of how much sarcasm dripped off my tongue.

"No, but..." His voice trailed off as he struggled to find a response.

"Oh, I know. It must be the way I look." I quickly interrupted him. "You took one glance at me and thought I came straight out of the jungle, didn't you? Is it that obvious?"

He smiled, and my heart felt like it was fighting to escape my chest.

Something strange is happening, like there's a raging storm inside me. If he touches me, I will dissolve like raindrops on this heated pavement. What the Hell is happening to me?

He oozed confidence that could only come from someone who knew how to ignite the firestorm in me. He wasn't making it easy to ignore him. There was something regal about his perfectly pumped physique, and he was unafraid to go toe to toe with me. I could tell he knew I was conflicted. His lips were inviting, and his easy smile came only from a man who knew his beguiling capabilities.

"Well, I see you have a sense of humor, brown-eyed girl."

"Something made you think I'm not from here. What is it?" I tapped my foot and stared him down. "Could it be that you can tell the visitors from the locals simply by looking?"

"I'm Jonathan. What's your name?" He offered me his hand. His smile had not faded. He looked arrogant and flashy, like a city slicker, a heartbreaker, a definite womanizer. After all, Gloucester Avenue was fertile ground for skirt chasers and loafers, with nothing to do but whistle at every female who passed them, tourists included.

"Let me ask you, Jonathan," I said, aware of all the cheesy pickup lines a pretty boy could say to me. My least favorite was, *mi woulda deh wid yuh enuh.*' Nothing he could have said would make me smile, hinting that I was attracted to him or even wanted to listen to what he had to say, as gorgeous as he looked.

He pulled the shades from his eyes after realizing I was not budging on the handshake. I had never seen eyes like his, and they threw me off my guard. They were sparkling, seductive, bold, and mysterious simultaneously. I took a step back, away from the glare of his eyes, trying not to let them consume me any more than he had, and I couldn't escape them.

"A man with your looks and style, why do you have to loaf around to pick up girls so early? You do not strike me as a guy with trouble getting women."

"But I am not interested in just any girl, Miss Pearson. Is it?" he asked, flashing another seductive smile as if he was sure I'd confirm it.

"If you must ask, then you don't know me as well as you think you do," I replied. My eyes were locked with Jonathan's. It was as if I could see deep into his soul. "Are you offering to show me around the city? Or take me on an adventure?" I scoffed.

The recent memory gain of my childhood trauma and my encounter with the creep in the taxi were front and center of my mind, and I was determined not to become anyone's victim again, whether he was a gold-teeth-grinning creep or a silver-tongue devil.

But I couldn't shake the feeling that somehow I knew him.

"I could arrange that," he laughed, lighting up his eyes.

"You are not a tour guide, are you, Jonathan?" I narrowed my eyes on him. "You do not even sound like you're from here. So, tell me, truthfully, where do you live? Let me guess. New York."

"Look who is talking. You're the one with the accent," he chuckled. "I live here," he boasted. "You can tell, can't you? Otherwise, I may be overdressed."

"Maybe?" I giggled. "That's not a maybe. That suit has no place in this heat unless you're off to church or a board meeting somewhere. And you shouldn't be idling by the side of the road, making small talk."

He shifted out of the glaring sunlight that hovered over us and moved closer to me.

"If you live here, you should know not to park here. You cannot block the entrance to the store." I pushed him out of my space to get some breathing room.

"I won't be long. I'm here only because of you."

I pulled my eyes away from his stare, looking around to see if he was referring to someone else. "Me?" I pointed at my chest.

"Yes, you," he laughed.

"Why me? There must be other girls you could harass. Don't think I'm easily fooled by your charm, suit, and silver tongue," I said, wagging my finger at him.

"Maybe my charm. Is it working?"

"No, Mr. Silver-tongue," I said immediately.

"Seriously, I chose you because you're the most gorgeous girl I have ever seen. I want to know you better. Is that so bad?"

"Well, bad enough for you to think I'd be interested. I see a man creep up behind me and ask for my name, and I want to know why. A stranger said he knows me, and you've got my full attention. After all, isn't this where the good, bad, and the ugly congregate? My parents warned me that the devil comes in all forms."

"Which one am I? Good, bad, or ugly? Or am I the devil incarnate?" His questions ambushed me, but I responded the only way I could.

"I wouldn't know," I said. "You see, Jonathan, I'm not like you. I can't tell just by looking."

"Wow!" he laughed. "I deserve that. I can see you will not make it easy for me. I just want to know your name today. Tomorrow, well, that's entirely up to you."

"Surely you have someplace you must be," I said, tapping my foot against the pavement, anxious for my boss to open the store.

"I don't. I'm exactly where I am supposed to be."

"Let me be upfront with you, Jonathan." I stepped closer to him without a second thought that he had almost a twelve-inch advantage and might not take kindly to my assertiveness. "I will not have time for you. I am on a mission, and you seem like just another handsome distraction." I looked him up and down, then rolled my eyes away from his stare and hissed.

"If you don't tell me your name today, I'll be back tomorrow and the day after that, and I'll ask again until you tell me. I am that persistent. And for your information, I already know more about you than you think."

"Then, why are you here wasting my time, asking for my name? Since you know so much about me, you should also know my name."

"I'm not lying," he said cheekily, like a guy not used to getting such harsh pushbacks. And even though his smile captivated me, his eyes hypnotized me.

"It seems you're up to some shenanigans. Whatever it is, you should know I'm not into playing games. Especially with a man I have no interest in knowing. Be careful who you sneak up behind next time; you could get clobbered."

"Go out with me some time," he said, radiating confidence and a calm vibe as if expecting me to say yes. But I was not an ordinary eighteen-year-old and was not easily impressed by a charming twenty-something who might be stalking me. But gosh, he was handsome.

"What part of not interested don't you understand?"

"You could have fun, you know." He peeked at me from the corner of his eye and smiled.

"You are wasting your time. Please do not waste mine. You cannot give me the kind of attention I deserve. You are arrogant and overconfident. Look at you; you are a better dresser than I am, for God's sake," I laughed.

"You're even more beautiful when you laugh, so I'm ignoring that crack about me being pretty," he said.

My eyes flickered up and down his tall, perfectly built frame, lingering on his mesmerizing eyes. "Did I hit a nerve?" I managed to ask.

He rubbed his chin, then nudged his head forward. "I'll live. I have thick skin."

"Jonathan, you are barking up the wrong tree," I said.

But getting so close to him was a mistake. I realized I had stepped inside a danger zone. Red lights were going off in my brain like crazy. But I couldn't move away from him, as if my foot got stuck on the concrete.

"Am I?" He beamed like he was having a breakthrough with me. But I couldn't have predicted I'd be so captivated by this stranger who was making me lose my cool.

"What?" I asked the minute I realized he could tell I was taken in by his private conversation with me with his eyes.

"Barking up the wrong tree," he said. "You said I'm barking up the wrong tree, but I don't think you believe that."

My heart fluttered, seeing how confident he seemed. That was when I realized that it would not be our last encounter. "Is this how you pick up girls? I can see I'm not the first one you try out your tired lines on." I pulled my handbag close to my chest, hoping he wouldn't hear the throbbing of my heart.

He curved his upper lip, and his eyes became more radiant. He seemed to be having a lot of fun at my expense.

"How could you not know how relationships start? I'm a guy, and you're a gorgeous girl," he emphasized the word gorgeous, then bit into his lower lip as if he wasn't already stirring up feelings in me that should have been illegal. "I'll get you to go out with me. It's that simple."

He winked at me as if I should find it sexy.

No, he didn't just do that. Does that even work on any girl?

I didn't see that coming. He was way too handsome for that, but what did I expect? He was a city boy, after all.

"But for you, Mr. dreamy-eyed lover-man," I wagged my finger at him, trying to regain some of my lost confidence. "There's always an agenda with guys like you, and I hope you don't think you're the one to enlighten me. I do not need a lesson on relationships from you."

"I didn't think so; you seem to have it all down. Beauty, brains, and a smile I could never get tired of waking up to. But in all seriousness, give me the chance to get to know you better. I am much more than this suit."

"I would hope so. Otherwise, that face on you would be a waste."

"Does that mean yes? You won't regret it." He straightened himself and flashed his million-dollar smile, hoping he had made a breakthrough with me.

Cars zipped through the narrow, two-way, single-lane street, which frightened me each time a driver honked his horn as if it got stuck. "Beware of this *jungle girl*, she will scratch you," I said as soon as Mr. Khan opened the door.

Chapter 8

Eyes That Smile

Vivienne

I shuffled through the rush hour traffic and returned from my weekend in Greenspring to find Jonathan outside the store. He was standing next to the front door. He pulled the shades from his eyes to reveal the spark in them and smiled at me teasingly.

I smiled back, releasing an avalanche of emotions I had suppressed since we first met.

"Hey, Beautiful," Jonathan approached me.

My heart pounded. My skin felt like tiny feet were crawling beneath it. His sneaky glances drew out a smile against my better judgment. His gaze was hypnotic, like a magnet, pulling me closer to him as if it were about to lift me off the ground.

I understood why my father warned me repeatedly against giving into the "temptations of the flesh. This intensity was not something I was prepared for. And while Jonathan's smile tugged at my heartstrings, and my nerves failed me, I resisted every urge to take him up on his offer. I was unsure how much longer I could resist him, though. He was wearing me down.

It had been a month since we met, and just like clockwork, Jonathan was at my job as if he did not have a care in the world or anywhere else to be. Like all the other times, his tailored suit looked like something out of a magazine. His shirt was crisp with the first two buttons opened. He looked flawless, with no crease anywhere on him.

He looks like he has a dutiful wife who cares for him. What does he want from me? He must think his good looks and charm easily fool me. I hope he doesn't think he'll get lucky with me.

"Seriously, man, you must have a wife, a job, or something better to do with your time. You are always immaculately dressed, so I am going out on a limb to say you have a job; from the looks of it, it seems like an important one. Either that or you secretly own this place," I said, pointing to the souvenir store.

"I do not own this store, but I am gainfully employed. You do not have to worry about me. But I will not stop coming here until you tell me your name and agree to go out with me. One date. That's all I ask. As for whether I have a wife, we'll talk about it on our date." He leaned against the store, crossed his legs at the ankles, and smiled. "There is a movie showing this weekend. Should I reserve tickets?" he asked with pleading eyes. "What do you say, Beautiful? Take me out of my misery. Whenever I think about you, I lose control of myself, and it's getting harder to breathe whenever I'm around you."

"You take rejection very well. I have a feeling that your heart will be okay if I don't fulfill your lusts," I said. "You are relentless. Is that a male thing? Or is it that you're unable to differentiate yes and no?"

"You are worth it. You stimulate my mind and body. So no, I do not have anywhere else I'd rather be, and I know the difference between yes and no. If you don't give me a chance, I don't think I'll—"

"What? Survive?" I asked, cutting him off before he could finish his pathetic plea. "You won't die, so get it together and stop embarrassing yourself."

He shrugged, uncrossed his legs, and moved closer. "You hear that?" he asked, his voice desperate. "My heart beats like this only for you. No one has ever made it rumble like that. There must be a special connection between us. Each time I see you, my heart speeds up. My mind accelerates like a bullet train when I'm not around you. Whether my heart or my brain, they have never responded to anyone the way they respond to you. Go ahead, ask me any questions. Don't be shy. I have no secrets," he bragged.

I could have been up against a persistent narcissist with a way with words and more time on his hands than should be allowed. I was damn sure not about to become his victim.

"Beware, people who declare they don't have secrets usually have a few tightly locked closet doors," I chuckled.

"I'm an open book. But seriously, before you rush to say no, again, think about it. Already, I see your lips moving to form the word." He grazed my chin with the back of his hand, held on to it, smiled again, and a warm sensation spread through my body, causing my heart rate to skyrocket.

But then he said the strangest thing I had ever heard in all my eighteen years. "I'd like to be your bodyguard."

I burst out laughing. I must admit, I had not heard that pickup line before, and I thought I had heard all the cheesy lines men used to lure their victims. "You mean you want to guard my body," I replied after recovering from the laughter.

"See, there. That's a good one—your sense of humor. I love it. But I was only thinking about what you said—someone tried to assault you. I want to make sure it never happens again."

"You men in the city are all the same. You're obsessed with women's bodies. You must stop stalking me."

"I mean it," he said. His countenance reflected a seriousness I had not seen before.

"I don't doubt that. But guarding me will never happen. The sooner you get that, the better for you."

"If you ever feel unsafe, I'm here for you. I don't want you to go through another day like the one you had. Men in the city can misbehave. I want you to be mindful of that, and even though you think I'm stalking you, I can protect you."

"No need. I'm not as alone as you may think, and I am not a damsel in distress for you to rescue. Stop coming here every day. You said you know me, and I don't know who you are."

Jonathan had a certain kind of swagger; he knew it too and constantly flaunted it at me. "You wouldn't need to get tired of seeing me only if you had given me your number, and since this is the only way to talk to you, I'll see you again tomorrow. As for how I know you?" He rubbed his chin and grinned. "If you think hard enough, it will come to you," he said as he jumped in his car, blew air kisses at me, flung his glasses back on, and sped off before I could utter another rejection.

"God help me. This man is relentless, and I'm unable to help that I am falling for him," I muttered as I walked away. "Those eyes and that smile, Lord, are piercing through me."

I opened the door, hurried behind the glass counter, and flung my handbag inside one of the cabinets as I prepared to meet shoppers. Reality had finally compelled me to admit that Jonathan was getting under my skin. I wanted to accept his movie offer, but my father's warnings would not allow for such a risk-taking venture. I would not budge.

I greeted Donna, the bubbly girl at the cash register. "Look who's dating Jonathan Hastings!" she declared gleefully. Her elbows rested on the display, hands holding up her chin.

"Do you know him? I can't seem to get rid of him."

"He's here every morning, waiting for you. I assume you're his girlfriend. You don't know who he is?" Her eyes widened with disbelief.

"Should I?"

"If you don't know, I'm certainly not going to tell you."

"Donna, has it ever occurred to you that he has nothing better to do with his time? What man positions himself at my job every morning? You don't see him dropping me off, do you? So no, he is not my boyfriend," I said, knocking her hands out from under her chin.

"One who's clearly into you. I can't believe you don't know Jonathan Hastings." Donna scrambled to prevent herself from collapsing onto the showcase. "Men are not supposed to be so gorgeous. I wish I had someone so handsome interested in me the way he is in you," she said after regaining her balance.

"You can have him. He's all yours." I slid the showcase door open to straighten the items. "Mr. Khan will not take kindly to us gossiping if things are out of place," I said, intending to change the subject.

"Yeah, right. That guy wouldn't see me even if I threw myself at his feet. You are who he wants."

"Shouldn't he have a job or something more important to do with his time? I feel like he's stalking me. But what do I know about men? I'm just a country girl."

"A country girl who is drop-dead gorgeous. That's why he's sniffing around you."

"Donna, here's a thought. A man that pretty, with so much time on his hands, is nothing more than a player who's looking for someone he can turn into his plaything. I'm not about to become his toy or victim. If I had known you were paying so much attention to him, I would have directed him to you." I rolled my eyes at her.

"Seriously, Vivienne, I think you're clueless about men. When a man like Jonathan Hastings sets his eyes on a target as beautiful as you, nothing can pull him away. Do you think he's stalking you now? Wait, you haven't seen anything yet."

"There's the operative word, Donna, *target*. Think about that the next time you think of running blindly into the arms of a stranger. It can't be good if I'm his target. Why are we wasting our time talking about him anyway?"

"Because he is Jonathan frigging Hastings, girl! I can't believe you don't know him."

"Then why don't you tell me who he is instead of letting me make a fool of myself? If you tell me, I'll know what I'm up against."

"Then that would ruin the look on your face when you find out, wouldn't it."

"Mr. Khan should be here any minute. You better help me straighten up before he returns. You know how grumpy he can be. Help me stock these shelves, will you? Instead of thinking I should be drooling over a man stalking me."

But at midday, I daydreamed about Jonathan's eyes and how they'd smile at me whenever he came by the store. I pondered over the perfect specimen waiting to see me in the mornings and how his body looked like it belonged in a museum. His eyes sparkled like a gem. His cologne lingered in the air long after he was gone, and I realized I was in trouble.

Chapter 9

For Your Eyes Only

Jonathan

I sat in the back seat of Dale's car for ten minutes after it pulled up to the blue and white iron gate. Dale was my part-time driver. I called him up whenever I wanted to keep a low profile.

With one foot in front of the other, Vivienne gracefully made her way down the steps, and I couldn't stop smiling at the beauty coming toward me. The evening sea breeze slightly lifted the hem of her dress. I tried not to stare but couldn't avoid her smile.

"Damn, Jonathan!" Dale's eyes widened. "Is that the girl? She is not Montegonian. I would have seen her before. You're right. She is beautiful!" He quickly turned his head to look at me. "I'm guessing she doesn't have a clue who you are," he laughed, as guilt washed over me. "How long before she finds out and runs in the other direction?"

"Mind your business, Dale," I said, pulling on my sleeves to straighten my shirt, grinning from ear to ear. "I mean it. You don't repeat what you see here tonight. I'm trying to keep a very low profile. You're not supposed to discuss this evening with anyone."

"My lips are sealed, man. Do you know me to gossip? Just go get your girl," he said, smiling, then turned the keys in the ignition.

I could always rely on Dale for discretion. But I had to make sure he knew my date would not be the topic of discussion by him or anyone. I couldn't let her be picked apart or become a target simply for going on a date with me. I had enough of a tough time getting her to tell me her name. She didn't seem like the girl who would stand for everyone's obsession with me. Their obsession with everything Hastings was one of the reasons my relationship with Jennifer didn't stand a chance. I held them partially responsible for how the relationship ended, making me fret whenever I thought of breaking the news of dating Vivienne to Sean. It was a good thing he wasn't home.

I met Vivienne at the bottom of the steps, smiled at her, took her arm, gently placed it between my elbow, rubbed my left hand across her wrist, and led her to the waiting car.

"Thank you, Jesus," I mouthed, turning my head toward the sky. "I think I'm in trouble." I helped her inside the back seat, sat beside her, and smiled like a schoolboy with a crush. "You could not look any more beautiful this evening."

She looked at me and furrowed her brows.

"One date, remember?" she said after seeing the ear-to-ear grin that lit up my face.

I weaved my fingers through hers and brought her hand to my lips for a kiss. I took a deep breath and whispered, "I'm sorry, but one date won't do, not when I've found the love of my life."

"Charming and funny. You should be a comedian," she said.

"Before the night ends, you won't be so cynical."

She locked her eyes with mine. "Let's get out of here before I change my mind," she said.

For the next fifteen minutes, I couldn't stop staring at her.

"Butter on your popcorn?" The attendant at the movie theater concession stands enquired.

"No butter," I said. I could hardly take my eyes off my date.

"Will that be all, Sir? Or would you like a drink to go with your order?" The cashier brought my attention back to her.

"Soft drinks," I replied.

A minute later, I headed toward a large room already blasting clips of movie previews, Vivienne Pearson lovingly on my arm. I wooed her for weeks, sometimes on bending knees, until finally, she took pity on me.

We sat outside the wide hallway that led inside the cinema. The windows swung back and forth to let in the evening breeze. Young couples paraded up and down the corridor, and teenage girls giggled at their rowdy boyfriends' playful gestures. Being close to Vivienne sent impure thoughts and emotions surging through me. At times, nervous excitement as she locked her eyes with mine. The smile that melted my heart every time and the physical attraction I had developed was not only perplexing but damn near mesmerizing.

"So, Jonathan, are you ready to tell me how you know me? It's been over a month since you told me you know me, and I haven't figured out who you are. Everyone I asked seemed guarded, and I'm beginning to feel a cloud of suspicion around you. So now that I've allowed myself to spend time with you, I need to know. Who is Jonathan Hastings? How do you know me? And why is everyone afraid to talk about you?" she whispered, leaning into me.

I took her hand and smiled, thinking of the worst scenario that could come at the end of my first sentence. More than being the guy who rescued her, I was the talk of the town.

Where do I begin? Telling her who I am will send her running, just like Dale said, and I don't want our date to end or to have to lie to this girl. Judging from how confident yet guarded she seems, lying is a non-starter, and telling her people think I'm a womanizing playboy would be counterproductive. If I do, it will come back to bite me. But how can she not know who I am? She must be playing with me.

"I know your brother," I said as I lifted her hand to my lips, my eyes fixed on her.

She turned her head fast and narrowed her eyes to me. "You do? How?"

I liked the fact that I was unknown to her. I could be whoever I wanted and not constantly worry about being judged.

"Sean and I go way back." I pulled my eyes away from hers. "But he didn't tell me he had such a lovely sister," I said.

She inhaled the gentle breeze coming in through the open window. "Oh, stop." She smiled and sipped the drink to hide the blush creeping into her eyes.

I leaned over and moved in for my first kiss.

"Tell me more about your relationship with my brother. How well do you know him?" she asked, pulling away.

"I'd rather talk about you." I rubbed my hand across her shoulder.

"I am not that interesting. You, on the other hand, seem both interesting and intimidating. How do you explain that?"

Her eyes followed mine as she slowly released the straw on which she had been sipping.

I lifted her chin, still wanting my first kiss. My head and heart were in a tug of war. One warned me to wait for a signal from her, to take it easy and go slow, the other pounding in my chest from anxiety and want. From the first day I saw her, all I could think of was when I'd get to kiss her. Now was the perfect time, but I had to tread lightly; otherwise, I would never have relieved the distrust in her eyes. I had already made plans for the upcoming holiday, and if she didn't kiss me soon, that would mean she was not into me as much as I was into her. I couldn't let her think I was just a slick-talking city boy who refused to take no for an answer.

"What made you change your mind about me?" I asked, pushing the strands of hair out of her face.

"I don't know. There's just something mysterious about you, so I thought, why not?" she laughed.

Her sarcasm and sense of humor were why I couldn't get her out of my mind. I couldn't believe it when she told me she'd go to the movies with me. I was up against a flawless girl with a smile I couldn't get out of my head, but I was willing to do everything I could to win the battle for her heart.

Her decision to see a movie with me was one thing. Getting her to sleep with me was an entirely different story, and I was in no hurry except to get past the awkward first kiss. Something about her told me we would be in it for the long haul, or it could be wishful thinking. We would go our separate ways when the movie ended. I could tell she had no intention of sleeping with me, not now or anytime soon.

I pulled her closer and smiled. "You have no reason to fear me," I said after sensing her lack of interest in kissing me. "I should be the one afraid of you, Vivienne." I shook my head. "I hope I'm not intimidating you the way you're scaring the hell out of me. I am gentler than I look, and I know you'd rather be anywhere than here with me. Do not let this body fool you. I am a lovable teddy bear." The stiffness in her shoulders stopped me each time I got close to her.

"So, what you are telling me is that you are not only a charmer, but you are also tender too?" she asked, gently pulling out of my grasp.

I was playing with fire. A stare like the one she was giving me could light the spark within me and send the wrong signal, and I couldn't let my lips tell her one thing, and my body scream another.

"Come on, it's time to go in," I said, helping her off the bench. "You'll see. I don't have to brag." I smiled and ran the back of my hand against her cheek.

We walked toward the wide door, and the volume from the soundtrack hit us with full force when we opened it, like an explosion. *"For Your Eyes Only"* had been showing all week, a re-run from an earlier release. Strand Street was famous for its movie theater and overcrowded taxi stand, but attending a James Bond movie with Vivienne seemed the perfect way to break the ice between us. Even though I had to push through a crowded street to enter the building she once called the devil's playhouse.

Ticket holders occupied their seats. Others loitered on the steps, waiting for the movie to start. We shuffled past the couple at the entrance of the row at the back of the theatre. My hand locked with Vivienne's as the endless loop of movie previews rolled across the enormous screen preceding the feature presentation.

"Are you okay?" My voice rose above the noise as I handed Vivienne the bucket of popcorn.

"I am," she replied with a smile. "But it is a bit noisy. I hope it quiets when the movie starts," she shouted over the volume of the soundtrack.

I rubbed the back of her hand, lifted it to my lips, and kissed it. "It usually does," I assured her. I was more into her than what was showing on the screen.

Sitting next to her, I experienced a phenomenal connection. It was as if a part of my heart leaped out of my chest and latched onto hers.

Two hours later, as the credits rolled, the theater doors swung open, and patrons scampered out, causing a mini stampede. I held Vivienne's hand and went through the back door. We hustled into Dale's car, waiting outside, away from the long lines of cabs that wrapped around the building where they parked, waiting for patrons to descend.

I was not ready for our date to be over, especially since it had gone off without a hitch, so I took Vivienne back to my house. She was poised and confident, with curves in all the right places.

She was intelligent and seemed like the girl who wouldn't crumble under the barrage of my mother's interrogation. My hand hardly left hers, and occasionally, I'd wrap it around my waist and smile at her. She returned my smile, sending electricity through me, and the Bad Boy in me crumbled.

Chapter 10

Alone in the Dark

Jonathan

Dale pulled up at my gate in what felt like an instant. The fifteen-minute drive to my house felt more like five. I got out, walked to the other side of the car, helped Vivienne out, and led her through the walkway to my house.

"Did you enjoy the movie?" I asked over the waves roaring in the distance as they crashed against the rocks, creating the perfect mood for a romantic night.

The stars blanketed the night sky, leaving a soft glow that shone around us. It was precisely the ambiance I needed to convince Vivienne we had made a connection. Nights like those were made for a memorable first date.

"I did," she said over the sound from the ocean waves. It's better than I had expected." My hand hung from her shoulder with our fingers locked as we slowly walked to my gate.

"Since you've never been to the movies, I didn't know if you'd like it. I'm glad you did."

"If I'm honest with you, Jonathan, the company wasn't bad either." She rubbed her thumb across the hand hanging from her shoulder, causing my heart rate to speed up.

"You know, Vivienne," I chuckled, relieved. But however desperate I was for her to fall in love with me at that moment, I could not let her know the real me just yet. "When I met you, I thought you were the feistiest pretty girl I had ever met. You rolled your eyes at me, hissed, gave me the cold shoulder, and accused me of thinking you were a jungle girl. Oh, lest I forget, you threatened to scratch me." I flung my head back and laughed. "I must admit, you are one gorgeous jungle girl."

"You thought I was feisty?" she asked, pulling on my fingers playfully. Butterflies clicked in my stomach. At times, I was entirely confounded by her presence as her gentle tug sliced through me like razor blades.

"Either that, or you did not like me." I barely got that out. No one had ever affected me with so little effort, and I had been around beautiful, confident women before. Granted, no one was as lovely as her.

"Well, here I am with you, alone, in the dark, and it's almost midnight. Any concerns I had must have disappeared." It was odd how more relaxed than me she seemed. I was crumbling inside, or melting was more like it. I loved being with her. There was a sudden burst of reality at that moment I couldn't deny. I loved her. And I wanted her to know how desperately I wished to cradle her into my arms and kiss her. I had never felt this emotionally invested in a girl or completely conquered by one. It scared me.

"Well, V," I said after I closed the gate behind us. "While you're here with me, I want to make tonight count." I needed to kiss her soon, but I would have to hug her for now. I couldn't afford to make her think all I wanted was to sleep with her.

"Do you live here by yourself?" she asked.

"Sort of," I said.

"What does that mean? Either you do or you don't."

"Patricia takes care of me,"

"Who is Patricia?" She looked at me worried, and I knew I had better explain before she got the wrong impression.

"She is my housekeeper and my second mother," I said. "She doesn't live here, but she comes in every day. She's very protective of me, but she'd love you."

"Isn't it odd for you to be living by yourself in such a big house? Aren't you a bit too young to be living like this? How old are you anyway?"

"Old enough," I said.

"Old enough for what, Jonathan? Do you always take your dates here?"

"Let's talk about you. Tell me about Vivienne Pearson," I said. If I was to answer her honestly, I was sure this would be our last date. I could feel where the questions were heading. I couldn't afford to veer into my checkered past.

"I remember you telling me you know more about me than I think. How much more would you like to know?"

"I'd like to know everything. How long you'll be in town? Any boyfriends? You know, little details like that."

"Well, you are a bit mysterious. I am not sure I should be telling you everything about me. I would rather keep my guard up."

I turned towards the swooshing sounds coming from below my house. "Do you hear that? It's just you, me, and the waves," I said. "Whatever you tell me will be our little secret." I smiled.

"You're funny, Jonathan. You and I won't be having any secrets," she said.

"I would like you to know everything about me. For one, you're safe here with me; over time, you will see that I am someone you can trust."

When we arrived inside the house, the clock on the living room wall had struck eleven, and Vivienne must be home by twelve. Sean was home waiting, so my time with her would soon end.

"I have to leave soon," she said as if reading my mind.

I might not get another date if she broke her curfew on our first one. Sean was very disciplined, and dating his sister was already one strike against me. I didn't want to ruin their trust by ignoring his midnight curfew.

"You do know your house is around the corner, right? I will walk with you whenever you are ready to go. You do not have to worry."

"So, you and I are neighbors? Why didn't you tell me?"

"Well, I did say I know you more than you think."

"What else aren't you telling me, Jonathan?" She glanced at me, her eyes searching for answers.

I let out a long breath, her hand resting on my chest. If I revealed that I was the one who saved her from Pastor Nate, perhaps she could forgive me for that. But the truth of my identity could erase all my progress, making her question her trust in me. The omission felt like a betrayal that threatened to shatter the gains I had made. But for now, the details of my identity would have to remain hidden.

"I'm in love with you, Vivienne." I gently touched her chin, then caressed her jawline, hoping she'd feel all my sincerity. "You stung me, V," I said.

She smiled, cupping my cheeks, and my body vibrated. "That quickly, ah. You're kidding, right? Who falls in love that quickly? Shouldn't you get to know me before you make such an important declaration? Unless it's just another one of your pick-up lines. I didn't take you as someone who wears his heart on his sleeves." A warm sensation shot through me. "Hmm, city boy, take it down a notch." She had to have known what her touch would do to me because I became tongue-tied.

I could barely form a coherent sentence at the feel of her hands against my cheek. "If I tried to explain how I feel about you, you would think I'm an idiot. Of everything in my life, how you make me feel is the one thing I cannot control or explain."

"Well, I hope you can control this night and not let me stay out past midnight," she said.

"I know." I pulled her closer.

"That is part of my brother's rules," she said as she crashed into me. "I cannot behave as if I have outgrown them. My father would go nuts if he thought I disobeyed Sean's wishes."

"Then we better make the best of the next hour. I'm having an amazing time with you. It is only a pity our date will end soon. You have managed to do what no other girl ever did. You made me feel like there is love at first sight."

"The first time you asked for my name, I thought you were a player, just another skirt chaser. I'm still not convinced that you are the type to be with one girl," she said.

"I would like to see you again. You know, to convince you that I am indeed a one-woman man. Independence Day is coming, and I want to take you to Ocho Rios. That will give you more time to decide whether I am the guy you take home to meet your father."

"Why do you want to go there? What's so special about Ocho Rios?"

"Waterfalls, beaches, jet skis, you know, lots of fun things to do."

"You mean hotels? Somewhere far away where you can lock me away from Sean and have your way with me?"

I chuckled. "V, I'm a single man who lives alone. I do not need to take you to a hotel if I want to have my way with you," I said, then bent my head to kiss her. She stepped back and stared at me, as if unsure what to say next. "Ocho Rios has more to see than inside a hotel room." I caressed her cheek, then lifted her chin. "I want to spend the holiday with you. If you do not feel comfortable going to Ochi, we can go somewhere else. We can stay in the city if it makes you feel more comfortable to hang out at Doctor's Cave Beach."

"I might have misjudged you," she said.

"What did you think I would do to you? Take your mind out of the gutter," I laughed.

"I cannot answer tonight, but I will let you know after I talk with Sean unless you want to ask him if I can travel that far. You did say you know him well, so I see no reason he wouldn't let you take me. Unless he knows you'd be a bad influence."

I led Vivienne back outside after hearing another swoosh from the ocean as the waves washed against the shore, whistling in the darkness. I wrapped my arms around her, rubbing my face through her hair.

"There it is again, V. Whenever I sit under the stars and listen to the waves, the same feeling sweeps over me. Tonight, the feeling is ten times more intense, though. It's hard to explain how I feel right now. I get to listen to the waves with you in my arms. It's sensational. I am certain this feeling will not go away anytime soon."

"You are full of surprises, Jonathan Hastings. You seem like a true romantic, like my friend, Jas," she said.

Everything about this girl amazed me. It wasn't just her beauty. Her whole being had my heart fluttering like a fish out of water, gasping. Suddenly, I needed her touch so I could breathe. "It feels like a volcano is erupting in me," I said, unable to claw myself back from the flames of her overwhelming presence that had engulfed me.

She flashed me a smile, then released herself from my arms. "Take it easy, Lover Boy. It's just one date."

"No, it can't be just one date," I said, then pulled her back into me and wrapped my arms around her to prevent every organ in me from shifting out of place. "Someday, when you are my girlfriend, we'll walk down to the beach, and we'll lie on the shore until the sun comes up," I said, hardly able to control the involuntary movement sweeping through me.

"Aren't you a bit presumptuous? Girlfriend? What makes you think I want to be your girlfriend?" she asked, giving me the side-eye.

"My heart says you will be, and it's never wrong. It's telling me that someday soon, you'll be my girlfriend. I can feel it, and I'm sure you feel it, too." I placed her left hand on my chest so she could feel the effects she was having on me.

The sound of the ocean swelled around us and became paralyzing. She rested her head against me, and I inhaled her seductive fragrance. I gently lifted her face, caressed her lips, and pulled her into me. I rubbed my nose against her nose, then moved in for my first kiss. Again, there was the magnetic pull as my tongue gently touched her lips. Her sweet strawberry breath tickled my nostrils and stimulated my already sensitive nerves.

I had wanted to kiss her since the day I met her downtown. As our lips pressed tightly against each other, I heard the throbbing of her heart, and I groaned as if I were a nerd kissing the prom queen. I held her tight, and she grabbed me tighter, igniting the flutters crawling under my skin and radiating throughout my body. I curved my arms around her, slightly lifting her off the ground.

Her fingers clutched my shirt. They felt like they had flints sparking from them.

The ocean roared again, and my entire body shivered. But not from the chill of the night air but from her lips on mine. I had been fighting the urge all night, afraid not to overstep. I already knew how it felt to want her. I never imagined it would be this intoxicating to kiss her.

"What just happened?" she asked, biting into her upper lip, slowly backed away, and then sprinted toward the edge of my garden as if trying to escape the feelings I had awakened in her.

"I felt the earth quaked too, V," I said as I hurried behind her. "That's how it feels when two people belong together. Please don't run away from me."

"I think it's the wave. It did something to me. It's been doing ungodly things to me since I moved here," V said, burying her face into her hands as if unfamiliar feelings erupted inside her from our kiss.

"Nah, that's not it." I pulled her back into me. "I think you know the train has left the station. There is no turning back now, V," I said, caressing her cheek.

"I can't," she protested.

"Please don't fight it. If you do, the feeling will eat us alive. Don't let me beg. I've never had to," I said.

My heart pounded, the sensation spreading all over me. It was as if every emotion was escaping at once, and I didn't know how to control them so I wouldn't cross the line. I wasn't used to feeling this way, ever.

My fall for Vivienne Pearson was complete. It was as if I dropped sixty feet into the padded arms of the girl I pursued relentlessly, and I was hooked, like a Red Snapper.

The tranquilizing sound of the ocean waves and her warm embrace did it. I finally wore her down to kiss me.

"Sorry, I didn't mean to be so clingy," she said, brushing her hair out of her face as she pulled away again.

"Don't be. The same thing happened to me the first time I saw you, and I haven't been the same since."

"This was not what I had in mind when I agreed to take you out of your misery, Jonathan."

"You mean you didn't think you'd fall for me?" I asked playfully. I lifted her off the ground and rubbed my nose against the edge of hers. "You can't go back now. You wouldn't want to be responsible for breaking my heart. Would you?"

"I'm starting to believe you planned this. You know what kind of effects the ocean waves would have on me. That's why you brought me here."

"I brought you here because I couldn't spend one more day without you, and yes, hoping to convince you to be my girl." I kissed her again. This time, with less nerves and more passion. I wrapped one arm around her waist and curved the other under her armpits, and our heartbeats synchronized.

"This is our first date and may be the only one. I cannot afford to rush into a relationship with you. To be your girlfriend after just one date would be unwise," she said after I let go of her lips. "Whatever you think is happening between us, sex cannot be the result tonight. Can you please take me home?" she asked.

I reluctantly loosened my arms, took her hands, and led her down the hill. I was disappointed the night was ending, but if she'd stayed longer, there was no telling what else might have happened between us.

I kissed her goodnight and watched her close the burglar bars behind her. I stood in the middle of the road, alone in the dark. I could still feel her lips on mine. I slapped my hand against my forehead, trying to calm the war that had broken out inside me. I didn't want her to go. She had unearthed feelings in me that I didn't even know existed.

Chapter 11

Throwing Shade

Vivienne

I was beginning to develop unfamiliar emotions whenever I was in Jonathan's company, and the vibes he let off were forcing me to take a chance on him. On the surface, he looked like the guy my parents would approve of. He was tall, dark, well-dressed, courteous, and handsome. Just the type of guy Jasmine had been daydreaming about since we were in grade nine.

But with my childhood trauma etched in my parents' minds, I doubt any man would have an easy time waltzing in on my arm, posing as my boyfriend. But I couldn't shake the feeling that underneath Jonathan's good looks and charm, there was a hidden secret no one was willing to talk about. I wasn't eager to ask my brother about him. He would follow me around like he did when we lived in Greenspring. I didn't want that. I didn't want him hovering over me like a helicopter.

Everybody treated Jonathan like he was a god or something, not to be spoken ill about, as if he would banish them from the city.

I arrived at the souvenir store a little earlier than usual to prepare for the Monday morning rush, when tourists stormed the store for one last-minute shopping spree before boarding their ship or plane.

I hurried towards the door, and there was Jonathan with his winning smile and hypnotic eyes. "I thought you had enough of me, Jonathan," I said as I approached him. "How much longer are you planning to show up at my job? You asked me for only one date. Why are you still coming here?"

"Not true. You promised me a trip to Ocho Rios. Have you changed your mind?"

"Your relentless pursuit of me will have to end at some point. You can't keep coming here. People will start to spread rumors about us."

"Let them. I'm used to people making up stories about me anyway," he laughed. "I need to hear you say you'll come with me to Dunn's River Falls."

"And if I don't?"

"I'll just have to have a conversation with Sean."

"You wouldn't dare." I smiled and rolled my eyes at him. "Bye, Jonathan," I said.

"I'm not giving up, V," he said, giving me a quick kiss on the cheek before he jumped in his car.

When I arrived inside the store, I began stacking the showcases with new products, filling the shelves with beach towels, sandals, sunglasses, and sunscreen. Donna hung large straw hats on the rack in the corner. I opened the window to let in the cool breeze from the ocean, just a couple of steps away.

Summer was in full swing, and Gloucester Avenue bubbled with excitement. Tourists were shopping, sunbathing, bumping, and grinding or barhopping along the strip, with grifters on their heels, trying to be their tour guides as they hustled for their next meal. I had little time to pay attention to the men who whistled at me. I focused more on the tourists who walked through the doors to find souvenirs, sought shelter from the sweltering heat, or listened to the reggae beat that blasted inside the store.

They'd dance to the amplified sounds of Burning Spear, Bob Marley, Dennis Brown, and Peter Tosh, trying to get a feel of the island vibes. Others searched for a hustler to sell them ganja while they sported their big cigars and paraphernalia, puffing thick smoke into the air. Rasta-man vibrations were everywhere.

Tourists swarmed the beach behind the store. White sand lodged in their wrinkles and bikinis or covered their bodies while sunbathing under umbrellas, sipping margaritas, piña coladas, martinis, or a cold Red Stripe Beer. Others nibbled on jerked chicken and oxtail. Half-drunk and semi-nude, they scattered along the crowded beach. Such a sight would be overwhelming for an ordinary young girl, much less one from the country. It was a lot for me to see. I couldn't get used to seeing the old and young nude bodies lying on the sand.

The locals' livelihoods depended on the tourists who descended on the island. They had come by boat or plane from all over the world: America, Canada, England, Spain, and as far away as Australia. Cruise ships sailed into the harbors and flooded Montego Bay with lovers, adventure seekers, and destination hoppers. Hookers on the loose on their heels, prowling in their skimpy clothes and six-inch boots. The ladies of the night, they called themselves. They pounced on drunken sailors or adventure seekers.

Against that backdrop, I must navigate what my father called a den of iniquity and come out unscathed. I had begun to think it might not be possible after all.

Now, with Jonathan in the mix, sweet-talking me, God help me.

Chapter 12

Knight Rider

Jonathan

On August 6, Independence Day had finally arrived, and at ten o'clock, the temperature had soared to eighty-five degrees, which was considered cool compared to the average ninety-eight degrees.

I wrapped Vivienne around my heart so tight I no longer had eyes for the girls gushing over me.

My heart throbbed as I rode up at her gate on my Kawasaki. How would I explain to Sean that I was there to take his sister to another parish? No one had ever accused me of being anything but solid, yet here I was, crumbling at the thought of getting into a fight over a girl I couldn't stop thinking about because her brother might think I was not worthy of her.

I soon realized I had a bigger problem.

"Jonathan Hastings! That was you?" V screamed as she approached me, looking like she had seen a ghost. The light slowly faded from her eyes, and my heart sank. I should have told her sooner that I was the one who had rescued her from Pastor Nate. I had always needed to disguise myself. I wasn't sure it would come at a cost this time. "Were you ever planning to tell me you were my 'knight?'" Her air quotes on Knight made me think twice about what I'd say next.

"As soon as you tell me how you ended up being chased by Pastor Nate," I said.

"I hope you know I'm not riding to Ochi on that thing." She pouted.

"That's the same 'thing' that saved you from Nate," I replied in air quotes with a chuckle. "Was that the first time you rode on a bike? No wonder you almost squeezed life out of me. Everyone I know has ridden on a bike, whether it was a small Honda or one like mine." It was a rite of passage for boys, and most girls loved the ride.

But not Vivienne. Convincing her that a bike ride was safe was like arguing over religion, an argument I couldn't win.

"That night, I was desperate. I'm not riding with you to Ochi!" She was emphatic. "So, take that thing back and get your car. Otherwise, *Bon Voyage.*" She waved me off.

"I pictured the wind in your hair and your arms wrapped around me. I like the way you make me feel with your arms around me." I smiled, leaned back, and tucked my hands under my armpits. "Please ride with me, I have my heart set on it, V."

"You will zigzag your way from Ironshore to Ocho Rios. There's no way I'm riding on that thing with you, Jonathan." She rolled her eyes at me.

"It's not like I'm riding an old jalopy. The ride is smooth and safe. Don't you trust me?"

"Trust you? Not when you show up on this...thing." She thrust her hand forward. "Is that something you regularly do? You are a regular damsel rescuer, aren't you? Or maybe the neighborhood stalker."

"If you don't trust that I could never hurt you, ask your brother about me. I'll ride off into the sunset if he tells you I'm dangerous. It would shatter my heart into fragments. Ride with me, V. I have been riding since I was a boy."

"What's going on?" Sean asked as soon as he came outside. The back and forth between V and me drew his attention.

"What's up, Sean?" I greeted him with a fist bump, trying to hide the discomfort on my face. Telling him I liked his sister would take more courage than I could muster. The good news was that Sean knew me well enough to put Vivienne's mind at ease about the ride. The bad news was that Sean knew me well enough to break up any relationship between V and me.

"Well, I guess you need no introduction," V said. "You know that run with the madman I told you about, Sean? Well, I just found out that Mr. Hastings happened to be the one who saved me from him. What are the odds that my good old Knight happens to be my date and your friend?" Her voice dripped with sarcasm.

"I should have said something sooner," I said.

"Did you tell him to shadow me or be my bodyguard, Sean? Is this your way of telling me I'm not mature enough to live in the city?"

Sean was not afraid to give you a piece of his mind or his fist. He said what he meant and meant every word. Although he usually said them without as much as a hint of anger.

"No, I didn't ask him to shadow you."

"She doesn't want to ride with me. I am trying to convince her that it's safe. But I'm not sure I'll be able to. Tell her there is nothing to worry about," I said.

Sean moved closer to V and put his arm around her shoulder. "Come on, Sis. You've seen me ride before. Danielle rode on them over a hundred times. Try it; it's the coolest thing ever," he said.

"Maybe it's cool to you, but I'm not about to risk my life for the thrill of a bike ride." She folded her arms and stiffened her lips. "He is not even wearing a helmet. That is so irresponsible. Please don't encourage him."

"You are looking for a way out of going to Ochi," I said. "Here is your helmet. I will put mine on soon." I handed her a red hard hat, the same color as the bike.

"If you feel uncomfortable after a mile, he will take you back but try it. I am sure you will love it," Sean told her.

The war that should have happened after he found out I was dating his sister was premature. Sean seemed cool with me taking her to Ochi.

"When the ride becomes uncomfortable, I am getting off, even if I have to jump in the middle of the road," V said with another pout.

"If it becomes too much, I will rent a car. But I was hoping you could ride with me. Jump on."

"I left my bag inside. I will be right back. And we need to talk about the madman some more. How you just happened to be there," V said, then ran to the house.

The weight of Sean's eyes bore down on me as soon as she left—the moment I dreaded. There was no pretending, especially since he knew everything I had been too scared to tell V.

"So, you and my sister, ah?" He shook his head, and my heart skipped a beat. I was sure he would tell me there was no chance in Hell he'd let me date his sister. I had too much baggage. "Judging from Viv's refusal to discuss you with me, I assume you haven't told her who you are. When she told me Jonathan Hastings asked her to the movies, I told Danielle there was no way it could be you; it must be some other guy. But the odds of two guys in Montego Bay with the same name had to be a million to one."

"Sean, I like her, please," I pleaded, clutching my chest.

"Jonathan Hastings, that's my sister! There will not be a happy ending to your relationship. You know that. Besides your name, what have you told her about you? Who are you pretending to be?"

"We're just…" I couldn't find the words to tell him what he needed to hear.

"Yeah, yeah, yeah. But have you told her who you are? I don't need you to stutter. She needs to know what she's getting herself into. You are not going to mess with my sister's head."

"I haven't told her yet. I am afraid that if I do, I might not stand a chance with her. I cannot risk that."

Sean looked up at me from the ground. He had been pretending to inspect my bike to hide his discontent with my interest in Vivienne. "Let me get this straight. You, the powerful, fearless Jonathan Hastings, afraid of my little sister? That doesn't make sense and is not a good enough reason. At what point is it okay for you to tell her? Either you'll tell her, I tell her, or she hears it from some chatterbox down the street, but she must know who you are. If you wait for her to hear from someone else, you will not have another date with her."

"Don't you think I know that? I can't tell her just yet."

"My father begged me to keep her safe. I'm not leaving that up to you unless you are honest with her. Whoever she chooses to be with is up to her, but I will protect her with my life." He took a deep breath, his eyes narrowed to me. "I'm going to ask you for three favors," he said.

Breaking up with the most beautiful girl I'd ever met because her brother said so, would be a challenge, and Sean knew me better than to think I'd back down from a challenge. But I didn't want to make him angry. We respected each other, but a fight over his sister was one I was willing to have.

"She cannot be your plaything. You must make sure she is always safe, and you must tell her who you are. No more delays, no deceit, and the minute you make her cry, I'll be on you so fast, your head will spin. I don't care that you are a Hastings, hurt her, and I'll forget all that," he said.

I exhaled. I was relieved that the conditions for dating his sister were straightforward. I had expected him to tell me there was no way he would allow me to date her, not after what had happened with my last girlfriend.

"Of course, I'll keep her safe. I promise you, Sean, she is not a plaything. This is real for me, and I will tell her who I am when the time is right. You have my word on that."

"There is no right time. Do you think people will wait for you to tell her before they blab? If you take her out in public, they will see you, and then it's not up to you anymore. She's not prepared enough to date someone like you."

"She's stronger than you think. That's why it's been eating me alive. I'm afraid to tell her, man."

Coming clean to Vivienne paralyzed me every time I tried. Since meeting her, I'd been too scared to tell her there was more to me than the guy she thought she met by chance. I tried several ways, and in my head, it ended with her leaving each time. I couldn't take that risk. Vivienne was the girl I wanted to take home to meet my parents. And fighting with Sean was not one I could get over in a week or so.

"I hear you," I said. His warnings stung me.

"Like I said, I know my sister better than you. Tell her who you are before you force me to do so. If she finds out from someone else, I guarantee you will never see her again. I'm giving you one week to come clean to her."

***

An hour later, Vivienne and I were in Ochi. Dunn's River Falls was our first stop. We joined the long line outside the gate. Beyond the security booth, adventure awaited us. I was a happy-go-lucky guy; hardly a dull moment around me.

Deep pockets of water covering Vivienne were nestled between the rocks on the 600-foot-long waterfall. We waded in and locked our lips before climbing the falls.

Water splashed in our faces as it gushed over the protruding rocks we used for easy climbing. Halfway up Dunn's River Falls, I hitched a safety harness onto the zip line and glided with her onto the beach two hundred and fifty feet below. Her screams rang in my ears and clogged it for the next five minutes.

We returned to finish climbing the falls, exploring what made it a magnet for tourists and locals alike. We ditched our plan to go to Puerto Seco Beach and settled for the one a few hundred feet below the falls.

Vivienne battled with the giant waves that washed against us as we lay on the shore. I smiled as she struggled to keep them from pulling her underwater. As we sat on the beach, she clutched her cheeks, then covered her eyes, and peered through her fingers at the jet skis that whisked by.

"There's something I have to tell you, V," I yelled over the roars of the giant waves barreling toward us.

"What! I can't hear you!" she shouted, falling on her back as the waves pushed her over. I grabbed her and collapsed onto the sand, preventing the waves from taking her with them. I wrapped my arms around her, flipped her on top of me, and wiped the water from her face.

"What did you want to tell me?" she asked over the chaos of the water trying to swallow everyone on the shore.

My heart felt like it had pumped a million beats in the last minute as I wrapped my hands tightly around her. She lowered her head and kissed me, and warm, tiny particles spread throughout my body, consuming me like wildfire.

"Never mind," I said, not wanting to let go of her or the feeling to subside. "We can talk about it another time," I said between kisses.

Telling her my story would have to wait. I couldn't afford to let the waves or the revelation of who I was get in the way of kissing her.

She raised her head and stared at me. Questions were plastered on her face, but I couldn't answer them then. I couldn't tell her the most important thing about the man she was falling in love with. There was no way she could pretend with that much emotion.

She pressed her lips onto mine, kissing me without reservation. She locked her fingers through mine, spreading my hands above my head. I moaned softly and welcomed her lips fervently.

I closed my eyes and whispered, "V. unless you plan for me to take you right here right now, I think you better stop kissing me."

"Do you want me to stop?" she asked teasingly, squeezing my palms with hers.

I stiffened my body and dug my toes into the wet sand. "Oh, God, no. But we have to, otherwise, they will kick us out of here."

I wrapped my legs around her and rolled onto my side, bringing her with me.

After a good ten minutes, I dragged my body off the sand and pulled her onto her feet.

"Come with me," I said, then ran toward the beach shop. "Let's get one of those." I pointed at the wall.

"Surfboard? Jonathan, no. It's not safe out there," she said.

"What are you talking about? It's the best time to surf. Look at those giant waves."

"I can't watch you risk your life trying to impress me. Your stunts are making me nervous. Please don't go out there," she pleaded. "I've never met anyone who is as determined to kill himself. I hope you're not doing it to impress me, so cut it out."

"You like me." I tickled her. "Look at you; your face is red," I said, remembering the first day I introduced myself. There was no doubt in my mind that I impressed her that day, as hard as she tried to hide it, regardless of all the pushbacks she gave me, which were harsh and sometimes downright offensive. No other girl had ever challenged or questioned my sincerity like she did.

"Don't flatter yourself. I don't want to bear witness when you hurt yourself," she said.

I laughed, unable to contain my glee. "Nah, that's not it. Vivienne Pearson is in love with me." I lifted her off the ground and kissed her.

She clutched my cheeks. "Someone must watch out for you, even if you seem to have a death wish. I'm sure your parents want you around longer."

"Are you sure you don't want me to go out there?"

She shook her head vigorously. "Please don't go out there," she begged. "I can have as much fun just dipping my toes in the water. You don't have to jump off a pier or out of a helicopter. I'm already impressed with you. You're a one-in-a-million kind of guy. I wouldn't come this far with just anyone."

"Well, since you say you love me, I won't go out there," I teased.

"You wish." She poked me.

I pressed my lips hard against her lips, then stared into the eyes that captivated me that first day I saw her as if I was committing her face to memory. "Someday, I'll hear you say you love me. Until then, I'll settle for a swim. So, let's go. You're not coming this far to dip your toes in the water."

I ran with her towards the clear blue water roaring onto the shore. I held onto V as our bodies surfed the waves fifty feet out into the deep.

"Jonathan, I can't swim!"

Chapter 13

Big Brother

Vivienne

I woke up before dawn and headed downstairs to the kitchen. It was my day to feed the family. Sean barely said two words to me since I returned from Ocho Rios, which was strange. It was not like him to give me the silent treatment. He was known to go dark on people who offended him, so it made me think he wasn't thrilled about me dating Jonathan after all.

Sean walked in after I was done making breakfast—the perfect opportunity to talk. I had two bones to pick with him, but I didn't know which one to start with. There was an eleven-year-old assault he deliberately hid from me. Yet, somehow, I wasn't as angry with him as I should have been.

"Why didn't you tell me you know Jonathan?" I pulled my soapy hands from the kitchen sink and leaned against the counter. It turned out I wasn't comfortable dredging up the most horrific time of my life.

I dried my hands on the towel hanging on the oven door and faced him. The golden-brown fried dumplings were covered on the stovetop, and the steamed callaloo with codfish was just about done. They were sitting on top of the burner, steam spewing from the slightly opened lid. Sean liked the scrumptiousness of the dumplings as he sunk his teeth into the softcore after he picked one from the container. It was the way our mother made them. I didn't mind being the designated chef on Sunday mornings. It made me feel useful, even if my contribution to his household was minor.

Sean looked at me like he was in no mood for conversation. He was more focused on the food.

"Jonathan Hastings?" He gave me a side eye, brushing the crusts off his fingertips.

I wasn't expecting that reaction. Things were supposed to be cool between Jonathan and Sean. They knew each other well. But now, his drag on the name Hastings with the questionable frown made me think he wasn't so thrilled about us being together.

It was one thing to scare off the boys back home when I was younger. It's quite another at eighteen. I would have to push back at my big brother objecting to me dating Jonathan unless he was a danger to me.

Sean led me outside onto the veranda as if to give me a stern talk. I was not prepared for that kind of reaction either.

"Viv, what do you know about Jonathan? Better yet, what did he tell you about himself?" he asked, folding his arm above his chest as he leaned against the rail. His bare foot rested against the veranda wall. He had a "not over my dead body" look.

"Is he married?" I asked immediately, beating him to the punch.

"You need to give me more credit. You think I'd let you date a married man?" He brushed his right hand over his forehead.

"Then what is it? You don't seem pleased. The look on your face scares me. It's as if you want to warn me about him. Is he a criminal or a womanizer? What is Jonathan not telling me, Sean?" I had become impatient.

"Jonathan needs to tell you himself," he said, refusing to look at me, a dead giveaway he was hiding something.

"So, you're not going to tell me? Then why did you bring me out here as if I'm one of your daughters you want to scold for drinking out of the milk carton?" I furrowed my brows and folded my arms across my chest.

He seemed unsure of what to say.

"Jonathan is..." He stopped himself and squeezed his eyes shut.

"Jonathan is what, Sean?" I yelled at him.

He took a deep breath and walked over to where I sat on the long veranda chair, growing more frustrated. He rested his hand on my shoulder. "There will be no fairy tale ending for you and Jonathan," he said softly.

"I'm taking him to Greenspring next weekend," I said. "Since you are unwilling to tell me what you know about him, I see no reason not to."

"If you're going to continue to date him, I may not be able to stop you. But you can't say I didn't warn you. I hope you know what you're getting yourself into."

"I don't know what I'm getting into, Sean!" I snapped. "You seemed unable to talk to me about important things, just like what happened in Dallas. Yes, the memories did come back. Instead of talking to me like an adult, you teamed up with our parents to keep me in the dark. Being with Jonathan helps me to forget what happened to me. I don't have to think about that day with him. But if you tell me not to see him anymore, I won't, because I trust you that much. Should I end my relationship with Jonathan? Now is the only chance I'll give you to tell me what you know about him. You don't get another. It will take one phone call, and he and I will be over."

Sean let out a nervous laugh, then took another deep breath. "No, Viv, girls don't easily get over Jonathan, and it won't be any easier for you. Jonathan Hastings needs to tell you who he is, and when he does, I'll be here if you need me," he said, tucking his hands inside his pockets as he walked back into the living room.

Now, I was mad at my brother for making me doubt myself. If he thought I made a mistake getting involved with Jonathan, why wouldn't he say so? And what's with the 'girls don't get over Jonathan' crap he warned me about? It couldn't be good if he thought I would need him after Jonathan told me who he was.

My brother forced me to re-evaluate my feelings for the most drop-dead gorgeous, sophisticated, loving man I had ever known. Granted, I didn't have any other to compare him to, but Sean was either testing my commitment or setting me up for disappointment. And the Sean I grew up with would never put me in such a precarious situation. Since he didn't demand I end my relationship, I was determined to keep seeing Jonathan.

Chapter 14

Enter the Jungle

Vivienne

Jonathan and I were coming off a high from our getaway to Ocho Rios when I took him to meet my parents, determined to cram in all the fun before the summer ended while I shoved Sean's warnings to the back of my mind.

"My Lord!" he screamed. His eyes shifted from left to right. "You come from out of the jungle, V. This place is totally off the grid." His jaw dropped. His car rocked from side to side, struggling to get through the small boulders in his path. It was the first time he had driven on unpaved roads.

He peered through the car window, trying to capture the mile-long journey through my village. He seemed to have yet to learn about places like Greenspring. The clustered trees in this rugged community, with its scenic beauty, littered with wildlife, and the sounds of swallow-tail hummingbirds fascinated him.

"You make it seem like you landed on Earth yesterday. There's no way you didn't know there are people who want to preserve the environment and not chop down every tree in the name of modernization. The people here are humble and believe we live longer when our air and water are clean. Ten years longer than those in the city was the latest estimate," I told him.

"Then how do you explain how you dress?" he asked. "I would never have guessed you came from here. You certainly do not dress like a country girl."

"What does a country girl look like? We like to look our best, you know. Living here does not prevent us from having nice things."

"I don't think your parents will like me very much. They'll take one look at me and think I'm no good for their only daughter. You should have warned me. I would have dressed more appropriately. First impressions are lasting, and I can't afford for them to think I'm no good for you," he said.

After we exited the car, I took Jonathan's hand, wove my fingers through his, and headed toward my house. "Well, my parents know how to spot a fake, so if you'd like to turn back now, I wouldn't hold it against you. Not everyone is brave enough to tell my father they'd like to date his baby girl."

"You should have warned me, V."

"Well, brave heart, it's too late to turn back now." I smiled at him. "Lighten up. My parents will love you. And if at first, they don't, I'm sure you'll pull out your irresistible charm. You're good at that."

"Do you think I should have brought them a gift?"

"Why? They are humble, not greedy." I rubbed his arm to calm him. "Relax, don't be nervous. My father is like a bloodhound who can smell fear from a mile away. You are a little over-dressed, but you'll be fine if you relax."

"I blame you. You should have prepared me better."

"You've never met a girl's parents before? Stop pretending as if you are a virgin, chosen for sacrifice."

"That's exactly how I feel."

He exhaled, then smiled at me as we landed at the top of the steps to my house.

My dad stood at the entrance to the living room, waiting for us to arrive. "Come here, baby girl. I missed you." He pulled me in for a minute-long hug.

He then turned to Jonathan. "Welcome to our home." He smiled and shook his hand with vigor.

"Thanks for having me, Sir. You have a lovely home," Jonathan said as he surveyed the modest structure.

"Jonathan, come inside." My mom beckoned to him after she pulled me out of my father's arms for a hug. "Relax, feel at home." She led him into the living room. "I'm Cecille, Viv's mother. Nice to finally meet you, Son. Viv told us so much about you. It is nice to put the name to a face finally."

"It's truly an honor to be here, Ma'am. The drive was utterly amazing coming up."

"You haven't seen anything yet. I'm sure Viv will give you a tour later. You won't want to leave here," she said.

"I'd love a tour." He smiled at me. "I'm yet to do any of the things kids usually do. I have never climbed a tree or gone birdwatching or anything like that."

"And you are not about to start today. Well, maybe bird watching," I said.

"You didn't tell me your mother was white," he whispered.

I held his hand and squeezed it. "Is that a problem?" I whispered.

"Oh God, no, V. I didn't know, that's all."

"Then stop whispering. It will make her uncomfortable."

When we entered the living room, the aroma of my mother's curried chicken smacked me. Preparing a meal was one of the things she loved to do whenever I visited.

Jonathan's eyes roamed with amazement. "I've never been so up close to nature. Look at those Iguanas hanging from tree branches. He peered out the window. "Wow, those big black crows, I've never seen birds that big," Jonathan said. "I'm falling in love with the countryside, V."

I smiled at Jonathan's newfound love for my village, and by the end of the visit, he was already making plans for his next. Since my spat with Sean over Jonathan, I hadn't allowed myself to doubt my feelings for him, and as I watched the man who captivated me marvel at my home, I was sure he couldn't be all bad.

I had already convinced myself that if Jonathan was a danger to me, there was no way my brother wouldn't move heaven and earth to stop the relationship. So, I took comfort in knowing that what Jonathan and I had was real, and nothing could make me change my mind about him.

I was hooked on his presence, handsome face, kindness, tenderness, and the unusual ways he said my name. And his magnetic eyes, I did not want anyone or anything to take them away from me.

****

Two weeks later, we returned. Jonathan was determined to climb to the top of the fifty-foot mountain. He was a risk-taking city boy who was not afraid of the ruggedness of the countryside. We found the perfect spot to watch the sunset. The tailored suits he usually wore didn't tell me much about who he was, but he came prepared for the exploration.

"The view is amazing from here, V," he said, proud of himself as if he deserved a gold medal after the climb.

I smiled at him and locked my fingers between his fingers, taking in the spectacular view while describing everything as far as our eyes could see. He smiled and rubbed his hand over the back of my hand.

Below the mountain, the river flowed through the meadow and spanned miles, ending in the ocean five miles away. The fish below the clear water's surface were perfect for a postcard. A hundred feet further down from where we sat, a four-foot body of water was warm to the touch, like nature's spa, beckoning us to jump in.

We moved down the river to the boundaries of Greenspring and Ridge Mount Hills, running through the wide-open spaces of the grassland and taking time to eat mangoes, apples, or jelly coconuts. It felt like we were in the Garden of Eden.

Chapter 15

Greenspring

Jonathan

Greenspring may have been a jungle to those in the outside world, but its natural beauty was a hidden treasure that belonged on a postcard.

The sunlight flickered off the water's edge, descending behind the hills, creating a glowing sunset backdrop. I lay next to V and reveled in the spectacle. We were inseparable. Two hearts, one love, seemed like a match made in Heaven.

"I will marry you one day, V. I'm sure of it." I stroked the strands of hair that hung down her face, pushed them away from her eye and off to the side, gently brushed my thumb over her lips, then kissed her softly.

"Marriage is serious stuff. It would help if you were not so cavalier with throwing it around," she said.

"I'm old enough to know when I've found the one for me. In my heart, I know that you are the one." I raised myself off the grass and hovered over her, forcing her to look into my eyes.

"I'm a free spirit, Jonathan. It'll be at least a decade before I become anyone's wife, if ever, so you might want to run away now."

"There is no doubt in my mind. Soon, you'll be Mrs. Hastings and, with God's blessings, the mother of my seven children." My light kiss on her lips sealed my declaration.

"Seven kids! Whatever do you mean, kind Sir?" she scoffed. The seven kids had just sunk in. "Why stop at seven?"

"Ten?" I chuckled, knowing she would freak out over my plan for the size of our family.

"Well, I'm glad you find that funny. You can search for the love of your life willing to bear your seven to ten kids."

She snuggled up to me again, bracing against my chest. Her knees crossed. I ran my hand through her hair, brushed it away from her face, and kissed the top of her head.

"Not long ago, Jasmine and I argued whether there was such a thing as soulmates," she continued. "She constantly daydreams that the love of her life is around the corner, coming to sweep her off her feet at any minute. She thinks I'm crazy to think that's a myth. Is that who we are?"

"I've been trying to tell you that since we met, V," I said sincerely. "Since I met you, I haven't thought about anyone else. The more you ignored me, the deeper my feelings became. You have not left my mind for a minute. Yes, you and I are meant to be together." I wrapped my hands around her, gently rocking her from side to side.

"You believe there is one special person for everyone?"

"I saw you the day you moved into your brother's house. From that day, I knew you were the one for me. I couldn't go up to Sean and ask him for you."

"Jonathan, you know I'm not from the city. Is there anything you're not telling me? Sometimes I get a bad vibe about you. For some reason, a cloud of suspicion won't go away. Why?" She spun around and faced me.

I took a deep breath. "There's something you ought to know about me." I held her hand, locking my fingers with hers when the smile disappeared from her face. It should not have been this hard, but Sean's warnings nagged me and stuck in the forefront of my mind since the day we went to Dunn's River Falls.

"If you let her find out from someone else, she will look for the exits," he had warned. Since then, I had dreaded the day Sean's prediction would come true.

Vivienne gently pulled her hand out of mine. "You're making me nervous," she said, eyeing me suspiciously. Her smile turned into sadness I had never seen. I rested my arms on the grass, pulled up my right knee, thrust my head backward, and sighed. "Jonathan!" she snapped, bringing me back into focus. "Who the hell are you, and why can't I get a straight answer from anyone about you? Do you even have a job?"

If only you knew how much courage I need right now.

"Vivienne." I sighed again, struggling for the words to come off my tongue.

"There is no way you could dress like this. Drive around like you own the damn place and do not have a job. Unless." She narrowed her eyes to me. The sparks had long disappeared from them. "Are you a drug—"

I cut her off before she could finish her question. "Heard of a little place called the Hideaway Resorts?" The drug dealer label was not the brand I needed.

"Should I? I'm a country girl, remember?"

"I work there." From the corner of my eyes, I waited for her reaction, dreading what would happen next. But keeping my identity from her for as long as I did create the self-inflicted tension. "My family owns Hideaway Resorts, V," I said reluctantly.

"Hideaway, Hideaway, Hide-a-way." She stroked her chin as if trying to remember why the name sounded familiar. "Do you mean Hideaway, Hideaway? One of the biggest resorts in Jamaica? That Hideaway? No way. It can't be. Can it?" She leaned into me.

I hung my head, waiting for the moment she'd freak out. It hadn't hit her quite just yet. "But that's where Sean works. That would make you my brother's boss?" She pointed at me. "You owned those resorts, Jonathan?"

"My family, not me," I said cautiously, as if that was supposed to make a difference.

"You didn't think you should have said something to me about that little nugget of your life?"

"Like what, V?" I pulled my head forward, knowing how this would end.

"How about, I don't know, welcome to Montego Bay, Beautiful? Do you want to date a millionaire? You conveniently left off the last part. My God, Jonathan, you deceived me. You are an heir, for God's sake."

"Be serious. No sane person would say that, and I didn't deceive you."

"What would you call it!" Her voice rose as she flung her arms in frustration. "You certainly don't trust me, that's for sure. If I didn't ask, I would be running behind you like a blind fool without a clue. I'm quite sure everyone in Montego Bay knows you. Everyone except me. I am just a country bumpkin you happen to stalk."

I wanted to hold her close and beg for forgiveness. I could have avoided what was happening if I had heeded Sean's advice. "Vivienne, please."

"Don't Vivienne me!" She grabbed her backpack to leave. "For you to take this long to tell me that your family owns a chain of resorts on the island means you don't trust me. Oh. My. God! Wow!" she chuckled nervously. "It can't be. You and I cannot be a thing.

"Jonathan Hastings, in my backyard? So why haven't I seen you with your Entourage? How did I not recognize you as the precious future head of Hideaway Resorts, who runs the entire chain? Isn't that what they say?" V's sarcastic jab pierced me.

"You're blowing things out of proportion. I don't run the resorts," I said, my feeble attempt to calm her.

"You don't want to split hairs with me now. The less you say, the better. You strung me along for so long, and it never dawned on you to tell me who you are. That's dishonesty on its face."

"Strung you along? Come on, V. I told Sean I'd find the right time to tell you. And this is exactly why I didn't sooner." I took a deep breath. "When we first met, you told me you didn't know me, and I was relieved. I thought you wouldn't have a preconceived notion of who I was. That is why I am always at ease with you. I can be myself with you and not think I'd be judged. But here we are, judging me, and I don't know why my family offends you so much."

"You took me gallivanting all over the country. You had many opportunities to tell me that you damn near own the entire island. You dragged this out because you don't trust me. I will have to re-evaluate this pretense we have going. I'm a laughingstock." She buried her face in her hands. "Oh no, this can't be happening to me."

"I didn't mean to deceive you," I said. I was not prepared for that kind of reaction. Granted, Sean did warn me, but I didn't listen.

"You know everything about my family from day one. You stalked, caught, wined, and dined me for an entire month, yet you couldn't find one moment to tell me the most significant thing about yourself?"

"We were having so much fun." My heart was breaking, and Vivienne no longer had the smile I had come to adore. It was the first time she had looked at me with disappointment. "The day we went to Dunn's River, Sean told me to tell you who I was. I couldn't find the right time."

"You mean the guts." She cut her eyes at me.

"It would take more than one conversation to tell you my story, and I didn't want to have to rush. If it makes any difference, I regret not telling you sooner."

"That's what you were trying to tell me?"

"Yes," I said, hoping she'd see I didn't mean to deceive her.

"You didn't try hard enough!" she fired back. "So, that makes you how old, Jonathan, ah? You look twentyish, but with you, nothing is what it seems. You could be in your fifties for all I know."

"…. Twenty-two," I said reluctantly. V still held resentment with the fifty-year-old comment.

"My God, you are a twenty-two-year-old heir? Did Sean tell you how old I am?"

"No, but I'm not a fool. I can tell you're not a kid. If you were, I'd be in deep trouble," I said.

How could I forget to ask how old she was? Could I have been so taken in by her beauty and appearance of maturity that I didn't think she might not be old enough to date? The last thing I wanted was for her to tell me she was underage. My heart raced, and my mind was a whirlwind of anxiety.

"I'll leave you to ponder how much trouble you put yourself in. You dug this hole yourself. You didn't think I should know that you are a rich, entitled brat, hoping that a silly country girl like me would fall for your charms," she said, her voice tinged with a mix of anger and disappointment.

She gazed up at the flock of birds as they flew over her head, tightening her grip on the straps of her backpack. She was serious about leaving me to find my way back to her house, her resolve unyielding.

"Come on, drop this country-girl routine. Please be reasonable. You don't believe that."

"You want to tell me what I believe now? Just answer me this. How long did you give yourself before you moved on to your next unsuspecting victim? Would it be right after you defile me?"

"Why are you talking like this?"

"I always wonder why you stalked me, and now I've gotten my answer. I was just a damn catch to you." She stomped her feet, then snarled at me. "Did you put a bet on me when I'd give it up?"

"I will not dignify that with an answer, Viv. Just tell me how old you are," I pleaded.

"You don't get to call me that! You are not the man I thought you were, and I'm beyond disappointed right now."

"How old are you, Vivienne Pearson?" I asked again. This time, more politely.

"I think you should figure that out on your own. Or better yet, why not call Sean and ask him? He should know whether you are dating his underage sister."

"Sean offered to tell you, but I told him you should hear it from me."

"Isn't that rather convenient?" she said, her voice oozing with bitter sarcasm. She cast me a look filled with a mix of anger and hurt. "You, in cahoots with my brother to deceive me? I had higher expectations, especially from Sean," she scoffed. "And here I was, genuinely liking you. I believe Jasmine's nonsense about you being my soulmate. You had me completely fooled."

Being in love with Vivienne was the easy part. I could be authentic around her, free from worrying about being with me for my family's wealth. The hardest thing was witnessing the anger she directed at me in real time as she was tearing our relationship apart.

"Please, don't be mad at Sean or me."

"I'm mad at myself for not seeing your privilege from the start. One day, you're in a new car. The next, you're parading around on a brand-new bike. Honestly, for a while, I worried you might be a drug dealer. But I figured Sean would have my back and warn me if you were." She picked up a couple of stones and threw them in the river.

"If you're underage, I must know. It would crush me, but you must tell me, V." I followed her to the riverbank, tripping over the rocks in my path before regaining my balance.

"Relax. I'm eighteen. Unlike you, I have a conscience. I'm not in the habit of leading anyone on. Did your parents not tell you to be honest? What happened to the home training they gave you? Did they tell you not to reveal that you were an almighty Hastings? I could see the hurt in her eyes, which pained me to know I caused it.

I exhaled. "You can't blame me for what my parents have."

She rushed over to me, stoned-faced. "Oh no, I don't blame you for that. I blame you for not preparing me for the onslaught that's about to hit me. This is not a game, Jonathan. Dating the heir to the Hastings fortune? I can't do that. I don't want to do that. I don't think you and I are going to work out. You lied to me about who you are, and I can't process that right now."

"I told you to ask me any questions. There was no topic off limits. Please don't blame me because you never did. And to be clear, I've never been, nor would I ever be, a drug dealer."

"Well, that's good to know. But you and I still won't work. We're from two completely different worlds."

My heart sank. Her words crushed me. "By what standard? Money?" I asked.

I had only myself to blame for V's reaction. It was my fault, even though I didn't know why her response was so explosive. I wasn't so bad she'd find me repulsive.

"Money, fame, lies, stalking, take your pick. I'm down to earth, not some stuck-up chick running behind some rich pretty boy."

"Is that what you think? I know I didn't misjudge you. What is wrong with having money? Isn't that what you aspire to have? Why go to college? If not to make a better life for yourself, then what? You are not narrow-minded. The fact that my parents are successful doesn't make me or them bad people."

"You think that's the entire reason I'm mad at you? Boy, you are even thicker than I thought."

"Then there must be something you know that I don't. Why would you be so devastated? We're not crooks or oppressors. My family owns a chain of resorts, so what?"

She then leaned into me. Her eyes seemed cold and distant. The hint of green that was usually prominent had disappeared from them.

"I'm upset with you because you thought you had to hide who you are from me. You had me running behind you with no idea who you were. What does that say about you? More importantly, what does that say about me? I should have known you were too good to be real. I'm seeing our future, Jonathan, and you're not in mine. I cannot tell you if it will be now or a month. You and I will not be together."

"You can see the future, my future, our future? What are you now, a psychic?" I didn't know what to make of her remarks because I was sure she was my future.

"What am I to you, ah? What does Vivienne Pearson mean to Prince Jonathan Hastings? Will you sneak around with me in these bushes until you get tired of me? Is that why you love coming here? Or will I ever meet your rich, powerful family? I want to know how much or how little this bush girl means to you." She stared at me with one of her signature stares. "You know what, let me make it easy for you. I don't want to know them because you and I are done. You probably are just one big bunch of liars anyway."

"Vivienne, you can't mean that." I held on to her.

"Don't touch me." She snapped. "You will have to find your way out of this jungle alone. Let's see how well you lie your way out of here."

"Vivienne!" I called out to her when she disappeared behind the trees.

Chapter 16

Peas in a Pod

Jonathan

"Jonathan Hastings, I'm still mad at you."

V found me an hour later sitting in the same spot she left me, lamenting that I might have sabotaged yet another relationship.

I did not have what it took to navigate a jungle.

Vivienne narrowed her eyes to me. "My dad said I can't leave you to find your way back. Be thankful my parents like you," she said.

"I'm sorry for concealing my identity, but I wanted you to love me for me and not because of what my family has. I messed up. I know that now."

"And I'm sorry I called your parents liars," she said as she knelt beside me. "Do I have anything else to worry about, Jonathan? A baby mama or two, perhaps?"

"You are the prettiest, funniest, and feistiest girl I've ever met, Vivienne Pearson. That's a bad combination. But I couldn't love you more if I tried," I laughed. "You'll be my only baby mama."

"There you go again with your seven to ten kids, crazy talk."

"I'm only messing with you, Professor Pearson. I'd like you to meet my parents before those babies come."

"I'm serious, Jonathan. What else should I know about you? If you have other skeletons, I suggest you tell me now. I'm not one of those girls who will forgive you whenever you apologize for your mistakes."

"I have one older brother. His name is Damien. My parents live in Greenwood. You know the rest regarding our hotels. If you think about it, my baggage is not as big as you think."

"It's big, Jonathan. I had no idea what I was getting into when I accepted your date. Now you have got me tangled up in one of, if not the richest families on the island. Consider yourself lucky I didn't hitchhike back to Montego Bay."

It took a minute to respond to her. I bit my lips and stifled a smile. I leaned closer to her. I needed her to know I meant every word I was about to say. "If we didn't resolve this issue, and you never wanted to see me again, it would have gutted me."

"In all fairness, you have yourself to blame. You have enough confidence to fill a stadium. Are you afraid of little old me? I don't believe that."

"The sooner I take you to meet my parents, the better I'll feel. I don't think your opinion of my family will change unless you meet them. My mother will adore you."

"Meeting your parents would be a huge step. I'm not ready for that." She looked up at the sky-high trees surrounding the river, noticed a flock of about twenty black crows perched on the branches, and realized we had an audience.

"My happiness is the most important thing to them. I like myself when I'm with you, and my parents will thank you for putting a smile on my face. Granted, you almost took it away. You'll be the first girl I'll bring home, and that says a lot."

"You're joking. Are you afraid of your parents? Wow! Are you a virgin, Jonathan?" she asked teasingly. "Jonathan Hastings is a virgin. Well, it will be a bit challenging for me to break you in." She laughed, and I felt embarrassed. No one had ever implied, let alone had the nerve to accuse me of being a virgin. If anything, everyone assumed I was banging every girl in the city. For V to suggest I might be a virgin somehow made me blush.

I looked around to make sure no one was in the viewing or listening range, and when the coast was clear, I pulled her down on top of me onto the freshly cut grass and kissed her softly. "Would you like me to prove it?" I whispered. "Let's risk it. This moment calls for making up, don't you think?"

"Right here, out in the open, just like that? You, city boys, have no scruples." She took my face in her hands and gazed into my eyes with a stare that sent an electric shock through me. "One day, I'll take you up on your offer, but it's not today," she said. "You're just going to have to wait for me to deflower you.

"Vivienne Pearson," I said, my arms wrapped around her. I flipped her on her back, then slid below her waist, trying to conceal the effects of what she was doing. "I am not a virgin. I've had several girlfriends. But until you stole my heart, I'd never met the right girl to bring home to my parents. There's some crazy chemistry going on between us. I've never had such connections with anyone."

I did everything to hide the way she was making me feel. I was embarrassed that she made me feel such burning desires, and I hated that I wasn't better prepared for the rush of emotions that came out of me.

I brought my hands forward, rested my elbows on the grass, and pulled her in for a kiss. Then, I forced myself off the grass and pulled her to her feet.

We ran down the mountain holding hands as we landed in the valley. We explored the forest while our feet crushed the dried leaves beneath them as we made our way through, trying to find an open space on the other side. The orange grove across the river spanned acres. Fallen tree branches lay in our paths. We held hands and jumped over them to go through the thick shrubs and hanging trees with birds perching on them, making it easy to touch the dried nest. I had no idea such an experience could be so fulfilling and calming. I had never gone on such an incredible adventure.

It was my first time exploring a jungle, and I loved it. Beyond the mountains, I discovered that the river flowing miles into the sea stretched throughout the forest from the waterfall. Greenspring was no doubt my new favorite place for a retreat. It was tranquil, memorable, serene, lovely, scenic, and romantic, and I loved its ruggedness.

We lowered our voices after discovering one remarkable insect after another. I clutched V's hand, trying not to disturb the wildlife. The tall trees blocked the sun's glare, forming a protective shield.

"Is that a cave over there?" I asked, brushing the hanging branch away from my face.

"The only one around this neck of the woods. Rumor has it that Neanderthals once lived in it. When we were younger, my parents warned me not to go inside. But you know, kids, we just had to disobey grownups."

"What's in it?"

"Bats. Big enough to lift you off the ground. You can't see anything inside. It's dark, dingy, and cold. That's why we only went there once. The shrubs around it were not so thick back then."

"Let's see what's inside." I was anxious to explore it.

"You? A city boy? You wouldn't last a minute in there. I don't think so. It's creepy inside," she laughed.

"I wished I had taken my camera," I said. "Do you know how much money tourists would pay to explore this? This place could easily be a safari."

"You see dollar signs in everything, don't you?" She smiled at me, my hand gripping hers as she guided me through the dense forest.

"That's what makes the world go around, V." I lifted her chin with my left hand, holding on to a branch with my right. "But seriously, this place is mind-blowing. There is history here. This looks like somewhere the Arawak once lived. Someone ought to do something to highlight it."

"If only we had a historian that documented this place, they'd discover that there was one more place they could drive out its residence in the name of modernization. I'm not so sure I want tree-loggers to come here. They would ruin everything, and the residents would rebel if the government should approve logging."

"Your sarcasm knows no limit," I laughed.

"We may be poor, but we would rather starve than allow outsiders to strip Greenspring of its natural resources in the name of commerce. I wish I had documented my early years here because I know one day, they'll eventually use this place as a source for lumber," she said.

"I want to come back another time. There is a rich history here, and I want to explore more."

"Let's go back, *Columbus*." She smiled at me teasingly. "It's getting dark, and my parents may begin to worry."

Chapter 17

Blood is Thicker than Water

Vivienne

It was one of those days when the weather was perfect for lounging on the beach, but Jonathan had other plans.

We drove through the Hastings estate with high gates and a security booth. I couldn't shake the feeling of being out of place.

It wasn't quite a sense of danger but rather a discomfort that this environment was too lavish for me, an unsettling conflict of belonging.

The enormous estate stretched across the beachfront property at the border of St. James and Trelawny. It spanned over acres of beautifully manicured lawns with rows of trimmed crotons, hibiscus, and large palm trees from the entrance to the stunning twenty-bedroom concrete structure.

The garden came alive with its breathtakingly vibrant colors. Each row of flowers was more stunning than the last. Gardeners in khaki uniforms with tree trimmers greeted us as we walked through the lavish estate. Their warm smiles added a soft touch to its serenity.

"Are you sure about this, Jonathan?" I asked, clutching his hand as we approached the main house. "I'm starting to think this was a bad idea," I said.

"I assure you, V, you have nothing to worry about." He squeezed my hand. "Wait, you'll see, my parents will love you as much as I do."

"Tell me why I agreed to do this?" I muttered.

"The sooner you meet them, the quicker we'll get it out of the way. My parents are like anyone else's parents. Don't let all this fool you. These are material things that they deserve. They've worked for every bit of it," he said as he pulled up in his assigned parking space with his name painted in large letters.

When we exited the car, Jonathan lifted me off the ground, kissed me, and ran up the steps. He placed me gently onto the porch, then entered through the front door into the spectacular living room surrounded by glass. My eyes fixed on the lofty ceilings that held the elegant chandelier. On the far left was a black marble piano at the entrance of the lavish dining room. In awe of its elaborateness, my eyes lingered on the family portrait on the wall. In it, Jonathan seemed to be around three years old, sitting on the floor in front of his parents, his brother seated next to him. He looked like he was about six or seven. As I held on to Jonathan's hand, about to comment on the portrait, voices came from the grand hallway to my right. I drew closer to him and waited to see who would appear.

"You must be Vivienne. It's nice to meet you," Jonathan's mother greeted me with outstretched arms. He did not get his height from her. She was barely over five feet five inches tall, and even the heels and the Afro she wore didn't get her past five feet seven inches. She wore an elegant long dress and a sparkling diamond necklace. She looked gorgeous.

"Wonderful to meet you, Vivienne," his father extended his hand as he welcomed me. Jonathan got his height from him. The good looks were a blend of both parents. But Jonathan's charm came from his mother.

"Nice to meet you both. Thank you for inviting me. You have a charming home," I said, casting my eyes throughout the house.

I was pleasantly surprised to see that Jonathan's parents were not the hoity-toity, stuck-up people I had expected them to be. His mother was warm and friendly, and his father was polite to me. But his brother Damien was entirely different.

"You didn't tell me you had invited your brother." I pulled Jonathan aside, my voice a whisper.

"I didn't. I think my mom did," he said.

"I don't think he likes me. He kept giving me a weird look."

We sat at the long table thirty minutes after arriving, and Damien's fixation with me had only worsened. "So, tell me, Vivienne. Where are you from?" He tilted his chin with a sneaky grin.

"Greenspring," I replied, aware that would be the first of many questions.

"Where is Greenspring?"

"Hanover."

"You're a country girl?" he asked immediately, his voice filled with deep suspicion. His eyes had not left mine. "So, how do you find life in the city?"

Yeah, he didn't like me. His questions had judgment written all over them. It seemed he had a thing against country girls. "How did you meet Jonathan?" Damien picked up his wine glass off the table and took a gulp.

"I'll let him tell you. It's a long story."

His stare made me uneasy. I knew what jealousy looked like, and Damien's stare was unmistakably devious.

"We have time," he said.

I narrowed my eyes on him. "You seemed different from your brother. You guys are not alike at all."

"What do you mean?" He placed the glass back onto the table and leaned back into his chair.

"For one, he's charming. I get the impression you don't think much of country girls. That's all I'll say."

"What did he see in you that makes you different from all the other girls he banged?" His voice was mean, as if he meant to hurt me with his comment. "Don't think you're special."

"Damien! Where's your manners?" his mother snapped.

"I'm only making conversation, Mom. She seems like a smart girl who can hold her own."

"You don't need to answer him, V," Jonathan said, frowning at his brother. "Do you always have to be such a jackass? Why are you trying to intimidate my girlfriend?"

"Jonathan, I am fine. I can handle him. He is curious. When it gets to be too much, I will let you know," I said.

"Damien!" Mr. Hastings' thunderous roar shook me with a force I had never felt before. "Do not come into this house with that kind of behavior! You are a grown man. We raised you better than that," he scolded him.

"Why are you always reprimanding me and not Jonathan?"

"Look around you and tell me who acts like a petulant child. With all the home training you got, you're still unable to get yourself together."

The back and forth between them went on for another five minutes.

After dinner, I thanked Jonathan's parents for hosting me and gushed more about their mansion. Umbrellas lined the large swimming pool, and lounge chairs had towels flung over them. Two smaller cottages were nestled between a running brook that separated a golf course at the back of the primary residence.

I have nothing in common with these people. Will I even like the pampered life? Or, more appropriately, will Jonathan's parents accept me for who I am, the country girl overwhelmed by the luxury of their life?

"Thank you for coming, Vivienne. You should come more often. If Jonathan can't take you, give me a call. I'll send someone to pick you up. My niece will be here next Saturday, and I'd like to introduce you to her. She's about your age."

"That's very gracious, Mrs. Hastings. I'd like that very much," I said as I hugged her.

"Let me give you the grand tour of the property." She locked arms with me and led me away from Jonathan.

"Take it easy on her, V!" Jonathan yelled as I looked back. He laughed, giving me two thumbs up.

I sat by the large swimming pool while Mrs. Hastings enjoyed a glass of rum cream, and I nibbled on the Guineps from the basket on the table. She had much in common with my mother, although they're from different cultures. They were both big reggae music lovers and felt passionate about their children.

We spent the next few hours getting to know each other.

Later that evening, Jonathan found us sitting by the pool. He excused us and led me into a room filled with photographs of how his family's business started, dating back to the early 1970s.

But that did little to eliminate the unease gnawing at me all day about his brother, Damien.

Chapter 18

Déjà vu

Vivienne

The pitter-patter on the rooftop had always calmed me, especially when I was wrapped up in my bed in the middle of the day, watching television or listening to music. My taste in music ranged from the soulful melodies of Country, R&B, and Reggae to the infectious beats of Disco. Each genre had its place, and the right mood would transport me into its unique rhythm. But despite the music's power, my mood seemed trapped in a cycle of regret, a feeling I couldn't quite shake.

After the thunderstorms dissipated, I gathered my books, packed them in the green and white backpack, and smiled, thinking of the many times I fought with Jasmine over leaving

Greenspring and how she could not stay mad at me for ten minutes afterward. She was the sister I didn't have. Even with her loose lips, she was the best friend any girl could want.

The countdown had begun, and with only a few weeks to go, my classes at New Oasis College were on the horizon. The excitement was palpable, and everything was in place for what I hoped would be a smooth first day.

I eased up off my stomach and sat on my legs, admiring the new outfit I purchased with the money I earned from my summer job. My journey to becoming a professor would finally start, a dream I had cherished since grade six.

Since arriving at Sean's house, I packed and repacked my backpack at least once a week.

I wish Jasmine were as lucky as I am. If only she had the means, we would be classmates. Man, poverty is indeed a crime.

The grin on my face disappeared. I had to leave my best friend in the country, probably to have babies with a poverty-stricken farmer who believed he could give her the world with the little pennies he earned, and here I was, a brand-new college-bound city girl and loving it.

In her attempts to scare me from moving to Montego Bay, Jasmine had warned me I'd see houses jammed up against each other, close enough to hear my neighbors' whispers. But except for my encounter with the naked madman at the grove and the creep in the taxi during my first week in Montego Bay, Ironshore was not so bad, and it was not even close to looking like a ghetto.

"Oh, Jas, I wish you were here," I murmured, my hands resting on my knees.

I cleared my bed of my school supplies and closed my backpack just as the black rotary telephone on my nightstand rang. I lunged across the bed and snatched the receiver at the first ring. "Jonathan?" I was sure it was him. I had been waiting to hear from him all day, and it was getting close to our meeting.

But as soon as I answered, my heart sank.

"Hello, Vivienne," the voice roared in my ear and unnerved me. I sat on the bed, disappointed, trying to understand why in the world he would call me and how he had gotten Sean's number.

"What do you want, Damien?" I could barely finish the question when he sniffled. "Are you crying?" I paced the room, wondering if he deserved my pity. But then, his words became more explicit.

"Jonathan had an accident."

I couldn't hang up now even if I wanted.

I scrambled back to my bed and grabbed the headboard to avoid collapsing. I slapped my hand over my mouth to suppress a scream.

"Can you come?" he asked, my heart pounding in my ears.

From the day I rode with Jonathan to Ochi, I had always dreaded the moment I would receive news that he had crashed.

"Is he okay?" I asked as the phone rattled in my hand.

Jonathan was the bravest guy I had ever met. He needed speed, especially when riding his Kawasaki. He rode that bike like Superman.

"How quickly can you get here?" The voice jolted me back. My mind had gone in many directions before settling on the possibility that I might have lost Jonathan.

"Five minutes," I said, my hands were still shaking.

I hung up the telephone and ran to the living room to find my sister-in-law. "Danielle, Danielle, Jonathan is hurt." My voice cracked beneath my sobs. "I don't know what happened, but I bet it's that damn bike he rides. I'll talk to you when I get back."

"Do you want me to come?" she asked.

"No, the girls need you. Just let Sean know where I am," I said.

I hugged her, then dashed out the door with my uncombed hair flying over my face. I hurried up the hill to Jonathan's house at 101 Valence Avenue, unaware of the condition I'd find him, whether fractured legs, broken arms, collarbone, or worse. If the accident stemmed from his motorbike, it could kill him.

The closer I got to the house, the louder the waves roared below the concrete wall that separated the main road from the beach as they crashed against the shore.

I sighed. *Oh God, please let him be okay.*

The swooshing sound took me back to the night of my first kiss. Electricity sparked when Jonathan brought me home from the movie. The roaring waves and his warm embrace mesmerized me. That was the night I fell in love with him.

Oddly, the call did not come from Patricia, Jonathan's long-time loyal housekeeper, whom he relied on for everything. Patricia was a guiding figure who had a hand in raising him. Watching Patricia prepare Jonathan's meals was like watching my mother.

Jonathan's kitchen was Patricia's safe space, where she poured her heart into every dish. He needed nothing, whether it was groceries or a freshly ironed shirt. His dapper appearance was all thanks to his energetic housekeeper. She could find water in the desert if he asked her to, a testament to her unwavering dedication to him.

"Don't break his heart. Or else you'll have to answer to me." Patricia pulled me aside when Jonathan first introduced us. Not that she needed to protect him from me. Patricia liked me, and Jonathan didn't need a defender. But she took one look at me and thought I had the potential to break his heart, although she was not as hard on me as she could have been. Her words were a mix of warning and acceptance, a sign that she saw something in me that she trusted with Jonathan's heart.

She would come in every day at seven in the morning to take care of the house's upkeep and ensure Jonathan had everything he needed for work. She was loyal. She spoke highly of him and called him Jon. It was an easy job for her, too. She didn't have to deal with a house full of rambunctious children, a demanding wife, or a violent husband. Jonathan was a single guy who was hardly home except in the late evenings, and by then, she was either gone or getting ready to go home.

Even so, he liked to clean up after himself, so Patricia had little to do. She didn't have to deal with girls coming in and out of the house to see Jonathan. That was more Damien's style. But he didn't live there anymore, so Patricia didn't have to deal with him or his girls.

I pressed my finger against the keypad, and immediately, the gate slid open.

"Come on up!" Damien yelled.

I hurried through the gate, stopping in front of him. "How is Jonathan?" My voice broke from anxiety.

"Banged up, but he'll live," he said, holding a beer with one hand and smoking a spliff with the other.

I was relieved. "What happened?"

"Chill, chill. He'll be okay," he assured me after seeing my tears.

"Is Patricia here?" I asked, wiping my eyes. Patricia would drop everything to take care of Jonathan if he were hurt.

Damien took a sip of his beer. "Patricia is in the kitchen," he said. His lips hardly left the bottle when he took another puff off his ganja cigar.

I fanned the smoke out of my face as it seared into my throat. "Can you not blow the smoke on me?" I asked after recovering from a cough.

"I didn't mean to." He took another sip. "I know we have our differences, but we need to be civil," he said, convincingly. "We must be able to get along better, for Jonathan's sake. I'll admit I haven't been cordial to you as I should, but I mean you no harm." He sounded reasonable amid his half-drunken state.

"So, all that hate you usually heap on me, what was that all about? Am I supposed to believe you had a conversion or even a heart?"

I stepped onto the large veranda decorated with potted plants in each corner. The sunset cast a shadow on the two long chairs on either side, and a small table was stacked with empty beer bottles. Stereo speakers were blasting dancehall's latest hits, with an ashtray with ganja butts on top of them.

Damien slammed the burglar bars, locking it behind him. The sound reverberated like the gates of a maximum-security prison, and a deep fear suddenly engulfed me.

The clock on Jonathan's living room wall ticked as I waited for Patricia to appear from the kitchen, each tick amplifying my sense of entrapment.

Five minutes passed, then ten, and I began to feel annoyed by Damien's small talk.

"Patricia!" I called out when she was taking a long time to come out. "You said Patricia was here." I turned to face Damien.

"Oh, about that," he said, dragging his words. "Patricia already left."

"You lied to me? Where's Jonathan? Is he hurt? Or is that a lie, too?" I asked.

"I wanted to see you. That was to get you to come. You have been on my mind for a long time." He flashed his lighter to relight his blunt.

"If you used Jonathan to lure me here, then you are more pathetic than I thought. Forget you don't like me. I didn't know you'd stoop so low."

I couldn't defend myself against this large man if he forced himself on me. With Patricia gone and Jonathan not around to shield me, I was sure I was heading toward a collision with my past.

"I wasn't here the last time you guys hung out. Now I get the chance to hang out with you one-on-one," Damien said. "Tell me, Vivienne, how does a country girl get to be so damn beautiful?" His head bobbled as he struggled to sit beside me.

The Saturday nights I spent with Jonathan and his friends in that house were some of the most memorable. None of the guys had ever made me feel as uncomfortable as Damien did. They welcomed me into their brotherhood with open arms and treated me like their little sister.

I shoved Damien onto the other side of the chair. "Ew! Get away from me. You smell like a drunk," I said, jumping.

"You are a hard one to catch, Vivienne," he said. "It's not fair Jonathan gets to be with you when I saw you first." His smoke-filled eyes filled me with dread.

"What?" I asked, confused.

"Nate. He was supposed to bring you to me, but the crazy son of a bitch couldn't follow simple instructions. How do you think it made me feel when Jonathan showed up with you on his arm, boasting that you are his girl? You should have been mine." He coughed, filling the air with moisture that landed all over me.

"You sent a madman after me? You sent a madman to kidnap me?" I yelled at him, unable to control my anger. "My God, you are evil. I thought I was going to die that night. An insane man running me down with a machete was your idea of what, exactly. What was he supposed to do if he had caught me?"

"Bring you to me," he said flatly.

My face hurt as I remembered what I went through the night Nate chased me into the ditch.

"They say you catch more flies with honey than vinegar," he chuckled.

"He had a machete, you, sick freak!" I yelled.

If I could evaporate, this would be the moment I'd choose to do it. The country girl in me wanted to curl up into my mother's arms for safety. There was no way I could be victimized again. I swore I was going to implode. I glared at him, my hands in a fist to stop them from shaking. "You tricked me into coming here, using Jonathan as bait?"

"You don't like me at all." He took another puff of the ganja, blew the smoke into the ceiling, and laughed at me. "How old are you anyway? You seem like you are still in high school," he said.

"Right now, you seem like a boy masquerading as a man who used deception to get what he wants. I don't think you can have a mature conversation with me. I don't know your intentions, but you and I will not discuss my age." His bloodshot eyes shot a wicked glance, which told me I should get the hell out of there as fast as possible.

"I always get what I want, Vivienne." He flashed another sinister smile. "My type or not, I want you." He pushed up to me while I fought back tears, trying hard to block the memories of Denton Reese as they shot to the forefront of my mind. "You're a beautiful girl, sassy as hell but pretty. I like that. I know I'd be a better fit for you than Jonathan."

Denton Reese was a giant compared to me, but this man is a giant's giant. There is no way I can survive him if he attacks me.

My fears deepened. I was defenseless against a man who locked me inside the house and was evil enough to lure me about his brother's nonexistent accident.

"What do you want from me?!" I screamed at him, frustrated that he had tricked me and I was no longer interested in conversation. He didn't seem like he wanted to be reasonable, and talking to him calmly couldn't convince him to let go of his idiotic fantasy.

"I want you, Vivienne. It's that simple. I wouldn't have gone through this much trouble if I didn't."

"Well, since we both know that you will not get me, you can just stop with the craziness," I said, hoping I could appeal to whatever little shred of loyalty he had. "Open the gate. I want to go home. I never knew you were this creepy, stupid, and evil."

The wounded child in me was screaming inside. My mind spun in so many directions. I wanted to run, but where would I go? The enclosed house with iron bars from one end to the other seemed futile if I made a run for my freedom. I wanted to claw Damien's eyes out. He might have been too drunk to feel it anyway. And I wanted, more than anything else, for Jonathan to walk through the gate.

Damien placed the beer bottle on the small table, then lunged at me. He pressed his lips hard against mine, swallowed my mouth, and forced his tongue inside.

My past was crashing into my present. I talked myself out of options, and now the words lodged in my brain as Damien sealed my fate.

He pulled me off the burglar bars and hauled me by my hair through the large living room. My feet dragged against the white tile, my shoes leaving skid marks leading into Jonathan's bedroom. Damien flung me onto the bed and ripped my blouse. He grabbed my breasts like he was a ravenous wild beast tearing at raw meat.

"Damien, please stop," I cried. "You are hurting me! Help!" I bit him as hard as I could. I scratched and clawed, pushing him off me. I dashed through the door into the room next to Jonathan's. He cornered me and dragged me back onto the bed.

I was in the claws of a giant, loaded up on marijuana and alcohol.

Damien was like a Frankenstein monster. His eyes bulged, his breath exhilarating, and I was no match for his tree-trunk masculinity.

He pushed me up against the bed and swallowed my body. My head hit the headboard hard. There was no more resistance, no movement, and Damien was free to do whatever he wanted.

***

It felt like something in me had ruptured. It might have been my pancreas or liver. I couldn't tell since I had no medical training. But judging from the excruciating pain in my abdomen, I was sure it was my pelvis.

My hands shook, and my mind couldn't concentrate as I stumbled through the veranda gate. My knees buckled as I choked on the smoke of the newly lit spliff between Damien's oversized fingers. He stretched his left hand across the long veranda chair and braced against it, crossing his leg above his knee while he blew another puff of smoke into the air. Satisfaction flashed across his bloated face as he watched me fall through the veranda gate.

And there it was, the familiar look of contempt appeared beneath his grin, and I remembered why I kept my distance from him.

I limped down the hill. I must get home before I lose consciousness again.

Chapter 19

Ochi Night

Jonathan

I grabbed a bunch of red roses from the gift shop downstairs and laid them on the back seat of my car. I added a white one, something special for standing V up. Although, if anyone were to blame, it would be my mother. Calling me at the last minute to fill in for Damien was a gut punch. I did not even get a chance to let V know I was going to Ochi. The least I could do was to apologize to her profusely for canceling our date night. I should have brought her with me instead of Blaise; then, I wouldn't be in a hurry to drive back to Ironshore.

By the time everything had calmed down, it was close to midnight, and I was in no condition for a two-hour drive. I threw my keys at Blaise and jumped into the front passenger seat. "I swear Damien is allergic to work. It can't be a coincidence he went to Negril the same night a busload of tourists showed up," I said. "He must have known they were coming." I had forgotten how difficult it was to register so many people in one night.

My work at the Montego Bay location of Hideaway was managerial. Overseeing heads of departments was far less taxing on my feet. It was good that I took Blaise with me, although he spent half the night hanging out by the pool, sipping on Margaritas.

With the midnight wind on my face, Blaise floored the car on the deserted road back to Ironshore. "When will you talk to Vivienne about Jennifer?" he asked five minutes into the ride. He gripped the steering wheel, his eyes fixed on the road with a mischievous grin. "I hope you know it will come back to bite you if you don't tell her your last girlfriend tried to kill you."

I had planned to ease my relationship with Jennifer in one of my conversations with V. I dreaded the fallout that was bound to happen the longer I waited to tell her. I couldn't afford for her to think she might have been wrong to love me after finding out my last relationship was toxic or that she should constantly be watching over her shoulders for a scorned girlfriend.

Blaise had already informed Pierre, Noah, Jude, and Fredrick that our Saturday night meeting was canceled, and I was mad at myself for not telling V I wouldn't see her. We'd meet for rounds of dominoes and board games or to catch up with the latest of who was stung by the love bug. Noah couldn't stop talking about Andrea, the Anita Baker look-alike new girl at his job. The guys teased him mercilessly that he didn't stand a chance with her.

The laughter and teasing were part of what made our brotherhood full of excitement. None of us were into the club scene, so my house on Valence Avenue became our hang-out spot. We didn't smoke or drink heavily. We'd have one Red Stripe beer or a Heineken, and that's only on the nights Patricia left a bucket of fried fish for us when we were celebrating a birthday or a promotion. The guys always raved about Patricia's cooking. They were big eaters, especially Jude. He had an appetite for someone three times his size but never gained a pound from his ravenous appetite.

"I don't know if I should tell V about Jennifer, Blaise," I said.

"I think Vivienne is the one for you. You've hit the jackpot this time. Jennifer is a lost cause."

Blaise was what I called the real irie one out of all of us. He was a cool guy, the laid-back and easy-going type. But he was badass as hell with his martial arts skills. He loved V the instant he saw her. Even though it didn't take long for the other guys to fall in love with her. V had that effect on everyone. Even my mother. Except for my brother, who didn't seem to care much for her.

"Where is that coming from? You know I don't like to discuss my relationships."

"Since when? That's all we talked about when we hung out. The first time Vivienne went out with you, you couldn't shut up about it," he laughed.

I rubbed my hand over my head and smiled.

"You may not like this, but I'm going to give you some free advice," Blaise said. "Tell her about Jennifer before someone else does. A woman scorned can be your worst enemy. Everyone except Jennifer knew she was bad for you. If I were you, I'd ensure your new girl is not blind-sided by your old one."

"You're right. But I don't know how V will react to another secret about me. The last time I had a heart-to-heart with her, it didn't go well."

"Be that as it may, you'd be wise to tell her."

"She didn't make it easy for me at all. But we were fighting a losing battle after our first date. So, I'm not about to risk her telling me she hates me because of another woman."

"It's worth the risk. Jennifer will see Vivienne as the obstacle to getting back with you."

"But she and I have been over for a long time now. She is going to force her way back in after what she did?" I asked. "Even she has her limit. She knew I could have had her arrested. I did not tell you that before she tried to run me over, she stalked me. The car incident was just the last straw."

"All the more reason to warn Vivienne about her."

"Well, you might be right. Let's hope V forgives me for coming to Ochi."

It was an uneasy ride back to Ironshore. Blaise was spot on, and I wished he wasn't so damn right all the time.

Chapter 20

Running Out of Time

Vivienne

I prefer Damien had killed me instead of leaving me half-dead as I lay broken, battered, and alone by the side of the road.

"I will not die tonight. I can't die here tonight," I mumbled as my breath slowly seeped out of me, and I slurred into silence.

I will die tonight, alone, in the dark, and tomorrow, when the day breaks, they'll find me. My mother will die from heartbreak, and my father will hate himself for being right.

I staggered off the ground with what little strength I had as the thoughts seeped into me. My legs wobbled, and my clothes hung like rags from my arm. One hand covered my breasts, the other tucked between my legs, my poor attempt to cover up my nakedness. My bra hung from my hand over my heart, and the blue and white panties I wore to the house that evening were nowhere in sight but lost during the thrashing, and I didn't want to spend another second searching for them.

A steady streak of blood oozed from my forehead as I convulsed. My vision blurred from the blood streaming down my face, mixed with my tears. I staggered, stretched out my hand for support, caught a glimpse of the clothes hanging from my arms, and let out a soft cry.

It was good that it was dark, and no one could see I was completely naked. My knees buckled again, and my legs gave out on me as I descended the hill. I was sure I was about to die alone on the curb in the middle of the night. My father's worst nightmare came true. His warnings suddenly crept into my mind before the light in my eyes went out, and I fell to the ground.

But how did I get here, taking my last breath and wrestling with the realization that my life was over? It should not be ending like this. The old Jamaican saying, 'Hard ears pickney dead a sun hot,' seemed to apply right about now. I did not cause this to myself, but it wouldn't have happened if I wasn't so hardheaded. I didn't deserve to lose my life because I didn't heed my father's warnings. The last thing I wanted was to break his heart.

With my body battered from one end to the other, I tried to remember the last time my dad cried and couldn't. Not even after so many of his siblings died long before their time. He had never yelled at my mother, not even once. He never punished my brother, even when he left home before the ink had dried on his high school diploma in search of his independence, and if you were me, you'd scream at him for the way he pretended as if I was his fragile little sister he couldn't let out of sight. Being a daddy's girl allowed far more leeway than I deserved. Yet, I was responsible for the broken heart my father had been nursing since I uttered three little words—New Oasis College.

"The city will swallow you, Viv. Please reconsider," my dad begged when I told him I wanted to move in with Sean. I hated how he swallowed hard to hide the pain in his voice. But it was too late to change my mind. Becoming a teacher had already been stuck in my brain for as long as I could remember, and he knew I was like a dog with a bone whenever I set my mind on anything. My obsession with New Oasis Teacher's College was just the latest.

Every day of my life in my small village was a blissful memory since we arrived. Whenever I closed my eyes at night, I could hear every creature within a two-mile radius. Night owls, crickets, dogs howling, chirping of all kinds, and even the mosquitoes buzzing in my ears sang beautiful melodies. I'd wake up at dawn with the cleanest air in my lungs as the sunlight peered through my open bedroom window. Most days, the sky was blue, gleaming from the sparkling Caribbean sun. The river ran through my backyard, and tree branches kissed the earth, tasting the early morning dew, with its lush green leaves swaying as the breeze gently blew through them.

Now, I lay by the side of the road, dying.

I scratched and crawled as I lifted my broken, bruised, and bloodied body off the ground. I pulled my dress over my head, but only after making several attempts. I staggered forward, barefooted, unsure whether I would reach my brother's house. It felt like a wild beast had torn me to shreds.

I braced against the small pear tree, and my body went limp. The only sound came from a stray dog sniffing the ground, his wet tongue slobbering my face under the tree where I fell.

"Please, God, don't let me die tonight. Not here by the side of the road," I mumbled.

I may have gotten a DNA sample from the brute while he was squeezing the life out of me, even though I had no intention of creating a firestorm or turning my assault into a big scandal by pressing charges. If my assault ever became public, the news headlines would not be kind to me. Nor did I have the money needed to go up against Damien's trove of lawyers who would enjoy putting the final nail in my coffin.

What he did to me was as vivid as each breath I craved to survive him. I didn't cause an oversized maniac to believe he had the right to take me while expecting me to be a good girl, and I wasn't the temptress he claimed. But my chance encounter with the *crème de la crème* of Montego Bay precipitated my demise. I should have run in the opposite direction the day I met Jonathan Hastings. But my feet felt stuck on the pavement, and my eyes glued to his stare. The magnetic pull that caused every cell in my body to come alive was bearing down on me like an albatross as I struggled to survive because I took a chance at loving Jonathan.

***

My bedroom door exploded and flew across the room at lightning speed after Jonathan kicked it in. I didn't think I'd make it past an hour, much less through the night. His fifteen-minute-long plea and threats to break down my door failed to register with me.

A familiar voice joined him, then another, and soon, a chorus of pleas begged me to answer. But no one knew I had lost my ability to control my limbs and lips. I lay motionless, unable to make even a whimper. Except for my ability to hear, I had lost all other senses, and it would have been a matter of minutes before I lost all of them.

Blood streamed from my head as Jonathan and Sean scraped me off the floor. My body hung from their arms. Danielle's voice echoed through the house, screaming at them.

Jonathan's quivering lips mumbled a prayer as he quickly laid me on the back seat of his car, and Sean jumped in beside me.

Would I survive? Or would I draw my last breath in the back seat of my boyfriend's car? I was sure I would die. My breath was leaving me. I was on my bedroom floor for almost seven hours, unable to move and running out of time. When they found me, I was sure I was about to lose consciousness for the last time.

I barely remember how I got into my brother's house. Perhaps I crawled. I had glimpses of being woken up naked from under a tree by a dog licking my face.

"Didn't you have an accident yesterday, Jonathan? Danielle told me you were hurt," Sean asked.

"I don't know what you're talking about," Jonathan said through sobs.

"Danielle said Viv left to see you because you were in an accident." Sean's voice trembled.

"I haven't seen V in two days."

"Viv has never lied to us. Danielle said she left the house yesterday crying. Now you show up with flowers as if nothing happened." Sean rubbed his trembling hand against my cheek as I struggled to breathe. "What happened to my sister, Jonathan?" he sobbed.

"Sean, I can't argue with you right now. As you can see, I am okay. Let's not lose focus on getting V to the hospital," Jonathan said, feverishly turning the key inside the ignition. There was no time to waste. It was a matter of life and death. My death if help didn't reach me soon. "I've already told you I didn't have an accident and haven't seen her since Friday," he said, speeding out of the narrow driveway and onto the Ironshore main road.

I was fading fast. My brain was shutting down, and I could no longer hear my brother arguing with my boyfriend.

"Stay with me, please, Viv, just stay with me." Sean's voice rose above his sobs and shook me. But the jolt of electricity from

Jonathan's touch recharged me for ten minutes when he reached over and placed his hand on me after I gasped for air.

Neither Jonathan nor my brother thought I'd make it to the hospital alive. The drive was rough. Jonathan sunk into every pothole in the road, and my body bounced against the black leather seat each time. But after Sean pulled my head onto his lap, it cushioned me.

Jonathan snatched me from Sean as soon as he stopped his car. "Get me a doctor!" he screamed.

Then, men in white coats grabbed me out of his arms and rushed me through the emergency room door. "Please don't let her die," Jonathan begged.

That was the last thing I remembered.

Chapter 21

Clinging to Hope

Jonathan

It had been an hour since the doctors pulled V out of my arms. I curled up in the corner of the ER. I thumped the floor, my fist bruised from the impact, and I pounded my head against the wall repeatedly. I could no longer stop my anger from showing. I was angry at Sean for not finding V sooner, mad at the doctors who seemed to have taken too long to come back with answers, and mad as hell at the unknown.

For the next hour, the hospital corridor had become an exercise route for me. I paced up and down the halls, awaiting an update on V's condition.

The hour stretched into two, which seemed more like ten, and I constantly nagged the front desk clerk for an update.

Later that afternoon, a doctor and an officer approached Sean, Danielle, and me. Danielle arrived at the hospital half an hour after we got there. They led us inside a small conference room down the long hallway near where the doctors had taken V, I had assumed they were taking us to see her.

"I know you. You're Jonathan Hastings from Hideaway Resorts." The Police Officer immediately recognized me. He had one hand on the edge of his gun belt and a baton in the other, lightly wielding it around. "You brought in a patient earlier. Can you tell me what happened?" he asked as soon as we entered the room.

"I don't understand why you'd ask me. If I knew what happened, I wouldn't be driving myself crazy all day trying to figure out how she ended up battling for her life."

"She's not suffering from a natural disease, Jonathan. You saw how mangled she was when you brought her in," the police officer said.

"I visited her at her home this morning and found her unresponsive. I have no idea what happened to her. As soon as we found her, I brought her here," I said.

"Can we talk alone?" he asked.

"No need. This is Sean, Vivienne's brother, and his wife, Danielle. Whatever you have to say to me, they can hear."

"I am Officer Wallace, and this is Dr. Daley. Vivienne is in critical condition, and since you brought her in, Jonathan, I'd like to know what happened when you found her."

"What do you mean?" I narrowed my eyes on the doctor. "I'd appreciate it if you level with me. Whatever it is, I can handle it. I'm a big boy."

"The victim is unconscious. Her condition is quite acute, but we're doing everything to save her," the doctor said calmly, holding on to the stethoscope around his neck.

"Please, tell us what happened to her." My chest heaved as I exhaled through my mouth. "Vivienne was okay when I saw her on Friday. I got back from Ochi this morning, and Sean and I found her dying. I don't know what happened to her."

"Sean, what might have happened to your sister?" Officer Wallace asked him.

"I don't know. Viv was okay the last time I saw her yesterday," Sean said, his voice strained.

"Vivienne was raped," Dr. Daley said bluntly. "She had internal injuries, and whoever raped her was brutal. So, she won't be able to leave the hospital today or tomorrow."

I heard the Doctor utter the words *Vivienne and rape* and lost it. Vivienne and rape did not belong in the same sentence. Rape denotes force, overpowered, pain, and crime. At that moment, every word that was synonymous with sexual assault came to mind, and my blood boiled as each one registered in my brain. I closed my eyes and let out an audible sigh to cool the blood rushing through my veins, reminding myself where I was.

"When she's in better shape, she must give a formal statement to the police. What happened to her was barbaric, and we must find out who was responsible. You can leave your contacts with the receptionist, and tomorrow, we'll call with an update on her condition," he said.

"With all due respect, Doctor, we will not leave here until she does," I said.

Danielle pressed her head against the wall, then banged it against the door frame. She had a close friendship with V and talked about everything. How could she not know who made the call that I had an accident? Sean seemed to have gone into another world upon hearing about the rape. He plopped down on the floor as if a sense of helplessness overcame him. How would he explain to their parents that the daughter they entrusted him with had fallen victim to a rapist before her studies began?

"I'd like to see her, Doctor," I said, unsure I was calm enough not to rip the place apart.

"You can't right now, but I'll let you know soon enough."

The small room where we were had become a mourners' closet. Sean blamed me for what he perceived as my fault that V left his house to see me. Danielle blamed herself for not asking about the phone call, and I blamed myself for going to Ocho Rios and not calling V. Not knowing what would happen next became the all-consuming force that paralyzed us.

***

For the next two days, twelve hours and thirty minutes, I sat inside the tiny hospital room where V was hooked up to life-saving machines.

"Nurse!" My voice roared. My patience had run out for an update.

"Sir, what happened?" The nurse ran from her station, rolling a crash cart as if V's condition had worsened.

"Is it normal for her to be out this long?" I asked.

"We don't have any control over when she wakes up. But if it helps to forget such horror, I'd wish I didn't wake up if I were in her position. I pray the damage is not permanent." She was blunt with me. "But next time you holler for me, do so when there is an emergency. I have other patients to which I must attend. She may be dying to forget the assault. Give her time," she said before returning to her station.

I calmed down a bit after my spat with the nurse, and I began to question why God allowed such a thing to happen to V. I refused to leave her side, clinging to the hope that she would survive. I wrapped myself in the small blanket the nurse gave me and planted myself on the tiny chair next to V's bed. My eyes were swollen from crying and lack of sleep. Besides the small cup of coffee from the cafeteria downstairs, I was not in the mood to eat or even show up for work. I was desperate to know why V told Danielle she had left her house to see me.

The morning crawled into the evening, and the trip to the emergency room turned into day three. "When will she be well enough to go home, Miss?" I accosted the young nurse who had come in to change the bandages on V's head. The swelling on her face still had not gone down.

"Sir, Miss Pearson suffered severe injuries. To release her without addressing them would be negligent. The Doctor will inform you when she is well enough to leave the hospital. Be patient, please." She was firm but sympathetic.

"Did she tell you who attacked her? She has not spoken to me since I brought her in. Please, I need to know something," I pleaded as I rubbed V's forehead.

"I am sorry, sir, but that is a question for the Doctor. I am not at liberty to answer you. Give her time, and even if it takes longer than you expect, remember it may take time for her to talk about the assault. Please be patient with her. It can be excruciating for someone to re-live that kind of attack."

My heart sank when the nurse left the room. That was when I realized it was a real possibility I could go to prison for murder.

Chapter 22

The Half-Dead Girlfriend

Vivienne

I popped a stitch over my right eye when I woke up three days after Jonathan took me to the hospital. I scanned the two-hundred-square-foot room and saw him curled on the small chair beside me. An empty cot was across the room, with a neatly folded blanket on top of the fitted sheet wrapped around the narrow mattress.

It was not by chance that I didn't have a roommate, it had to be by Jonathan's design. He was the sophisticated boyfriend who would spare nothing to give me what I needed to get well.

I narrowed my eyes on my unwelcomed male companion and took a deep breath, my heart rate spiking, dreading what I'd say to him. He looked messy, totally out of character. Jonathan Hastings was a suit-and-tie guy, except for the times he spent gallivanting with me across the island. He didn't need to be formal at those times, but he'd still look dapper.

He had pulled his blood-stained shirt out of his pants, and tiny hair had begun to burst through his chin and upper lip. His snores sounded as if he had not slept for those three days. It would have been more comfortable for him to sleep on the empty bed.

But knowing Jonathan like I did, he was not in the mood for comfort while I fought for my life. He looked different from the last time I saw him.

My blood ran cold as memories of the Saturday night assault that landed me in the hospital became more explicit. The first memory trickled in was the telephone call that lured me to Valence Avenue. I grabbed onto the bed's railing to prevent it from vibrating. The last thing I wanted was to wake him up.

Oh God. How do I tell him his house is the crime scene? What do I tell him?

Everything about that night was rushing through my mind at once. I needed time to process the depth of my assault. It hurt whenever I breathed, and what felt like cracked ribs were making the pain more excruciating. I took shallow breaths, groaned, slowly leaned my head against my pillow, forced my swollen eyes shut, and stifled a cry.

Jonathan's love for me was no longer enough to get me through my agony. I needed him to leave my room. Get out of my life and disappear as if he had never met me. I wanted him to be gone by the next time I opened my eyes. I needed to think about what I'd say to convince him I didn't want to be with him anymore. Nothing I could say would be reason enough, but I must get rid of him, one way or another.

I tossed excuses back and forth in my head, but none would be enough to make him leave me. I needed to think and breathe, and I couldn't with him shadowing me.

Damien made sure I had to let Jonathan go. Not temporarily, not to take a breather, but a permanent break that could never mend.

I could tell Jonathan a beast had attacked me. Technically, it would not be a lie. I'd just let him believe the beast was a wild animal, which he'd find ridiculously unbelievable since no wild animals roamed the streets of Ironshore. At least not those on four legs.

I was not the only victim of my assault. While I may be the one with the fractured skull, cracked ribs, busted lips, shattered pelvis, and disfigured face, Jonathan was the one with the broken heart and the half-dead girlfriend.

Chapter 23

Over His Dead Body

Vivienne

It puzzled me why Damien battered me to near death. But, since the son-of-a-bitch was stupid enough to leave me alive, I was determined not to let him get away with what he did to me. Whenever I closed my eyes, I would re-live every second of the nightmare he put me through.

My parents taught me to beware of strangers, but Damien was no stranger. I never thought his hostility toward me would almost become fatal, and I had no choice but to keep this near-fatal encounter a secret from the one person who would stop at nothing to get justice for me. I wasn't proud of myself for ignoring Jonathan after waking up and finding him asleep, but I didn't have a choice. I was desperate and didn't know what to tell him.

I had a panic attack, dreading what to say, and finding him in the same spot, wearing the same clothes days after he brought me to the hospital, broke my heart. That's how I was convinced he would never leave my bedside, and I had to think fast.

"Nurse, what day is today?" I whispered to Nurse Blair. Her warm hands against my face, while she changed my bandages, were comforting. She was with me when I came out of unconsciousness, and I had asked her to keep Jonathan out of the loop while I figured out what to tell him. But I wasn't sure how long she'd be able to oblige.

"Wednesday. You came on Sunday, remember? We talked about this yesterday," she said, her lips brushing against my ear.

"I'm starting to remember what happened to me," I told her.

She nudged her head over at Jonathan. "When will you talk to him about what happened? He's been here for days, waiting for the moment you wake up. I'm not sure how much longer I can convince him you're still unconscious."

If only Nurse Blair knew how Jonathan Hastings and my assault were connected, she wouldn't be so eager for me to talk to him. But she saw a man who looked disheveled. The only logical conclusion was that he must be terrified that I'd die. And while I seemed insensitive, my reasons for ignoring him were complicated. If he knew I was awake, he'd want me to tell him where I got the bruises all over my body: fractured skull and gashes the size of raisins on my face, cracked ribs, busted lips, swollen beyond recognition as if a train had run over me, and I was in no mood to argue with him. I was sure he'd pepper me with questions I did not want to answer.

"You mean he has been here all this time?" It was a silly question. There was no way he would leave my side, not even if the hospital were under quarantine.

"Every day since. We didn't think you'd make it, and he'd be happy to know you're improving nicely. I'm unsure I'll be able to convince him much longer that you are still in a coma. He seems like a smart man."

"Oh, Nurse," I sighed. "You don't know him like I do. He can never know I'm awake." I could only talk through clenched teeth without feeling like the stitches on my lips would burst. "It hurts whenever I open my mouth."

"You haven't opened it for days. It's natural in your condition to feel a bit sore. The more you talk, the less painful it becomes." Nurse Blair held a bottle of water up to my parched lips.

"Are you sure they haven't wired my mouth? I can barely open it," I said through clenched teeth before I took a sip of the water.

"No, it's not wired. But do you have pain anywhere else?" She then lightly pressed onto my belly, and I twitched. It felt like it was on fire.

"The pain is excruciating," I told her. "Each time I move, it feels like my hip is breaking."

"Dr. Daley ordered tests, Vivienne. I'm taking you to get them done."

I struggled to open my left eye. It felt like someone glued the lids together. "Do I have to?" I whined.

Jonathan's snores grew louder.

"I can keep him out of the room if you want," Nurse Blair said.

"You can?" I became intrigued and wanted to laugh, but I couldn't. There was no way she could get rid of him that easily. "I'm just curious. How would you get him to leave?"

"It's not visiting hours, so he's not allowed to be here," she said.

"Do you think there's a chance of you putting him out? Over his dead body would he leave," I said, trying not to cry.

"Is he family?" she asked.

I appreciated that she was still whispering. One loud sound could wake him, and I was in no mood to argue.

Nurse Blair unlocked the wheels on my bed, pulled up the blanket, and tucked it under my armpits. "Kind of. Well, no, but you can't tell him he is not my family," I said. "He brought me in and has been here every day since. What does that tell you?"

"Only immediate family can be here when it's not visiting hours."

I was in pain and didn't want to worsen it. "If you say so," I said.

Getting Jonathan to leave my hospital room wouldn't be easy. He would evacuate and pay for the entire floor if asked to leave. Nurse Blair wheeled me out of the room without waking him or causing me additional suffering.

"You will have to tell him something soon. He seems like a good guy, but you may have your reasons for not wanting to talk to him."

I let out a soft sob, then pressed my feet against the bed's metal frame as if pressing on a car's brake. She halted, and I grabbed onto the rail. "Just a little longer, please don't tell him I woke up. Tell him I'm not responding well to treatment or something if he asks. I'll keep my eyes closed to make it believable."

"Should I call the police?" She sounded concerned like a mother, and suddenly, I was missing mine. Jonathan hadn't left the hospital since he brought me in, so he had not spoken to my parents, and they hadn't come to visit, so they had no idea what had happened to me. I needed my mother. She would have nursed me back to health immediately after she exploded from seeing me in such a dire condition. No amount of sedative would calm her. But I didn't need the drama.

"You do know who Jonathan Hastings is, don't you?"

"No, the name doesn't ring a bell."

"Well, everybody in Montego Bay knows him. I'm sure his face will come back to you. All I know is that the army couldn't make him leave. No police, please."

"He does look familiar, but I don't care. He was with your brother and his wife yesterday, but if you don't want him here, he can't be here," she said.

"Sean was here?" I almost pop another stitch. I hadn't thought much about him or Danielle.

"You have a family who is very worried about you," she said.

The ride relaxed me, and Nurse Blair made me feel like she cared. "Jonathan wouldn't hurt me." I slowly raised my arms and placed my hands under my head to cushion it.

We moved along the hallway and shuffled past the nurses who popped out from their stations to look at the distorted image passing them. They were young, dressed in white uniforms with tiny white hats pinned to the sides of their heads. I could read their lips and faces through one open eye. I was ashamed and wished Nurse Blair had drawn the sheet over my head. That way, they'd think I was dead.

"Why is it so difficult for you to talk to him?" she asked.

Jonathan will not go home until I talk to him, and if I die, he will not forgive himself for as long as he lives. But he should have left me to die from my injuries, and then I wouldn't have to face him to tell him who tried to kill me. I may feel differently years from now, but telling my boyfriend his brother raped me? Well, that will never happen.

"I'm not ready to re-live every detail of my assault. It's a story I cannot tell Jonathan. He'll want to know the full account of what happened, and if I tell him, he'll want a pound of flesh. Furthermore, I cannot re-live so much horror."

The nurse rolled me along, and my half-open eyes caught a glimpse of the clock on the wall, and my body shuddered. It dragged me back to Valence Avenue. It resembled the clock in Jonathan's living room. I could hear the loud tick as I sat on his veranda chair, waiting to see him. I turned my head away. The memory of Saturday night was flooding my mind.

Sean and Danielle had not visited me all day. Unlike Jonathan, they had small children at home who needed them, so I didn't expect them to plant themselves at my bedside. But like Jonathan, I had not spoken to them since, either. My brother thought my father had given him guardianship over me. He made it a habit of acting like my father, and I was not looking forward to talking with him.

We arrived at the Radiology department in less than five minutes. The equipment in the room intimidated me, but anywhere was better than being in the same place as Jonathan and explaining what had happened to me.

Nurse Blair pumped the brakes on my bed and handed me off to the technician. The coverings on his head and shoes made him look like he was wearing a hazmat suit. Luckily, I didn't have to leave the mobile bed the nurse wheeled me in on, and she didn't leave me alone with him. I appreciated the care I received from her, and although I wanted to tell her my story, I dared not try. I wouldn't get past telling her about the phone call that led to my assault without weeping. All I could think of was how my story would obliterate Jonathan's world.

"David, you will have to perform the exam where she is. She is fragile, and it's best if you do not move her," she told the scrawny-looking technician. He looked thirtyish with his big Afro, which made him seem older, or he could be an old soul.

"We don't normally do the exam that way," he said. "But she seemed in terrible shape, so I'll try to work around her."

"I know it's possible, so do your best," she told him.

I sensed everyone in the hospital had heard of my predicament. As I passed them in the hallway on my way to the exam room, the frightened looks on their faces were a dead giveaway. They whispered about who tried to kill me. One of them argued with another that it must be a jealous ex-boyfriend. The other replied that I partied too much and went home with the wrong guy. One nurse folded her fist to her chest and mouthed, "Be strong." Others stared at me until I was out of sight. I rolled down the hallway, not wanting to survive the next hour.

I was half dead when Jonathan brought me in. If not for him, I wouldn't have been alive to watch the pity on everyone's faces. Another fifteen minutes on my bedroom floor and I would have been dead on arrival at the hospital, and I was not the only one who thought so. Damien had rearranged my face. I had suffered blunt-force trauma. The nurses and doctors felt sorry for me, especially since the swelling still had not completely gone after four days.

And, waiting by my bedside for answers, was the one person who would move mountains to protect me, but I wished he would go away.

The cold metal object on my belly hurt with the slightest movement as the technician rubbed it back and forth. I tensed and bit into the soft tissues of my lower lip. I tasted blood. I groaned as he pressed harder to get better reading, but I didn't need an ultrasound or x-ray to confirm that my rapist broke something inside me.

I didn't think I'd fall victim to a rapist if I were a delinquent. At least delinquents know how to spot a predator. Street-smart women could easily detect predatory behaviors, but a religious country girl? Not so much. I was not used to the struggle it took to survive city life.

I returned to my room two hours later, and Jonathan was gone. And while part of me was relieved, the other part was devastated. It turned out I would miss him if he left me there. I looked at where he had sat for days. Now that he was gone, I hoped he'd return, even though I had silently prayed for him to leave me alone.

My heart sank, thinking I had gotten my wish. But he was back an hour later after searching the hospital for me.

"Nurse, where did you take her?" He rubbed his hand against my cheek. The warmth of his touch soothed me. I missed his gentle touches, especially when he rubbed his thumb against my lips right before he kissed them. I nearly gave away my ruse and almost leaned my head against his hand, lost in our connection.

"She got an x-ray," the young nurse replied.

Nurse Blair's shift had ended, and her replacement was equally caring. She was also aware that I didn't want to talk to Jonathan.

I am unsure how long I can keep pretending to be in a coma. If I keep up this deception for another day, he may lift me out of here to another hospital. I better not push my luck.

I was nervous thinking about what story I'd tell Jonathan. It couldn't be the truth. That much was clear. My rape went beyond hurting only me. I had been pretending to be in a coma since I came out of unconsciousness and saw him sleeping by my bedside. But there was no need to delay the inevitable much longer. The "together forever" he promised me would never happen, and I must convince him our love had run its course. It was okay to go through a puppy love phase.

But who was I kidding?

I opened my eyes after Nurse Blair closed the light blue wooden door behind her. She had been prodding me to talk with Jonathan instead of letting him believe my health was not improving. She had warned me my deception could backfire, and that's when I remembered how hurt I was after I found out I was dating Montego Bay's most eligible bachelor. But I also told Jonathan our relationship would not last. I didn't know when, but I never imagined my near-fatal assault would be what it would take.

I couldn't let Jonathan move me to another hospital. I liked the nurses taking care of me. It would take getting used to a new set of nurses who might treat me as if getting mauled by a human

Pitbull was my fault. I wasn't willing to take the risk. So, I faced my fears head-on.

I sat up and took a deep breath, ready to face Jonathan. "Why are you here?" My voice was full of disappointment.

"Hey, V!" Jonathan rushed over to me. "How are you feeling, Babe?" The sparks returned to his eyes.

"I'll live." I pulled myself closer to the top of the bed. "You don't need to be here," I said.

"Where else should I be? I am not leaving you here alone." He gently rubbed my forehead below the bandages over my eye.

"I'm fine, please go home. Look at you. You're a mess. Don't hang around here and harass the nurses. You will only do more harm than good."

"How much harm could I do right now? I have been sitting here for five days, praying, hoping, and waiting for you to wake up." He stroked the back of my hand before putting it up to his lips. "Do not waste your energy because I'm not leaving you here. Please do not tell me to go home. I am trying not to lose my mind because someone turned our world upside down, and I do not know who is responsible for you being here."

"You are responsible," I said immediately.

O damn. I didn't mean to say that out loud.

I pulled my hand from Jonathan's grasp. I regretted my answer the minute the words came out of my mouth. They sounded more believable in my head. I meant to say that I wouldn't have gotten mauled if I hadn't met him. "If you hadn't left me alone, I would not be lying in this hospital. You left me alone, and a monster viciously attacked me." I was surprised that my anger was still so raw. "I'm not sure our relationship can survive. I'm sure it won't," I said.

Jonathan's smile disappeared. "What does that mean?" he asked.

"It took us a long time to reach this point, but here we are. You can't say I didn't warn you. I didn't know how or what would happen, but I had suspected something would break us up."

I tapped a spot on the bed, then shuffled to accommodate him. "Sit, please. I have something to say, but I don't want you to overreact. Know that what I'm about to tell you is for your good and mine." I took his hand and gently squeezed it to calm myself. Suddenly, I became nervous.

"This will be the last time you get this close to me." I wiped my eyes as the tears started to build up. "I will always remember our time together. Greenspring is my favorite place to be with you. It was truly the best time of my life. But now I am afraid our relationship must end. I told you something would drive us apart. I didn't know what it would be."

"What are you talking about, V?" He gently wiped a tear from my cheek.

"Greenspring. You remember the conversation we had. Well, this is it. You will look back on our time together with fondness, but you will come to appreciate my decision today. I am sure you already know what happened to me, so you do not have to pretend we will be okay. I hope you'll understand my decision has absolutely nothing to do with the man you are. I cannot be with you anymore."

"You cannot mean that. It's the medication talking. You're just waking up from a coma, and you don't know what you're saying. Please, V, you can't mean it." He snuggled up to me on the small cot, gently lifted my head, and rested it on his shoulder. "This is so unfair. Why are you punishing me? You are casting me aside as if I did something to you. Don't you think I should know why you're dumping me the minute you open your eyes? You are being irrational. Please do not do this."

"I need time to think, Jonathan. It may take months or years, but I will need a long time to recover from this. I do not want to take my anger out on you. This is not something I'll get over anytime soon."

"Then tell me what I can do to help you." He stared at me as if searching for the girl who fell in love with him. "What am I supposed to tell your parents? They will think I am a no-good city boy who caused this on you. It's a very awkward position you are putting me in."

"My parents can never know what happened to me. Please, Jonathan, you must not tell them. They only agreed to send me to the city because I convinced them I'm responsible enough to attend college here. They can't go through this again." I held onto his hand. It was a desperate plea that I knew was too much to ask of him.

"Again?" His eyes widened with confusion. "This has happened to you before?" he asked, as if unsure what to make of what he had just heard. "So, I wasn't the only one keeping secrets?" He furrowed his brows.

"It's not the same, so don't give me that look," I said. "I was seven years old, Jonathan, I didn't even remember about it until recently. If you tell my parents about this, it will kill them. I beg you. They don't need to know."

"Don't you think Sean already told them?" He gently stroked my face with the back of his hand, then rubbed his thumb across my swollen lips before gently pulling me into him.

"They would have visited me already. I don't think he told them."

"That's not a promise I can make to you. Lying to your parents about something so serious. Come on, you cannot ask me to do that. You said you would need time to recover. What about the rest of us?"

I pulled away from him. "You don't want to worry yourself with my shame. If you're around, I'll never get over it anyway. Sean won't hold it against you if you stop visiting me," I said.

"Sean? I don't care about Sean's feelings right now. I care about you, and I will always worry about you. I get it that he's devastated, and he may never speak to me again, but I can't worry about that right now. Your parents will ask me how you ended up in a hospital, fighting for your life. I don't have the slightest idea what to tell them." The damage had been done to Jonathan's bubbly personality, and the sparks that usually lit up his eyes had disappeared. "You are breaking up with me, and I do not even know why. Now you want me not to tell your parents that you almost died. I'm not sure what makes you suddenly think that I'm the enemy. This makes no sense, and I'm having a hard time understanding why you would want to throw away our relationship."

"When the doctor discharges me, please don't visit me at Sean's," I said, staring at the open space beside my bed.

"That further proves that you're punishing me for what someone else did to you. Was I wrong to think I meant something to you? How can you shut me out completely? Something horrible you think I did must make me the target of your anger."

"I have made up my mind, Jonathan. Please do not be mad at me. I cannot see how we can recover from this."

"What exactly are you blaming me for, V? Please tell me if it's something I did because I haven't the slightest idea."

"Nothing you did," I said.

"Then it must be something deeper and hidden, like you now realized that you didn't love me. Please tell me exactly what you think I have done to deserve your anger."

"I cannot deal with you right now, Jonathan. Understand that I have been to Hell, and I'll never be back to normal. My decision is not because of any regret I have about us."

"Don't give me that. I'm not stupid. You're not making sense right now." He got up and walked over to the other side of the room. "Be honest and tell me why our relationship cannot survive. Why is it that you must sacrifice us?" He shoved his hands inside his pockets, his eyes beseeching.

"Because he broke me!" I clenched my jaw and screamed at him. The rage I hid had finally escaped.

"Then tell me who did, for God's sake," he said. The pain in his voice almost made me change my mind. "What did you expect me to do, V? Did you think I would run away with my tail between my legs and hide in a corner somewhere? What kind of man do you take me for?" His voice had escaped to the hallway.

"Can you sit? You don't need to broadcast my business to the entire hospital. I don't want to argue with you. I mean what I said, I have no more interest in a relationship with you. Over time I may feel different, but I am too angry to think ahead. I feel like you're suffocating me, and I'll burst if you don't go. It's what's best for both of us."

Jonathan stared at me as our world collapsed in that hospital room. It was the most explosive moment of our relationship. Nothing or no one could make me change my mind. I was done with him. There was nothing left to fight for, and I didn't have the strength to argue with a man unwilling to accept my decision as final.

Chapter 24

Don't Break My Heart

Jonathan

"May I come in?" Dr. Daley knocked and pushed the door open, not waiting for a response. He wasn't there to check up on V. He had come in earlier and was not due back for another four hours.

"Hello, Dr. Daley. I have been waiting for you to tell me I am all set to go home," V said, smiling. "I've been anticipating my discharge. I can't wait to get out of here. Although I couldn't ask for better people to take care of me, but I must prepare for school in a few days."

"I'm afraid there's a problem, Vivienne. We need to keep you a little bit longer," Dr. Daley said, looking at the paper in his hand.

"Oh God." V thrust her head back and sighed. "Why can't I go home today? It's been more than a week. What's the hold-up?" she asked.

"I'm sorry, but your condition is more complicated than we thought."

"Complicated? How so, Doctor?" I rushed over to him, wide-eyed.

"Don't answer that!" V said immediately.

"Vivienne! You can't be serious right now."

"Jonathan is leaving, Dr. Daley. There's no need to burden him with my health problems. Whatever you need to discuss, it can wait."

"In that case, we'll talk about it when I come back to check on you later." Dr. Daley shook my hand, gave V a nod, and left the room.

I took a deep breath, then narrowed my glossy eyes to V. My heart raced with a mixture of fear and sadness. "Vivienne Pearson!" I said, biting my bottom lip to prevent the tears that had built up from pouring out. "I have never met anyone so stubborn. I didn't think I could survive the week for failing to protect you. Our world is in turmoil, yet you choose this moment to shut me out. Why? It doesn't make sense. It doesn't matter what happened, I will love you forever."

"Why do you keep making promises you can't keep? For God's sake, haven't you done enough? I knew you were bad for me the first day we met. I didn't want to be with you. You're trouble, Jonathan Hastings. Just move on to your next victim and leave me alone. Please find someone else to pity. I've had enough of that since I got here," V said, taking a long breath.

My fingers brought her face to me. "Do you expect me to walk out on you now? Now, V? You can't be serious." I cradled her face and lightly stroked the bandages.

She grabbed my hand, pushed it away, and walked over to the other side of the room. She wasn't going to make it easy for me.

"I'm dead serious, Jonathan," she said. "Let's not pretend you don't keep secrets. You strung me along without telling me who you were. So, I don't have to tell you a damn thing."

I followed her and gently pulled her into me. "So, you'll throw it in my face whenever we argue? You can't compare me not telling you who I was to who brutalized you. What did I do to deserve so much of your rage, V? Please tell me."

The thread that connected us had begun to unravel. V was breaking my heart as if she had decided long ago that we were over.

"Goodbye, Jonathan," she said, avoiding my penetrating stare.

"It can't be goodbye." I rubbed her forehead, then buried my face in her neck before resting my head on her shoulder. I couldn't speak for over a minute. "You know why it can't be goodbye, V?" I exhaled again, and my heart raced. "Because, on Sunday morning, right before sunrise, I arrived at your house and found you unresponsive. Not even your brother knew that you were dying inside his house." I held her chin and stroked it, gently rubbing my fingers over the bruises on her lower lip. "I thought it would be the last I'd see you. Whenever I think about it, I feel like I can't breathe.

"For days, I glued myself to your bedside, pleading with God to bring you back to me, and he did. With all my flaws, He knew I did not deserve His favor. But I didn't have anyone else to turn to. I needed Him to bring you back to me. So, no, V, you don't get to say goodbye until you tell me who did this to you."

She stiffened her shoulders against the wall as if trying to disappear into the concrete. "Stop badgering me," she said through clenched teeth. Her eyes were swollen, her face battered and bruised. She peered at me through her half-opened eyes. Her lips quivered as she forced back tears. "You must stop asking questions you don't want answers to, please," she said. That's when it finally broke me.

I could say nothing to heal the wounds and erase the scars. Nothing to get a smile from her cracked lips. I felt like V was being punished for things I had done in the past.

"Who put you in the hospital?" I sobbed, tears running down my face as if I let out a facet. It wasn't because of the crushing pain in my chest that felt like someone was ripping my heart out of its enclosure, but because of the distorted face in front of me. I promised to protect her, and I could feel her slipping away. I was about to lose her. "I don't want to go, V. Please don't let me walk out of here without telling me how one night away from you nearly got you killed. I just want to know, please. I found you curled up on your bedroom floor like a water-soaked puppy, left in the rain overnight. God knows what might have happened if I hadn't found you when I did. Who are you protecting?"

"Don't ask me again. It doesn't matter if you ask me ten different ways. I'm still not talking about it with you," V murmured.

"Just answer me this. Did you leave your house on Saturday to see me?" I lifted her chin with my index finger and held on to it with my thumb.

She closed her eyes and exhaled.

"I'm not talking to you anymore." She wrestled away.

"Where did you tell Danielle you were going? You know I didn't have an accident, so who told you I did? Where were you attacked, V?"

"I'm not talking to you about it, so please leave me alone. Can you do what I asked?"

"I don't know who you're protecting, but it's unfair to you, me, or your family. Did he threaten you not to talk? If that's the case, I can protect you from him. You don't have to be afraid anymore," I said.

"Yeah, right. Stop making promises you can't keep." She pressed her lips together, shot me a dirty look, and hissed. "You can't protect me, Jonathan! Otherwise, we wouldn't be having this conversation now, would we?"

"Do you even care about your parents? Do they deserve to know what happened to their daughter? I fell in love with the most beautiful girl I've ever met. Where is she? What happened to her between the time I left for Ochi to now? I know you're in there somewhere, V."

"The longer you stay here, badgering me, the less likely I will tell you. Nothing you say to me will ever make me re-live the day you let a maniac maul me. Where were you when I screamed your name? You left for Ochi without telling me; now you are here, forcing me to recount the worst day of my life. You don't deserve any answers!" she yelled at me.

"You don't believe I left you to be mauled," I said, desperation creeping into my voice. "I got an emergency call to go to Ochi. I should have called you when I arrived but planned to return. Things got chaotic."

"I don't want to hear your excuses," she replied, her tone becoming sharper. "No apologies can change what happened."

"What will you tell the police?" I asked, furrowing my brows. You will have to tell them something."

"Let me worry about that," V said, stone-faced. "Do not come back here. You and I are over, Jonathan. I don't want to be with you anymore. Please, for God's sake, leave me alone! I wish I had never met you."

She stared at me. Her eyes were cold, as all the light in them had faded.

"Did Nate do this to you? Please, Babe, you must tell me."

"Goodbye, Jonathan," she said, turning her head away.

"Like I said, this cannot be goodbye, V."
I kissed her cheek and stormed out.

Chapter 25

Oh, Baby, Baby!

Vivienne

I scrambled to the hallway as the double door swung open. Jonathan didn't look back, and I fell to the floor, sobbing.

I picked myself up five minutes later, crawled back inside, and sat on the edge of my bed. I swung my legs back and forth and stared into space. I turned to my left, and the vase with a dozen long-stemmed red roses caught my eye for the first time. I had not seen them before, but Jonathan was the only person who could have brought them. Every visit he made to me at home, he would show up with a bundle of the same kinds of roses. I often joked that I might need to plant a garden so he wouldn't go broke.

I stared at the vase and let out a soft cry. "O God, what have I done?" I buried my head in my hands. I did not expect it to hit me so hard. I had convinced myself I didn't need Jonathan. How could he believe me if I told him who raped me? I kicked him out of my life without a proper explanation or goodbye. However, there would never have been a perfect time to say goodbye to him. I could no longer process the possibility of a future with Jonathan.

I pulled out one of the stems, smelled the petals, and rubbed them against my cheek. I slowly moved them back and forth between my thumb and index finger, closed my eyes, and sighed. I picked at each petal and placed them next to me. By the time the vase was empty, there was a complete heart shape. I curled up in the middle of the bed, faced with the enormity of what I had just done.

It was hard to watch Jonathan fall apart. But where would I begin telling him how my assault began? I hated seeing him distraught. He was not accustomed to losing his temper, let alone total control. I was making a colossal mistake. But I couldn't let him know I was crumbling. He'd know how much I didn't want him to go if I wavered. I'd have to tell him I had seen the white light as Damien's hands crushed my windpipe. How I bled on his satin sheet, and his house held all the evidence to lock up this menace for a long time. I couldn't tell him that the burn marks on my breast and between my legs would be permanent, and I would have to say to him I had seen the giant poster of us on his Kawasaki with my arms wrapped around him, and he would know I had finally seen the inside of his bedroom. I would have to tell him every itty-bitty detail and risk watching his whole life crumble, one sentence at a time. I couldn't do that to him. Losing me was better than losing everything he believed about the people in his life. But I was dying to tell him. At least I wouldn't feel like the world had abandoned me. I wouldn't feel like I had no way out of my misery. Either I tell Jonathan the whole story and risk tearing his world open to reveal the rot among him, or I break up with him. Either way, I'd end up the villain.

Dr. Daley returned about ten o'clock. I was anxious to hear about the complications. He seemed to have devastating news.

At first, Dr. Daley didn't speak. He pulled up the small chair Jonathan had slept on for days and sat facing me. He seemed different from all the other times. It was as if the news he would give me was hard to say. His visits to my room usually sounded cheery. This time, there was none of that, only silence with a look of pity.

He opened the manila folder he carried, pulled out a letter-size paper, dragged the chair closer, and cleared his throat. "Vivienne. I won't beat around the bush. There is no easy way to tell you. I won't beat around the bush. It's not good news." He shook his head, and my heart felt like it had dropped ten feet from my chest. My mind went straight to the possibility of an STD, irreparable damage to my uterus, or HIV, anything but what he told me. After all, Damien was a promiscuous, ganja-smoking alcoholic.

"You're scaring me, Doctor." I shuffled forward and sat on the edge of my bed, my hands resting on each side.

"You're pregnant, Vivienne. We ran tests, and they all confirmed it." My hands shook when he handed me the piece of paper. "I'm sure you didn't want this information under these circumstances, and I am so sorry I have to give it to you."

I shook my head, grabbed the paper from him, and stared at it. "Pregnant? That can't be. Can it?" I looked up from the paper at him. "There is just no way this is correct. Re-run the test!" I demanded.

"I'm sorry, Vivienne, but it is correct." He held on to my hands, as they wouldn't stop shaking. I didn't even make a sound when the tears poured out of my eyes.

"My life is over. All it took was an oversized, sex-crazed psychopath to destroy me."

"I know how you must feel," he said.

"You don't, Doctor. I can't be pregnant. I came to the city to start school in September. There is no way I can carry the baby of the man who raped me. No way under the sun." I shook my head as if I didn't know how to make it stop moving.

"You must take it out of me, Doctor. I don't want it. I don't want it! I don't want it inside me; please take it out, I beg you!" I screamed.

"There's no option other than carrying the baby to term, Vivienne. That may seem unfair, given what happened. I wish there were a way out for you. I truly do."

Since I woke from unconsciousness, Dr. Daley focused on my healing like a laser. He treated me like a concerned father, not just my doctor, and would check on me at least twice daily.

"I'll return later to update you when you can go home." A tear fell out of his eye when he turned to leave.

"I did not want him, had no interest in him, thought he was a big fat jerk, and wouldn't be with him if he was the last man on earth. That's what I told him," I said between sobs. "Guys in Greenspring know how to deal with that kind of rejection. Their egos are not as big as these men in the city. But I didn't realize that the girls who refused to play nice found out the hard way how vicious city guys can be." I grabbed a tissue from the table beside my bed and wiped the snot from my nose.

Dr. Daley wiped his eyes and faced me again. "Vivienne, if you don't tell us who raped you, he won't be punished. So, I'm begging you to please give me a name. The police would like to know who is responsible for putting you in the hospital and now fathers your baby."

I took a deep breath and straightened myself. I had already decided on the night of my assault that I could never tell anyone about it. And if not for the fact that the bastard almost killed me, I would have just licked my wounds like most victims who chose to stay silent. It was just my burden to bear alone.

"I'm sorry, Dr. Daley, but telling you will do more harm than good," I said after a long pause.

He lifted my chin and held on to it. "I'm sorry you feel that way, but he may do the same to another girl if you don't report him. It's your call," he said, then tapped my left shoulder.

Dr. Daley left my room, looking disappointed.

The paper in my hand confirmed the positive pregnancy test. I crushed it into a ball, hurled it across the room, and wept openly. I could not process the magnitude of being pregnant by my rapist. I had big dreams, which had become nightmares overnight. It was just too much, even after witnessing the tragedy of Monica Stevens. At least she didn't accuse anyone of raping her.

I paced every square inch of my hospital room, reflecting on how I got to this point in my life, and I empathized with Monica's desperation. Even though her decision to terminate her pregnancy turned tragic quickly, I understood why she deemed it necessary.

Monica never got a chance to achieve her dreams, and my rapist stole mine right from under me. No morning-after pills were available, and no laws gave me the freedom to decide whether I wanted a baby, constantly reminding me of the experience that nearly killed me. I was a long way from Greenspring without the protection of my family, so I concluded that no one could save me.

I lay on my bed contemplating my fate with only one choice.

Chapter 26

The Schizophrenic Nudist

Jonathan

I could have killed Nathaniel Walker, the schizophrenic nudist ex-pastor, after Vivienne threw me out of her hospital room. I went looking for him with a vengeance. I was sure he was responsible for attacking her.

Pastor Nate had become a nuisance to Ironshore. I was so close to putting him out of his misery. He was once the well-respected pastor of the church my parents once attended, and after he went off the rails, they started worshipping elsewhere.

In his glory days, Pastor Nate was one of the most celebrated young clergymen in Montego Bay. He built his church from scratch soon after he graduated from college. He was a dynamic preacher whom many touted as authentic. But as the years progressed, he started to ignore his teachings, and fornication became his biggest challenge. He couldn't keep his hands off the young girls in the church. He spiraled after the elders forced him out, and his fall from grace overwhelmed him.

Nate was the only person in Ironshore who called my next-door neighbor, Stephanie, Stephie. Not to be confused with the seventy-five-year-old woman living down the street who taught kindergarten for half a century. Her name was Stephie, and my neighbor was Stephanie, or Steph to her family, for as long as I was old enough to remember. But Nate would tell her he was not like the others, and she was his to call whatever he wanted. It annoyed her, and after he attacked her with a machete, she stayed clear of him. She was also a member of the church Nate once pastored, Saint Agnes Mission Tabernacle. Pastor Nathaniel Walker lost his mind one year after he lost his job.

The night I rescued V from him was all I could think about. I could not think of anyone else who was capable of such savagery. No one in their right mind could have inflicted so much damage on another individual, and I was determined to find him. The last time I saw him was two weeks earlier, leaning against the library, naked as on the day he was born. That was the first place I went after leaving the hospital.

According to Stephanie, Pastor Nate never felt any urgency except when he saw her. Her encounters with him were a little-known secret I latched onto. I had intended to seek revenge on whoever put V in the hospital, and Nate was my target.

I hurried to Valence Avenue when I couldn't find him, knocked on Stephanie's door, and beckoned for her to come outside. I didn't want anyone else to hear the conversation. Immediately, she could tell something was wrong. I had been crying. I never felt that emotionally devastated, but nothing ever pierced my soul like what they did to V.

"I'd like you to tell me about the night Nate attacked you. I've heard several versions, but I need to hear yours. You told me he was obsessed with you, but you never went into the whole story, and I'd like to know what happened the night he came after you." I calmed down a bit so I wouldn't miss anything she would tell me.

She closed the door behind her, sat on the steps, and looked up at me. She didn't have to ask why I suddenly needed to know. The news of V's assault had spread like wildfire.

I pulled out a brand-new pack of cigarettes, took one out, and flipped the lighter.

Stephanie snatched the cigarette out of my hand and crushed it. "Not in front of me, you don't. You're not starting that bad habit. I've known you all your life, you are not a smoker. You didn't come here to smoke. If you really want to know what happened the night Nate attacked me, I will tell you, if it means it will take that devastated look off your face."

My heart ached, and I was a shell of myself. Stephanie watched as I crumbled, plopping down beside her, while she told of the night she came to near death.

"'Step-hie, where are you? Come out, come out, wherever you are,' Nate cried, slapping his machete against the palm of his hand, sounding like one of those creepy voices in horror movies. His voice came from the living room at one o'clock in the morning. The closer he got to my bedroom, the more I panicked. I didn't know what to do, and I couldn't wrestle with this madman who was only a few steps away. So, I grabbed the small can of Mace I kept in my purse and tried to hide inside my closet. The Mace was for the pickpockets downtown. I never thought I'd need to defend myself from my former pastor inside my home.

"I covered my mouth to muzzle the involuntary screams that were escaping. I remembered that Preston always complained about me living alone, and when he realized I was not willing to live with him before we got married, he built an escape hatch. No one else knew it existed besides us and my father. Well, now you know, but I trust you with my life, so I don't have to worry about you hurting me." She rubbed my arm and smiled at me. "I crawled through the shower, pushed the rotating wall, and locked it after I got to the other side. When Preston introduced the idea of building the hatch, I fought with him. He and my father were becoming overprotective worry warts.

"I ran outside, pushed the back gate, and it could not open. I didn't have the key. But Nate had no idea where I was, so I had time to find another way out. I climbed over the three-foot fence and dashed barefoot to Clarita's house.

"The loud banging on Clarita's door must have alerted Nate. 'Step-hie!' I could hear him screaming for me as he ran back outside. It was dark, and I figured he was at least half naked, if not entirely. Clarita quickly opened her door, and I slid inside.

"Nate was chasing me, and I was out of breath. It haunts me to this day. I was frantic. A naked madman was chasing after me. Everyone knew Nate would turn on me eventually; they saw it coming, but I told myself that he was harmless as a former man of God."

I stared at Stephanie and noticed how calm she was talking about her ordeal. But whoever came after Vivienne stole more than just her innocence and was not as lucky as her. "The day Nate takes his last breath will be the day the people of Ironshore can live in peace. He's been a nuisance for too long," I said. Stephanie grabbed my hands. I had become jittery, seething with the need to avenge whoever was responsible for V's attack.

"My hands were still shaking, just like yours, when Clarita tucked me in the back room of her house. Nate was banging on her door then, calling out for me. At that moment, I thought about calling Preston from the phone in the room where I was, but I didn't want him to rush over and encounter Nate. I shuddered to think what he might have done to him," she continued. "It's been a year and six months since Nate broke into my house and came after me."

"How are you doing now? You seem like you've gotten past it," I said.

"Not even a little," she answered almost immediately. "Don't beat up on yourself. There was nothing you could have done to prevent what happened to Vivienne. What you can do now is make sure she gets the support she needs. She will need you around to help her through it."

I shook my head. "She broke up with me earlier today. She blames me for not being there when she needed me, and I can't disagree with that."

"Oh, Jonathan, I'm so sorry." She shuffled closer. "If it's any comfort, she'll come around. Just give her time," she said.

I wanted to believe V would come around, but deep in my gut, I knew otherwise.

"Be there, nonetheless. If you walk away from her now, it will be as if you don't care about her, and I know you love her. Stick around for her, she will need you moving forward." Her eyes pierced me as if waiting for confirmation.

I took a deep breath, exhaled, then nodded.

"Do you think it's my past catching up with me? I wasn't the most loyal boyfriend at times. But with V, she changed me. It's hard to explain, but I thought she was it for me."

Stephanie grabbed my chin with her right hand and laughed. "Dear sweet, gorgeous man. This is not your karma. You are one of the most handsome men I've known. If I were younger, I'd want you, too. You are not as bad as you think. You are young, and young people do silly things like running around. But if you think Vivienne is the one to make you settle down, you must prove it to her." She rubbed the top of my head and pulled me in for a hug.

"Do you think you'll ever get over what Nate did?" I needed to know, at some point, that V would get past her pain. If she couldn't, it would turn her into a completely different person, and I wouldn't change anything about her," I said.

"My trauma is one I wouldn't wish on my worst enemy," she said. "I still get counseling for his attempt on my life."

"How does it make you feel? Do you think that would be something I should introduce to V so she can move forward?"

"It can't hurt, but remember, not everyone wants to pour their heart out to a stranger, especially if it's something as horrific as what Vivienne went through."

"The fact that you're still getting counseling tells me that her experience might not be something she'll get over. Damn it, I won't get over it, especially if I lose her forever. I lost my girlfriend today, and everything in me screams revenge. I don't want to be alone tonight. Maybe I should camp out in the hospital parking lot. I will lose my mind if I'm not near her, but she won't even let me grieve with her."

I wanted to keep talking. If I stopped, I'd have to think about V's distorted face, which made me physically ill.

Stephanie went inside and came back with two beers. She handed one to me. "This will make you feel better," she said. "It relaxes me whenever I remember how close Nate got to me. Go ahead, I know you don't drink, but it will take the edge off."

"Thank you, but I don't know if anything will make me feel better."

I grabbed the bottle out of her hand and took my first sip, then a long, deep breath. For the next two hours, the moon kept us company.

Chapter 27

Ocean Currents

Vivienne

I grabbed the pill bottle off my nightstand before limping to the beach below Sean's house, Dr. Daley's pleas still ringing in my head days after begging me to give him the name of the man who put me in the hospital. Since he told me I was pregnant, the son of a bitch's name was the last thing I would disclose. All I wanted to do was get the seed he implanted out of me. Since Dr. Daley couldn't help me, the ocean had become my weapon of choice.

At last, I found a way out of my misery.

I gulped a couple of pills down. They lodged in my throat for a minute because I had no water to ease their way down. They did little to ease the pain that had been ripping through me for over a week. I should have doubled the dosage, but it didn't matter anymore. Permanent relief was in sight.

I took five steps forward, then two steps back, psyching myself up and deciding when to dive in. I dipped my toes into the warm water before sinking my right foot in—seashells lodged between my toes. The waves taunted me as they receded after beating furiously against the shore, and I wanted them to take me away.

I was done with Jonathan Hastings. I had run out of ways to let him know we were over. As for Sean, he was no better. If only he had acted like the big brother he was instead of my damn father, I wouldn't be trying to get away from him. There was much blame to heap on them. I could not endure one more day with either one. I could not tell them there was a life growing inside me, much less that I had no intention of carrying it to full term.

The seven to ten kids Jonathan wanted would never come from me, and I was painfully aware I would be robbing him of his greatest desire. My number one priority was to extract this seed out of me. But escaping Jonathan had become more challenging by the day. He was like a ghost, shadowing me. Since I got out of the hospital, all I could think of was to get the hell away from him as far and as fast as I could. He was the last person I wanted to see my body disappear beneath the surface. Losing me would be the one thing from which he could not recover, but loving him kept me from plunging in the minute I arrived at the beach.

Destroying Jonathan should not be the result of my unbearable pain. I did not mean to hurt him more than I already did, but I was consumed with too much shame, guilt, and grief to reason with him, and I was too far gone for him to save me. I could not pull back from the brink.

I plopped down on the vacant shore, fidgeting with the sand between my toes, picking out the seashells, throwing them back into the sea, and deciding when to disappear into the darkness. My anguish had boiled over, and my thoughts entered the deepest part of the sea, but if I stopped for a minute to listen, I would hear the seagulls squawking and the sounds of the cars above my head zipping by, but my mind was already at the bottom of the ocean. I just needed my body to get there with it.

It is the perfect place to escape from the world, my family, Jonathan, and this shame. There is no way I will give birth to this baby.

The water repeatedly washed against me, pulling me from the shore, and I closed my eyes, extended my arms, and let the waves carry me away. I finally freed myself from an assault that crushed more than my pelvis.

I freed myself from the shame, the struggle to breathe as my rapist wrapped his hands around my throat and squeezed, and squeezed, and squeezed, and squeezed, and squeezed until the light went out of my eyes. I would no longer see the smirk on his face as his sweat dripped onto me, and I would no longer smell the foul stench that seeped into my brain.

"Vivienne!" A voice cried out. "Vivienne, come back!" he yelled again, becoming frantic. There were about fifty feet between us as I drifted farther away from him while my mind traveled to Greenspring, blocking the sounds of sea creatures and his voice. I gently rode the waves as they carried me out into the deep. "Vivienne! Oh, God!" He dashed into the darkness while the waves pushed me back and forth.

His screams became more frantic and echoed throughout the deserted beach. My mind traveled to the countryside in Greenspring, and I remembered how I sat on the mountaintop and gazed at the sunset with him. Five minutes passed, and I drifted far beyond Jonathan's reach before the current gently pulled me underwater.

My future flashed before me. I searched for Jonathan, but he was not in it, only the scorn and disappointment from my parents, lamenting their decision to allow me to move to the city.

I was suffocating among the coral reefs, ten feet below the surface. Anything was better than bringing to term Damien's seed, and drowning was the only way to uproot it.

I repeatedly replayed every moment of my assault in my head. There was no way to tune out the brutality, no way to unsee his sweat dripping onto me. There was no way to forget his grunts as he forced himself into me. While mere feet above my head, Jonathan, whom I would rather die than tell who savaged me, scoured the sea, searching for me.

By the time I had decided to drown myself, I had lovingly tucked away the memories of our comatose relationship, and I no longer opened the door for him. The butterflies I usually felt whenever he was near me had long disappeared, ruined by an oversexed maniac, and replaced with the flutter of a heartbeat that anchored inside me.

Alone with my thoughts in the dark and underwater, my attempt at drowning my sorrow took Jonathan to the deep as he dived beneath the water and ransacked the ocean floor. If he were to find me, there would have to be a collision, or he would have to use his hands to feel his way through, and in that case, he could not lose focus. His fallacy that a rape victim with nothing else to lose would see reason took him to the bottom of the ocean, where I lay among the coral reefs. Either I was destined to ruin Jonathan's life, or he would die trying to save mine, but he was like a photoelectric sensor I could not evade. The magnetic force between us was bound to snap him to me eventually. It had been the closest he had gotten since I drove him out of my hospital room, and as I lay at the bottom of the ocean, I wondered what would happen to him if my life had ended there, with him being the only witness.

The night had camouflaged the white sands, and if Jonathan could not find me, the bottom of the sea was where he would want to be, but he was not about to concede defeat until he recovered me, dead or alive.

Chapter 28

The Drowning Man

Jonathan

Panic seized me when V's shadow disappeared from the water's surface. But without a moment's hesitation, I leaped in, not even considering the danger to my own life. All I could think of was that my girlfriend's life was in jeopardy as I witnessed her succumbing to the water's deadly clutches. The once serene surface had transformed into a snare and swallowed her whole. Every muscle in my body ached as I battled against an overwhelming force to reach her.

Time was ticking, a frantic race against the inevitable.

Amid the turmoil, I had to remain focused even as I struggled against the undercurrent, armed with nothing but my bare hands.

It was dark all around. It must have been divine intervention because I located V soon after I dived in.

I dragged V's waterlogged body up to the surface.

I clutched her, steadily pulling her toward the shore, hoping against all hope that I wasn't too late in these critical seconds where tragedy was perilously thin. Another rush of waves violently washed V out of my grasp, pulling her back out to sea. As I fought against the force, I swam after her.

I grabbed onto the tail end of V's dress just in time before she went under again. I wrapped it around my hand and pulled her into me just when another wave was about to hit us. I held on to her with all the strength I had as I fought against the roaring waves, determined not to let go of V. I slid under her, weaved my arms under hers before locking them across her chest, and gently pulled her limp body toward the shore, out of the clutches of the waves.

I frantically pumped her chest, praying for the water to spout out of her the minute her body hit the sand. "Is it so bad you'd rather die than talk to me, V? Please don't die on me tonight." My muffled sobs may have helped to jerk her motionless body forward and emptied her lungs.

I was exhausted as I lay on the shore, while the next few minutes felt like an eternity.

"Why didn't you just let me die? You keep interfering and prolonging my suffering," she said, barely audible.

I kissed her at the sound of her voice. I laid my face against her cheek, slowly moving it up and down to soothe her. "I can't,

V," I whispered, my voice hoarse. I had been screaming her name since she left the shore. "I'm sorry, but you cannot tell me not to save you. I'm not leaving you to die here. Please don't die and leave me. Not tonight or any other time." I rocked her back and forth to calm her shivering body.

I sniffled. It sounded like a muffled sob. My heart was breaking. I did not expect I'd have to fish my girlfriend out of the sea. But I was determined to save her, and she was too stubborn to let me.

"Leave me alone, for God's sake," she cried.

I collapsed onto the shore beside her, breathing heavily, overwhelmed with grief. "You have to let me help you," I said, fumbling in the darkness until my trembling fingers contacted her cheek. I cradled her face then gently rolled her on top of me.

I cushioned her against my chest for the next few minutes without speaking. She buried her face in my chest while I wrapped my arms around her.

"Don't think because you pulled me from the bottom of the sea, suddenly that makes you my guardian angel. You cannot imagine what he did to me, so if you cannot make me whole again, I see no point telling you who raped me," she said, coughing up the last of what was in her water-logged lungs.

"You refused to let me help you. Why, V? It's not okay that you would rather die than tell me who is responsible for almost killing you."

"How will you help me, Jonathan? Are you able to make my pain go away? What about the shame, as if my life does not matter? Will you get rid of all my hurt? If not, what good does it do to tell you anything?"

In the dark of night, cars whisked by on the roadway above us, unaware of the chaos below.

"To start, you could tell me who raped you. I can't sleep, and I follow you around like a guard dog to make sure you're okay, and now I must worry about what you might do to yourself. How can I protect you from that?" I squeezed her tight.

"I can't tell you, Jonathan," she cried. "It's not your fault, and I'm sorry I blamed you. I wish I could tell you." She held onto me while I cradled her.

At the ocean's edge, darkness all around us, the whistling of the waves had begun to calm me, and as we lay together, I remembered the promise I had made to V on our first date.

"This was not how I pictured us on the beach, V. When the sun comes up, I will have to explain to Sean how you ended up in the water beneath the surface, drifting out to sea. Telling him you don't want to live anymore will not go over well with him."

"Daddy was right. I let the city swallow me; now the sea did, too. I am so stupid to think that someone like me deserves more than what is in Greenspring. I wish I had not left," she cried.

"If you hadn't left, I would not have gotten the chance to know you. There's nothing you could've done to deserve what happened to you. I just wish you'd let me help you."

"Why do you even bother with me anyway?" Her voice trembled.

"My heart belongs to you, V, that's why. It doesn't matter how hard you push me away. It will always belong to you. I will not stop searching for the son of a bitch who assaulted you."

"And what will you do after you find him, ah? Kill him? If you do, then what's next? There is no way forward, Jonathan. If I tell you who raped me, you end up in prison, I guarantee that would happen, and I will not have that on my conscience. So let it go because it will not end well for either of you if you do not."

I gently rolled her off me and jumped to my feet. "Let it go? Wow! After everything that we mean to each other. You do not know me at all. Let it go? I will never let this go. Someone almost killed you, and you want me just to let it go?"

The anger in me was slowly rising. I couldn't hide it any longer. I felt the unease swelling up in my throat. The one person who consumed my every thought for the past two months gave up on us and was giving up on life. I couldn't be mad at her and didn't know where to direct my rage. I had no one else to blame but myself. The helplessness that overwhelmed me threatened to explode. I didn't know how to make V stop hurting. She had redefined my whole world and was leaving me out to dry. I couldn't make her see there was another way out.

Was I the only one who cared if she lived?

I turned my eyes to the dark sky and screamed.

I lifted V off the sand and carried her to her house an hour later.

Chapter 29

Dear Jonathan

Vivienne

With my love life destroyed and my suicide attempt thwarted, leaving Ironshore was my only choice. I had to leave Sean's house. My arguments with him had become too frequent for me to remain there, and my fights with Jonathan were a daily occurrence. He refused to leave me alone. And the growing proof of my rape had compounded an already distressing situation. My decision to leave Ironshore was erratic and ill-considered. But I consulted with no one and relied only on my emotions to guide my choices. I wanted to sever all ties to Montego Bay and everyone connecting me to the city.

An assault that gruesome was more than enough to get me as far away as possible. I had enough reasons to escape Montego Bay. Jonathan and I were over.

I grabbed a pen and paper and began writing.

Dear Jonathan,

I will be long gone when you receive this letter. Please, I beg you, do not try to find me. I need this time to clear my head. When the sun rises, tell Sean I said it was not your fault I nearly died, and tell Daddy I'm sorry I couldn't live up to his advice. When the sun comes up, Jonathan, that will be our goodbye, and you will be free to look into someone else's eyes.

You said you love me. I don't doubt that, but I'm no good to you now. My heart is not in our relationship. Know that wherever I'll be, I will think of you and remember when you promised me you would say I do, but I cannot stay in Ironshore, not even for one more day. I'll only be torturing myself for not telling you the truth. Keeping it from you is cruel, and letting you go is foolish, but I'm giving up on my fairytale ending.

Someday, I hope you'll forgive me for not having the courage to tell you about the night someone brutalized me. I cannot imagine you would still be in love with me if you knew. I need to hold on to your romantic gazes. I know you well enough, Jonathan, that you will stop at nothing, and no matter how long it takes, you will find out what took place, which is why I must be absent. I must disappear somewhere far away to clear my head. I need to escape this horrible stench that keeps following me everywhere. I hope you will forgive me for leaving this way. Know that wherever I go, I'll tuck your memories deep inside my heart.

Your love,

Vivienne.

I folded the final draft of the one-page letter, tucked the envelope under the lamp next to my bed, Jonathan's name in bold print, and drifted off to sleep.

Leaving without telling Sean hung on my conscience. But I feared he'd lock me away to prevent me from going.

The next day, right before sunrise, I boarded a bus. With the backpack I should have used for college, I disappeared from Montego Bay.

Chapter 30

Three Broken Hearts

Jonathan

The hole in the painting on the wall of Sean's veranda shook me into focus. That was how desperately he wanted to punch me after he read the letter V left for me, but I was relieved his fist caught the painting instead.

A look of pity suddenly came over him as if he felt sorry for me. I was crumbling before him.

"I should have seen this coming," I said after finally getting my lips to form a coherent sentence. "I shouldn't have let her out of my sight."

"What the hell are you talking about, Jonathan?" Sean crept toward me, tightening his jaw. The muscles in his face bulged as he narrowed his eyes on me. I could no longer see the hazel in them. The hand he used to punch the painting now folded into a ball as he got closer. I kept my eyes on his fist. I couldn't let him hit me in the face.

"She's gone, man, she's gone," I said as he tried to process what I said. He looked like he was about to explode.

"I know she's gone. I read the damn letter!" Sean yelled. "Where did my sister go? You had to know what was happening to her. You were never apart." Sean gritted his teeth and moved closer. "Where, Jonathan?!" The blood had drained from his face.

I lifted my head. I no longer cared if he punched me since I had promised him that I would protect V. It was a heartbreak I had to endure in front of the one person from whom I could not conceal the truth about V's attempted suicide.

I struggled to compose myself. Where would I begin to tell Sean that the last time I saw his sister, she didn't want to live? That I pulled her from the bottom of the ocean, and how frantic I was as I scoured the sea trying to find her, and how I would have died if I didn't.

"Talk to me! I will not miss your face the next time. What happened to Viv?" He exploded. That was the second time I saw him get angry. The first time was the day we rushed V to the hospital.

When it came to Sean, I'd always had my defenses down. There was no need to fight with a man who was obviously in pain. Out of love for his sister and respect for him, there was no way I'd start a fight I couldn't lose.

I walked over to the other end of the veranda, hoping he'd calm down while I figured out how to tell him I pulled V from the bottom of the ocean.

"I don't know where she's gone. I'm just finding out that she left," I said. "Stop shouting. I can't think while you're yelling at me." I closed my eyes and rested my head against the wall as I focused on Maxi Priest's music coming from the house down the street. I hoped it would soothe me enough to muster the courage to give Sean the answers he desperately sought. But it only made me feel worse. They were playing my favorite song, but it didn't put me in the same vibe as when I was with V.

"I trusted you to take care of her. You promised you would. How can you not know where she has gone?" Sean paced the veranda, nervously gliding his hand over his head before pounding it against the wall.

I tried to be sympathetic, but I braced myself for what would come from what I was about to tell him. "A week ago, V tried to kill herself. I'm not so sure she won't try again." My heart pounded as I waited for Sean to lose his mind completely.

"A week ago!" He grimaced at me. "You are telling me now that Viv tried to take her life? What kind of game are you playing, Jonathan?" He pushed me up against the burglar bars. "This whole thing is your fucking fault, you know." He had his fist inches from my face, and the tears he had been nursing broke like a dam. "I don't know how yet. But I will find out why she left to see you the night someone raped her."

I have known Sean for a long time and have never heard him curse. A hollow feeling filled my gut because I was the first to make him use the F word. "I told you I wasn't home and didn't see her." I wiggled out of his grip and straightened myself. I was not used to being yelled at or manhandled, but as much as I could defend myself, I chose not to escalate an already tense situation. I would have been just as angry if someone had brutalized my sister, and I was more distraught about losing V than I ever could.

"Viv is not a liar!" he yelled. "If she said you were hurt, she believed it."

"I don't believe she lied, but she wouldn't talk to me, and I don't know what else to do."

"If you love her like you said, you will find who did this to her. You will find her, and you will bring her home. I'm beginning to think her attack was not random. If you hadn't gotten involved with her, none of this would have happened."

"You don't think I know that?" I walked away, then stuck my fingers through the burglar bars surrounding the veranda.

"Then what will you do about it?" Sean's voice cracked. "I always told you I was sorry for the poor girl who fell for you. Now you've got my sister missing, and I can't help but think her disappearance is not a coincidence with her attack. "Could one of your old girlfriends set her up?" he asked.

"I never professed to be an angel. God knows I've had my share of fun with women. Most times, I wasn't even the one pursuing them. They'd latch onto me for one reason or another. Even their mothers would chase me, thinking I was the perfect catch for their daughters. But even before I met V, I stopped messing with any of them. Why would you think one of my exes is responsible?" I asked. But I already knew what his response would be. I tried not to focus on the tumultuous time I had with Jennifer. I didn't want to remember how toxic the relationship was.

"Women fight over you all the time. You're not exactly a damn choir boy. Everyone is out to get her when you put Viv on blast. You made her an enemy of all your screwed-up girlfriends. One of them doesn't want her with you. Viv is in the way. Or, just frigging, maybe, you messed up. I know how bad your relationship with Jennifer was. You told me she stalked you for months. Find out where she was. You don't want me to confront her."

"You should know me better than to think I'd let anything happen to V."

My eyes caught Sean's when those words left my lips, and I realized they were not the best choice. He glared at me, his fist in a ball, as he inched closer. I straightened myself, our eyes locked, as I waited for the moment he raised his fist.

"But something did happen to her! Someone raped and beat the crap out of her. So don't tell me you won't let anything happen to her. It already did!"

I walked across the veranda, leaned against the burglar bars, tucked my hands in my pocket, and crossed my legs at the ankles. I tilted my head back and sighed. "She dumped me right before she left the hospital. I won't stop looking for her, but I don't know where to begin."

He loosened his fist, then ran his hand over his head to calm down. "Why did she break up with you? Is there something you're not telling me?" His voice was calmer now, and I was relieved we wouldn't come to blows.

"What do you think? She blamed me, just like you're doing now," I said, letting out the breath I had been holding. "She wouldn't talk to me. I pleaded with her day and night, and I couldn't get her to give me a name or tell me what happened to her. I know she's hiding something. I didn't know how to break through to her."

"I don't care how you do it, but you must bring her home. I am not telling my parents that Viv disappeared after someone brutalized her. You got that! Just find her, or else!"

The day could not have gotten any worse for Sean or me. So, when he punched his hand through the painting, it was his way of finally letting out some pent-up frustration about his inability to protect V. I couldn't give him any answers. His sister had disappeared, and we were both in the dark.

"When I told you to tell Viv who you are, you needed to tell her everything, not just about your family. I meant all of it. You should have told her about Jennifer. I blame myself for not telling her. I should not have relied on you."

Although my breakup with Jennifer was tumultuous, I refused to believe she could set V up. I didn't think she had that bitterness. But then again, this was the same woman who tried to mow me down.

I reflected on why men exercised their power over women through rape. It was the most disturbing act of violence against anyone and concluded that sexual assault should be one of those crimes that warranted unforgiveness. I wasn't about to forgive the criminal who tortured my girlfriend.

Sometimes, we convince ourselves that when we forgive, the benefit is not for the other person but for us and that it is better to forgive the person who has wronged us instead of holding on to old grievances. That is easier said than done.

There was a saying, "To err is human; to forgive is divine." It was hard for me to forgive someone who tried to kill the person I loved and took away her entire future before she could begin living. Nothing could be more brutal than that. Nothing was less worthy of forgiveness. There was nothing more difficult to forgive than that. To absolve the person who wrecked so many lives in just one night. Well, I was not that person. That sounded like a job for a higher power.

Sean looked at me with tremendous grief in his eyes. I had never seen him cry, and it was distressing to watch. For a while, he did not speak. He just stared at me. It hurt me to have to see him suffer. I wanted to tell him I'd relentlessly track down the creep that decimated our lives, but I could not ignore the dead look in his eyes.

Sean fell onto the veranda chair, and I realized he would have to take the long journey to Greenspring to tell his parents their daughter had vanished.

Danielle walked in from her trip downtown. She missed the scuffle but did not have to ask what was wrong. My face said it, confirmed by Sean's bruised knuckles and look of devastation. She knew the fight had to be about V.

She greeted me, set the grocery bags on the veranda table, sat beside her husband without saying another word, and extended her arms. She cradled his head in her elbow.

Something had to be done to turn the tide of misfortunes and catastrophes. Three heads, three broken hearts, and none of us had the first clue where to begin looking for V.

But I was sure I would find her even if I had to use every red cent.

Chapter 31

Lonely Won't Leave Me Alone.

Vivienne

I left Ironshore without saying goodbye to Sean. I was aware he did not deserve the way I sneaked out of his house, leaving him to explain to our parents that I had disappeared without a trace.

I boarded a minibus to Sav-la-mar before connecting to another heading to Mandeville. I was dressed in blue jeans, a red and white striped polo shirt, and the backpack I had brought with me from Greenspring. The three-hour journey gave me time to reflect on my life and the people I was leaving behind. The first thing that came to mind was the letter I left for Jonathan. It was the only sure way to end our relationship. It would never have happened if it were up to him.

The journey from Montego Bay wasn't just a physical distance. It was a voyage through the depths of my sorrow. Each item I packed was not just a piece of clothing but a fragment of a future I would no longer have. My backpack, heavy with regrets, held the crushing weight of loneliness and became the vessel carrying the remnants of my heart and the shattered life I had dragged behind me.

I sat at the back of the bus and placed my backpack on the empty seat next to me. I rummaged through the pockets and searched for the last letter I received from my aunt.

We drove past an orange grove leading into the community of about two hundred residents with the smell of burnt sugar cane wafting through the air, indicating the Frome Sugar Factory was nearby. We've passed the "You're Leaving St. James" sign a while back. The similarities to Greenspring were stark. Narrow, winding, and scanty roads for miles and no honking of horns, except for the old market bus with baskets of ground provisions on top heading to the farmers' market. Animals grazed on the uncut grass, nibbling around the blooms of wild Cerasee with their tiny green bumpy pods that turned bright yellow when ripe and felt like a crocodile's skin, spreading along the roadways, and overwhelming the nearby plants.

I rested my head on the windowsill. The wind blew through my hair as I stared outside at the mangy dog that whimpered and hopped away. It was as if I was driving home to Greenspring. A small blue and white post office served the community a mile further down. A rusty phone booth that urgently needed repair was next to the all-age school, closed for the summer. The large sign at the entrance stated that the newly built Housing Scheme was constructed for civil servants.

Across the road, women crossed the river with loads of laundry on their heads. Farmers loaded mangoes in hampers hoisted on their donkeys, stopping to let the bus pass. For how long it would take, this small countryside of Spring Valley, with its humble residents just outside Mandeville, would become my solitary confinement.

Greenspring and my parents had become casualties of my assault. I had abandoned my country road for somewhere untouched by my rape. The shame pushed me to find refuge in this tiny community. The guilt of blaming Jonathan for leaving me alone while Damien lured and raped me and the growing proof I could not tell anyone about had convinced me that Jonathan would never forgive me if he knew the truth. Our relationship was barely over two months old. How could I expect him to take my side over his brother's?

It was hard to pull my mind away from Jonathan for long. During the brief time we spent together, we did everything together, went everywhere together, and spent every minute outside work with each other at his house. The place that held so many precious memories had become my most hated. I couldn't go back there.

I stared out the window. The wind dried my tears before they had a chance to fall, and I closed my eyes and lamented the destruction of my future.

I hopped off the bus, looked around, and realized it was the middle of nowhere. I walked half a mile farther up the road before I came across the first building. The ten-year-old boy I met on my way had given me directions. All I had was a name and an address. Josephine Blagrove, Spring Valley, Manchester. The last time I saw Aunty Josephine, I was twelve years old when she visited Greenspring for my grandmother's funeral, and even then, she and my father had barely spoken. Their story was one my father refused to tell me. But, after graduating high school, I received a letter from my aunt congratulating me. I couldn't tell my father about it. I was afraid he would ban me from communicating with her.

I climbed the steps of an old wooden grocery store and went inside. No one was in sight. I turned to walk back out the door when an old lady walked in from the back of the building.

"May I help you?" She peered over her thick-rimmed glasses, the strings hanging behind her ears. She frowned, leaned forward, made her way toward me, and I realized her posture was permanent.

"I'm looking for Josephine Blagrove." My voice was low. I was afraid she'd tip over on me.

"You related?" Her eyes told me she didn't trust me, and her voice rattled like the wooden floor.

"Yes," I said cautiously. She didn't seem eager to tell me where Aunty Josephine lived. "My name is Vivienne. I've come from Montego Bay."

Maybe the distance convinced her, or it could be a sudden burst of pity. I looked exhausted, and directions followed swiftly. "Take the next right turn. Her house is the second one on the left. Watch out for the dog at the first house," she warned.

"That's the least of my worries," I grumbled, then thanked her for the directions. Fear of a half-starved, mangy dog? "How bad could he be?" I smiled, thinking about the last dog I saw on my way.

Here I was, penniless and pregnant, abandoning everything and everyone I loved. Getting mauled by a dog seemed fitting for what I had done to my parents.

***

Farmers wielded machetes early every morning as they whistled and hustled to their farms since I arrived. Children fetched water from the stream at daybreak before leaving for school. The early morning dew covered their bare feet. Insects sounded like cicadas, and birds chirped while they emigrated, adding to the bustling sounds of daybreak. The rugged little countryside, known as Spring Valley, was where I would call home.

Chapter 32

Hiding in A Bottle

Jonathan

"Another one." I beckoned to Chara, the petite bartender, as she leaned forward to collect the empty bottles.

Her jet-black ponytail hung over her left shoulder and rested on the countertop. I ignored her disapproving stare and lifted the almost empty bottle to my lips for one last gulp. I could barely get the two words out. My speech slurred, and my vision blurred. Tears rolled down my cheeks when I reflected on pulling V from the bottom of the ocean. It was the second time in a week that someone had looked at me with disappointment.

But I had far worse things to worry about than a bartender who had no business being concerned about the amount of Red Stripe I tried to use to numb me. My fingers gripped the photograph of V I had been carrying since Sean issued an ultimatum to find her.

I clutched the picture to my chest. "Why did you have to leave, V?" I moaned from the agony within me.

The clanging of the beer bottles sounded like shattered glasses and jerked me from the daze in which I had fallen. I wasn't quite sure how many beers I'd had. It could have been more than seven. I stopped counting after the second. Trying to drink myself into a coma wasn't my most brilliant move.

Chara stared at me, itching to reprimand me. I banged my head repeatedly against the countertop. I would eventually knock myself out if I kept hitting it against the countertop. When that didn't work, I attempted to pry open the tap from the bottle before me, and I couldn't.

"That's the last one I'm serving." Chara scoffed. "I get it. You miss her. Everything inside is screaming out for her to come back. But what would she think if she returned and found you in such terrible shape? And your poor mother. My God, you'll kill her if you keep this up. Everyone knows you're not a heavy drinker, but here you are, chugging down almost ten bottles of beer for the third night this week. I hope you know you're not driving home in this condition."

"Who will stop me?" I wagged my finger at her with what little strength I had. "Don't forget who pays your salary," I mumbled.

"Your family might own this resort, but your mother will thank me for kicking you out. Right now, you're acting like the other one," she admonished, scrubbing the beer-stained counter. "You're the good son, Jonathan. You can't let Vivienne's disappearance cause you to become like Damien. This resort doesn't need one more drunk Hastings. Pull yourself together, or I'm calling your father."

"Call him, and you are fired!" I slurred, then rose off the counter, snatched the bottle, and staggered to the sofa nearby.

"I'll let the concierge know so he can prepare a room for you. You can't go home in this condition."

Chara followed behind me, snatching me up right before I hit the sofa. She gently laid my head against the pillow and sat beside me.

"Why did she leave me?" I wailed. I pulled my shirt out of my pants, crumpled with beer stains. I hadn't worn a tie since V kicked me out of her hospital room. "She won't be okay out there on her own. Her brother hates my guts, and I swear he would have killed me if he could get away with it. You should have seen the way he looked at me as if I was scum. He thinks I'm the cause of everything that happened to V. He believes Jennifer planned the attack. You know her, Chara. Please tell me she's not capable of something so horrific. Tell me my ex-girlfriend didn't try to get back at me by setting V up to be raped."

"You didn't tell me she was raped," Chara said in a hushed tone as she tried to prevent her voice from traveling throughout the bar. "My God, Jonathan, I am so sorry. Last night, you told me someone raped her. I assumed you meant roughed up." She pulled me in for a hug.

Everything inside me screamed revenge for the bastard who mutilated my girlfriend.

"If Jennifer set her up, how can I live with myself, knowing someone nearly killed her because of me?"

"Jonathan, I knew you long before you got me this job. You went to high school with my boyfriend. You used to bring Jennifer around. We all know what she was like. But, as much as she is vain, she is not that evil. Sean is wrong about her, and you didn't cause Vivienne to be assaulted. Give yourself a break, but please do not return to this bar unless it's to say hello. I hate to see you like this." She wrapped her arms around me.

"Maybe you didn't hear that she tried to run me over. I don't put anything past her, Chara. Oh God, what have I done?"

***

It was ten o'clock the following day when I woke up. The sun peered through the thick glass window ten stories off the ground. Someone must have pulled the drapes aside. I raised my hand over my eyes to block out the glare as a hand tugged on my leg. I peeped over the comforter, and Chara looked down at me. She was adorned in her miniskirt and high heels, her handbag slung

239

over her shoulders as if she were about to leave. I pulled the covers back over my head, ashamed about what I had done the night before.

"I am leaving, Jonathan. I will make sure no one sees me leaving your hotel room. It would not look good if people saw me sneaking out of here. But, before I go, remember what I said. You are not the reason Vivienne disappeared. Jennifer did not set her up. So, focus your attention on finding her. For a non-drinker, the amount of alcohol you consumed last night could have killed you."

"What happened last night?"

"I had to pry you away before you drown yourself in alcohol."

"Did we….?" I asked, lifting the covers and peering down. "I don't remember how I got in here," I said after coming out from under the covers.

"What kind of girl do you take me for?" She pursed her lips together and furrowed her brows. "I would have to be desperate and unscrupulous to take advantage of you while you were hiding in the beer bottles. At your most vulnerable, even a bartender has standards. And I do have standards, Jonathan," Chara said as she waved goodbye.

Chapter 33

Misery Loves Company

Vivienne

Rage consumed me, which fueled my loneliness months later. I was in a strange place to have a baby fathered by my rapist with no idea what the next chapter of my life would be, and most heartbreaking was how I'd lament daily over losing my family.

My parents had invested everything in me. Jasmine had expected me to put Greenspring on the map, and I left my love behind to die from worry. There was not a day I didn't think about Jonathan, remembering his tenderness and kind eyes. It was another punishment I had endured.

I lay on the small bed on my back, my legs apart, waiting to expel the result of the worst day of my life. "Push, Miss, push!

De baby nah go come out if you nuh push." The midwife coached me in patois. She was in her late fifties, knowledgeable and skillful, but seemed to have no formal education or training. But that did not prevent the five-footer from expertly performing her task. "Weh di baby fada deh?" She inquired about the paternity of my baby while I groaned. She may have already guessed there was a dark story behind my pregnancy. I was a stranger and barely legal.

"She doesn't have one, Ma'am," I replied, then let out another gigantic scream. "It hurts," I cried, squeezing my auntie's hand as she tapped my forehead with a damp rag to comfort me. I had no idea labor pains would be so intense.

The midwife constantly reshuffled stacks of towels under me as soon as I wrestled them out of place to find relief. The pot on the small two-burner gas stove in the kitchen had the boiling water she used for sanitizing, as Aunty Josephine's house had become a makeshift delivery room.

Outside, curious neighbors occasionally peeped through the open window and cheered me on while they waited to hear the baby scream. After hours of screaming at the top of my lungs, a fully formed human being emerged, and just like that, I became a mother.

"It's a girl!" The midwife smiled as she held my baby in the palm of her hands, cradling her head as she moved over to the small table near the bed. "She is perfect!" she declared. A healthy baby with fully developed lungs, two eyes, ears, hands, and feet were in her hands.

Cheers erupted outside. "Here's your daughter." She handed her to me after she cleaned her off. It was the first time I smiled in a long time. I cradled the innocent life in my arms and realized what they said about misery and company was spot on.

As much as I must now bond with the result of such a horrible day—a daughter I named Shannon Jayne Pearson. I couldn't help but think how much my life would have been different if it were not for the encounter with my rapist—a brute who pounced on me during Jonathan's absence.

Shannon bore an uncanny resemblance to Damien. She had his eyes, thick black hair, nose, and unibrows. I realized that "blood is thicker than water and misery loved company."

To give my daughter the best care, I must separate her from what Damien did to me. If I didn't, I'd rob her of the security she needed to thrive. But amid all that, I found that loving my daughter was not just a duty but a joy, easier than I thought possible.

I've been trying to understand why my dad and Aunty Josephine didn't get along. She took me in, no questions asked. You'd think women with such maternal skills were bound to have at least a dozen children. That's why when I asked to stay with her, she didn't hesitate.

She'd wake up at six every Sunday morning just as I pulled the covers over my head after staying up all night with Shannon. I struggled to adjust to the cold early morning air. No one could explain why Mandeville's temperature was more frigid than anywhere else in Jamaica. Soon after Shannon was born, I'd get out of bed each morning to find a bowl of cornmeal porridge, a boiled egg, codfish fritters, and a cup of freshly brewed mint my aunt got from her backyard garden sitting on the table.

The days came and went in a flash. Some days, I was at ease, caring for the little bundle I was now responsible for. On other days, my heart was fighting with my brain like I had been punished for running away.

I hadn't considered the ramifications of my inconsiderate decision to extricate myself from the toxicity around me. However, if I hadn't, I would have succeeded where I had previously failed.

It was as if I closed my eyes, and when I opened them, Shannon turned one year old, another doze, and she was two. Before you know it, I had a three-year-old hyperactive, curious toddler, a daughter Jonathan knew nothing of, and I was determined to keep it that way. It was not easy to forget what he meant to me. His memories wouldn't leave me alone.

I still had not gotten past my assault. More than giving birth away from the chaos I left back home, I wanted to find a way through my trauma. I had a flashback to the night on the beach and recoiled, thinking how I almost got Jonathan killed trying to rescue me. I could still hear his pleas as I drifted away whenever I closed my eyes. I realized how my actions endangered his life.

Aunty Josephine did not contact my parents only because I begged her not to. I wasn't ready to face them. I was still too ashamed that I couldn't even last six months in the city before my life fell apart.

The struggle to forget Montego Bay took me down the street to the ragged old telephone booth near the all-age school. It was the only one in Spring Valley and not very close to Aunty Josephine's house, but I was desperate to hear Jonathan's voice again. I had so much to tell him. It had been almost four years without him, and it was killing me.

A motorbike barreled toward me as I dragged my feet inside the phone booth. I lifted the blue receiver to dial, holding the phone away from my ear. The female passenger wrapped her arms around her male companion, and I smiled. They were riding an old jalopy, yet the woman seemed comfortable. It reminded me of the night Jonathan rescued me from Nate. I also remembered my first trip to Ocho Rios with him and his difficulty convincing me that the bike ride was safe.

The couple was the same age as we were. As they disappeared around the bend and out of sight, I turned my attention to why I was there. Nervously, I dialed the number to the Montego Bay location of Hideaway Resorts, the first time I ever did. I figured Jonathan must be at work.

The voice on the other end of the line jolted me. *"Hideaway, how may I direct your call?"* The female receptionist was polite.

"Jonathan Hastings, please," I said. It had been a long time since I spoke his name out loud, and it frightened me to say it.

My heart sank when I heard Maxi Priest's newest hit; Some Guys Have All the Luck, come over the phone. It would be two minutes later until the baritone voice hit me.

"This is Jonathan." My hands shook—that was the effect he had on me. He cleared his throat. "Hello. Are you there?" He spoke again.

"Tell my parents I'm okay," I said.

My heart was throbbing beyond my ability to stay still when Jonathan's voice rose, and he became frantic. "V! Where are you?"

My eyes welled up. I quickly hung up the telephone and rushed out of the booth. Hearing Jonathan's voice was more difficult than penning the Dear John letter I had left for him.

I had not matured beyond my trauma, as I thought. For four years, my mind was stuck. It was stuck with my family, stuck on Jonathan, and stuck on August 24, 1985. The world had moved on and left me behind, and I had no idea how to get out of my misery. I realized the only way to communicate with Jonathan would be with a pen and paper. Even if it was only to pretend, I was conversing with him.

After reading bedtime stories to Shannon, I pulled her pink blanket over her and sang her a lullaby. I exhaled, then stared at the notebook on the table. I sunk my teeth into my bottom lip to find courage, then wrapped my fingers around the blue paper mate pen.

> Dear Jonathan,
> There's so much I'd like to tell you, but I need
> to figure out where or how to begin. Today, I heard
> your voice, and it scared me. I couldn't bring

myself to tell you where I was. Hearing your voice was very hard. I was sure I was ready, but the years apart didn't do a thing to change the way I feel about you. It's difficult for me to move on, and I am stuck in this never-ending loop of reliving the day I threw you out of my hospital room.

I'm ashamed of myself for the way I treated you, but I was tortured into thinking you bore responsibility for my rape. Running away from you was the easy part. Getting over you, not so much. I'd take one step closer to calling you, especially when I think about our time in Greenspring, and then the memory of my assault would drag me two steps farther away. I constantly feel like I'm in a tug-a-war.

I wanted to call you many times before, and finally, after finding the courage, I froze when I heard your voice. If someone had told me I'd be tongue-tied with you, I'd say they didn't know me. I always have a response to you. You told me that was one of the things you loved about me. The way I held my own in a conversation. What did you call me? The feistiest girl you've ever met. That was what you told me on our first date. But that was because my parents taught me to stand up for myself.

I heard Maxi's new song today. It took me back to when you introduced me to his music and said he looked like Sean. That's when I fell in love with them too. How is Sean? He must have been distraught. I didn't think that far ahead when I left you to explain to him why I tried drowning myself.

I know I messed up, leaving the way I did. I should have been braver to confide in him about what was happening to me. I hope one day he'll be able to forgive me. Hopefully, he didn't try to kill you. I'm sure you know by now that he is very protective of me. Surprisingly, everyone here is kind, even the young guys. They may have suspected that something terrible had happened. But I dare not tell anyone what I've been through.

I rarely have moments where I smile these days, but today, I did. Do you remember when I didn't want to ride to Ocho Rios, and you and Sean ganged up on me, trying to convince me that riding a bike was cool? Well, I remember that today, too. That's one of the reasons it's not easy to forget about you. God knows I wish it were easier.

We both know you're why I'm still alive, well, you and this little one by my side. I've got a daughter now. She will be the most challenging part of my trauma to explain if I get to see you again. It was the main reason I ran away. Maybe we could have found a way to get past my pain, but having to tell you that your brother is my rapist who fathers my baby? That would be too much, and I don't know if you'd even believe me.

Your memories keep me from losing my mind. I don't know what I'd do without them. The truth is, I'm still determining how much longer I'll stay hidden. Even though I've already said goodbye, these feelings I have for you refuse to die and are forcing me not to forget about you.

Some things will take a long time to explain, Jonathan, and right now, I don't know how to start the conversation. It might be too late now. You tried to get it out of me. I should have told you what happened long ago when you pleaded with me. I'm not even able to tell my aunt. She's never asked me why I ran away. She just knew she couldn't turn her back on me. She's waiting until I'm ready to talk to her about it. She reminds me of my mother. She is not pushy or judgmental, just kind and patient, and attends church just as often.

I got a job at the All-Age School last year. Although I couldn't start college, these little ones gave me a new purpose. I'm not giving up hope, however. There is still time for me to become Professor Pearson. But I'm stuck here until I can get past what happened or when these little ones don't need me as much. They hung on to me like I was their mama. Miss Vivienne is what they call me. Can you believe it? I feel like an old lady whenever they call me that.

I will not be calling you again. It's just too hard to hear your voice. So, from now on, I'll tuck you into my diary. That way, I'll write more letters whenever I am tempted to cry. I'll keep them in a safe place until I can see you one more time. I would never have written this letter if only memories would leave like people do. I'll write again soon, and who knows, someday I'll find the courage to give these letters to you.

All my love,

-Vivienne

Chapter 34

Memories Don't Leave Like People Do

Jonathan

I could hardly wait to give V's parents the good news that their daughter was alive.

A cruel game had been played on them. The years they spent mourning V were hard to watch. I thought, somehow, it was my fault.

I had endured a storm of emotions as I reeled from a mixture of disbelief, anger, and remorse.

V is alive! That's all that matters.

Hearing V's voice was indescribable.

I breathed in and out through my mouth. An overwhelming sense of relief washed over me, as if V's voice recharged my heart; feeling like it was exploding against my ribs. I paced the entire length of my office, slapped my hands against the wall, and screamed.

***

After I got off work, I made the hourlong journey to Greenspring. It was my second visit of the week. A flicker of light returned to Mr. Pearson's eyes when I told him I had heard from V.

My fears that she had succeeded in taking her life were gone, albeit briefly. My worries would never completely disappear until she was back in my arms or at her parents' house. I was running out of places to look for her since I had already scoured Montego Bay.

I couldn't wrap my mind around the possibility that our relationship could be over, but I must put that aside and focus all my attention on finding her. It didn't matter whether she wanted me back. All I wanted was to make sure she was okay. I had tucked the goodbye letter she wrote me inside my wallet, occasionally pulling it out and rereading it to find a sense of peace and clues about where she could have gone. She left the comfort of her brother's home without saying goodbye to him and went out into the unknown to fend for herself.

She was not usually irresponsible, but she was a young girl who did not know how to cope with such a traumatic experience, which time alone could not heal.

I walked down to the river in Greenspring after I told her parents the good news. In the vast area where horses roamed, and cattle grazed, there was peace—a spiritual healing to my soul that connected me to V. I called it my Wonderland, our Garden of Eden. I needed to feel V's spirit again, if even temporarily.

"Sometimes I'd come here too, Jonathan."

Jasmine sneaked behind me as I peered beneath the clear water at the fish below.

"You're not the only one that's missing her. Sometimes, I want to jump into the water and not come out," she said. Her voice was sorrowful.

I spun around and faced her. "Jasmine!" I said, frightened. "Please don't. I'd hate you not being here when V comes back."

We were outside V's parents' house the day I told Jasmine her best friend had disappeared. I had to pick her up off the ground, and it took me half an hour to console her.

"It's been years and no hope of finding Viv. Jamaica is not so big that she could disappear without a trace." Jasmine began to cry.

"Can you think of anywhere she might have gone?" I asked. I put my arm around her shoulder, trying to comfort her.

"What I'd like to know, Jonathan, is what happened between you and Viv." Jasmine wiped away tears with her thumb. "You were so crazy about each other, then suddenly you started coming here alone, and no one has heard from her since."

"I did," I told her. "I heard from her today. The call was brief, but she wanted me to tell her parents she was okay. She didn't say anything else. I'm trying to find her but running out of places to look."

I led Jasmine to the coconut tree and sat on one of the wooden benches scattered across the valley.

"How did she sound?" she asked excitedly.

"Scared," I replied. "The good thing is that she is alive. But I need to find her, Jas, or I'll dissolve into madness. There's a pain in the middle of my chest that grips me each time I think about her, which is all the time. I'm afraid my heart will eventually rupture and do me in. I must get her back, Jasmine. I will not survive if I don't."

"I know it wasn't you who hurt her. She loved you wholeheartedly, but I think something horrible happened. I wish you would tell me what could be so devastating that she ran away from you. There is something about your avoidance of explaining why she left without even saying goodbye to her parents. Every time I asked you what happened, you dodged the question. Please, Jonathan, tell me what happened between you and my best friend," she pleaded.

"I don't know the whole story. She refused to tell me."

"So, tell me the half that you know." Her inquisitive eyes gazed at me. "Why aren't you together anymore?"

I threw a couple of stones into the water. But Jasmine wasn't about to let me avoid her question for much longer. But I wasn't going to tell her V tried to kill herself because someone raped and tortured her.

"She was hurting the last time I saw her; that's all I can tell you. I couldn't get her to talk to me about anything," I said. I couldn't let Jasmine know the terrible shape her best friend was in. How she sank beneath the ocean's surface, trying to disappear from the world. I didn't think Jasmine could handle knowing that someone disfigured her face. "No matter how hard I tried, I couldn't get her to tell me what happened. I would love to tell her parents where she is, but I don't know. She left sort of a cryptic goodbye letter before she disappeared," I told her. Except for Sean and I, no one else knew about the letter. I didn't think it was wise to alarm her parents. "I'll admit, it's not like her to be this selfish, but I can hardly blame her."

"I know you miss her, but I feel you are still holding back from telling me what caused her to run away. You're saying a lot, but none of it makes sense. Viv and I used to tell each other everything. I was the one who convinced her to take a chance on you." Jasmine grabbed the small pebbles from under her feet and threw them into the river. "Now I'm starting to question whether I should have done that. She is a smart, responsible person. Something dire must have caused her to pack up and leave. I think you are missing a big clue. Viv would never have disappeared if what happened to her wasn't harrowing." She eyed me intently. "Abandoning her family for this long? That's not Viv. I can't imagine what her parents are going through. They didn't even want her to go to Montego Bay. I remember how she pleaded with them until eventually they relented," Jasmine said.

I realized I hadn't done nearly enough to find V.

***

The First Time Ever I Saw Your Face. That was the music playing the last time V and I were together at my house. Sometimes, I'd wrap myself in the lyrics not to forget her.

Like spring water flowing toward a river, which was how her spirit had consumed me.

I opened the veranda gate to find my friends sitting on the steps outside my house, staging an intervention. I had been avoiding them. I couldn't tell them what had made V disappear, what had happened to her, or that I could not protect her.

"You look like crap, man. What if she walks through the door and sees you like this?" Blaise accosted me after I let them in. I swung the wine bottle to my lips, ignored him, dragged myself to my room, and sunk onto the bed.

"Why did you come? I told you to leave me alone. It's my fault she's gone. Not yours." I wasn't interested in hearing another one of Blaise's pep talks about patience, space, or time. My brain was still wrestling with V's limp body as I pulled her to shore, the night that kept spinning around in my head like a hamster on a wheel.

"How is it your fault? You've been acting like a complete jerk. If you don't stop playing that damn song, it's going to drive you mad. Every time I see you, you have a memorial or something. We don't hang out anymore. Vivienne is not dead, so stop torturing yourself. You're digging your grave with alcohol and whatever crap you think will help get you through the day. You're not the first person to lose someone you love. Pull yourself together, man," he said.

I couldn't bear listening to Blaise's reprimand any longer. I would do something terrible if I had hung around for another one of his "get over it" speeches.

Ten minutes later, I sat alone in the dark, looking out where I pulled V out of the water. There was no way to escape the torments, and I could still hear Roberta Flack in my head. I couldn't forget the first time I saw V's face, nor could I block out the memory of the last time I saw her.

Chapter 35

Killing Me Softly

Jonathan

"I've asked you so many times, Jonathan. What happened between you and Vivienne?" my mother asked with deep concern.

I sat beside her on the bench near the gazebo entrance outside her house. I rested my head on her shoulder; my heart felt like it was about to burst through my chest. There was no way I could delay telling her what happened to V. I needed to talk to someone about my internal turmoil. I couldn't escape the images of the last time I saw V.

"Someone raped her, Mom, brutally. It happened the weekend you asked me to work for Damien," I finally said.

"Come again?" she leaped from her seat. I was barely able to keep myself from falling over. If one thing irked my mother, it was to see her children unhappy. That was why I kept V's disappearance from her for as long as I did. I didn't want her to make a big fuss. She was already hassling me about my dress code. I didn't feel like dressing up while my girlfriend was scratching to survive or, God forbid, lying in a ditch somewhere.

"I couldn't get through to her after the attack, and I think something terrible might have happened to her. I blame myself and don't know what I could've done to prevent it. If I were in town, it would have never happened."

"Let's go back to where you said your girlfriend was brutally raped. After four years of moping around, why didn't you think you could have shared that little detail with your parents? When you are not hiding in a bottle from yourself, you're arguing with everyone, and I know that's not the man you are. Watching you go from the confident young man I raised to you dissolving into this stranger you've become is painful. Now, to hear you have been battling this demon alone is not only disappointing but downright disrespectful."

"Here we go again!" I flung my hands in frustration and walked toward the gazebo. "Please don't make this about you and me. This is why I didn't tell you. I wasn't disrespecting you.

I didn't think that she would have been away for this long. I keep telling myself she needed time to recover, and she'd return after a while."

"It doesn't matter the length of time, Son. The fact that someone assaulted the person you care about is reason enough. Is it that you didn't think that we would care?"

"That's not it, Mom."

"Then what is it? Maybe you think little of your parents. I cannot tell you how disappointed I am in you."

"I didn't think my relationship with V was that important to you. You've only met her a few times."

"And I've known you all your life. That girl brought something you didn't have for a long time: peace. And whether it took only months or years for her to do that, if she means this much to you, she also means a lot to us." She got closer as if she wanted to hit me. Not that she ever would, but she was so angry at me for not telling her about the rape sooner. I didn't because I couldn't discuss it with anyone. "During the time you spent together, I saw how she revealed what we already knew about you, which you tried to hide from everyone else. You are the son I boasted about to everyone. A beautiful human being." She wiped my cheeks with the back of her hand.

"When she needed me, I wasn't there. It probably wouldn't have happened if I had called her to let her know I was going to Ochi that afternoon."

"Son, it's not your fault, please stop torturing yourself."

"She relied on me to keep her safe. I promised her I would, and I didn't. I failed her." My voice cracked under the weight of my sobs. "She was new to the city, and I should have expected that she might encounter evil people. They brutalized her. I hardly recognized her the morning I took her to the hospital."

"You do realize you are coming off incredibly selfish for not telling your father and me about it? Unless you think we did something to deserve seeing you suffer in silence, I'm not sure what would make you keep all of this bottled up. You were never this secretive. You've always had my unconditional support, Jonathan. You should have known that you could come to me for anything. I could have helped you to find her a long time ago. There are resources at your disposal that you can employ to find her; use them."

"I've already started to do an island-wide search. I'm not sure whether it will work, but I must do something so that I can sleep. I haven't closed my eyes for more than a few hours a night since."

"You cannot go on like this. It's breaking my heart. I can't believe you've been hiding this secret from me all these years," she grumbled, walking back to the main house and leaving me to wallow. She didn't even give me a chance to tell her she had called me. But since V didn't say much, I didn't have much to tell my mother about the phone call.

"Why does everyone look so gloomy?" Damien asked as he sneaked behind the orange tree next to the pavilion. The bright yellow shirt he had on blended with the multitude of oranges that caused the tree to bend, almost touching the ground.

"Ask your brother," Mom said, then shut the door behind her.

"Did somebody die? You look like hell," Damien said, then plucked an orange from the tree.

"Why do you care? This doesn't concern you." I leaned against the palm tree, both hands tucked inside my jeans, my right leg resting against the tree trunk as I repeatedly knocked my head against it like a woodpecker.

"Well, it looks like you're mourning," Damien said. "What's gotten you so down?"

"V is missing," I finally told him.

"The country girl? I thought you broke up with her?"

"I didn't break up with her!" I eased off the tree to face him.

"Why are you yelling at me? Please don't take out your frustrations on me. I didn't even know you still remember her." He glanced at me. "What happened between the two of you anyway?"

"She is not up for discussion with you. You never liked her, so I'm not about to spill my guts to you."

"So, we're not talking about her?" he asked.

"No, not with you. We are not talking about her! What makes you think I need to discuss V with you?"

"Because, little bro, like it or not, I'm your only brother. If you can't talk to me, who can you talk to?"

"Anyone but you!" I yelled at him.

I headed toward the house, then turned to address him again. "For weeks, I listened to you berate her for no reason. You called her a gold digger and said that I should be careful. Not because you have any legitimate reason to think of her that way. You looked at her and concluded she was not good enough for this family. Now, suddenly, you are concerned about her?" What do you take me for?"

"I regret that. I should have given her a chance. I can help you find her," he said.

"I don't believe you," I said through clenched teeth.

"What do you mean you don't believe me?" Damien was surprised.

"I don't believe you regret how you treated my girlfriend." I moved closer to him, staring at him. The anger in me was bubbling up to the surface. "She didn't disappear yesterday. It's been four long frigging years. Where was your concern then? Not once did you ever ask about her? I know you are a selfish son of a bitch, but my God, you should've been the big brother you were supposed to be. You can keep your sympathy and go back to the bottle you've been hiding in for the past seven years!" I yelled, walking into the house.

"I'm sorry, man," he said. "But have you ever thought you might be why she left?" Damien followed me, his hands still clutching the orange. "Maybe she realized you are not the knight in shining armor she thought you were. Or, maybe, just maybe, she found someone with deeper pockets," he said.

"Don't get me started!" I growled at him. "For all your life, you leaped from one woman to another. You wouldn't know commitment if it smacked you in the face. Except, of course, your eternal dedication to alcohol and weed. You're one to talk about commitment, especially V's." I grabbed my car keys off the corner table in the living room and headed to my car. I did not want my parents to witness another fight between us.

***

I listened to the news every day and fretted whenever there was a gruesome discovery of human remains. My chest would tighten until an identification turned out not to be V's, but I would remain trapped in a constant worry loop until I laid eyes on her.

The times I ran into Sean were some of the most painful. It was a continual reminder that I might have contributed to the misery of his family, and it was killing me softly.

Each day went by with more urgency than the last. I kept in touch with my staff for updates, but the disappointing news of no sighting became more difficult to hear. My search had come up empty, and after a long search to find her, I had begun to feel less hopeful.

Chapter 36

Evil Never Stops Hunting

Vivienne

I stood outside Spring Valley All-Age school grounds with Jessica, the grade six teacher, four years my senior. We watched groundsmen prepare the field for the upcoming annual track and field competition. Principal Nedrick had hired me two years before to teach Mrs. Gordon's Grade One students until she returned from maternity leave but kept me on as her assistant after she returned.

I didn't intend to make friends with Jessica; I was already punishing myself for the way I left things with Jasmine, and I didn't want to form another friendship and then be forced to flee from it. However, Jessica was especially warm to me when I started teaching, and I appreciated how she welcomed me on staff. I kept the circumstances surrounding Shannon's birth a secret from everyone. I still couldn't even share them with my aunt. And the five years that passed didn't bring me closer to telling her that the energetic black-haired girl she adored came through violence. I could not talk to her about August 24, 1985. It was too gruesome, and whenever I allowed my mind to recall that day, my body would convulse.

I hadn't spoken to anyone from my past since my failed attempt to communicate with Jonathan. The hurt and shame were just as raw as the first day I woke from my coma. My parents had no idea where I was or that they had a granddaughter. Shannon would have loved her two cousins, and I would have to grovel profusely to Sean and beg for his forgiveness. He would love his niece like she was his own. I often wanted to jump on a bus and return to my parents like a prodigal child, and then I'd think of Jonathan and realize he'd have to be a saint to want me back.

The painted tracks were coming into focus very nicely, and everything would be completed the next day.

Sports Day was the only time athletes could participate in several events. Whether the 100-meter dash, high and long jumps, or the marathon, they would get the opportunity to show off their talents as if they were auditioning for a spot at the boys' and girls' championships that took place every year in Kingston.

Spring Valley All Age had at least three alumni selected in the 1970s but none since.

I moved away from Jessica to inspect the ribbons and trophies among the prizes to be given to the winners in each category. I cast my eye over to where I last saw Shannon with her friend, Gayle, five minutes earlier, and when I didn't see her, I hurried to her classroom to see if they had gone back inside. It was lunchtime, and kids could eat in the cafeteria or classrooms, depending on their ages. Shannon wasn't old enough to eat with the bigger kids, so, usually, we'd eat lunch together in my classroom.

I rushed back outside in a state of panic after I found the classroom empty and saw a stranger lifting her and placing her in the back seat of a black station wagon taxi like the ones I took to work when I lived in Montego Bay. But I was too far to stop the man with dreadlocks from driving off with her. I hollered, but not loud enough to make the driver release his foot off the gas pedal. He fled before any of my colleagues saw him. Shannon looked back as I ran behind the car before falling on my knees.

It took Principal Nedrick ten minutes to pull me off the asphalt. All my strength had drained from me. My body limped each time she attempted to pull me off the ground. At that moment, I had lost all hope of living.

It had been one week since the stranger kidnapped Shannon. Poof, and just like that, she was gone.

Chapter 37

Drifting on a Memory

Vivienne

The minibus pulled up at its final stop on Barnett Street. One week after they kidnapped Shannon, I returned to the city that destroyed me, hoping not to run into anyone from my past. It would have been awkward having to explain where I had been. I had no idea what I would tell Sean or Jonathan, let alone my parents.

I rented a tiny one-bedroom in Catherine Hall, a few minutes from downtown. I wanted to be as far from Ironshore as possible. The last time I lived there didn't work so well, even though it was supposed to be safer than the city. What I didn't know was that it had a homegrown rapist.

Sean did not deserve the way I treated him. He was a good brother and deserved better from me. But I was a rape victim who tried to kill myself. I couldn't think straight, let alone cope with the brutality inflicted on me. What consumed me was a desperate need. I had to escape the toxic environment responsible for my demise, and I couldn't let him know I was carrying the baby of the man who tortured me.

I used what little money I earned as an untrained teacher to pay the rent for my new place, which could hardly be considered safe. The housing scheme was an access point to the more dangerous community of West Green, but I couldn't afford to pick and choose. I had answered an ad in the newspaper for one bedroom, first and last month's rent, with no job history checks. If you could pay, you were in; if you can't, there was no need to apply. I needed somewhere to sleep at night, but it didn't take long to realize that my mind had drifted in and out of reality. But I still couldn't block the memory of my brutal assault. It reminded me of why I had to run away everywhere I went.

Street people, mostly older, loitered across every corner of the city. They always looked filthy and lonely, as if they had reached the end of their ropes. Their bare feet took on the color of the asphalt they had trotted on night and day. Their heels cracked and blistered from continuous walking. From the farthest corner of the city, Barnett Street, to Harbor Street, throughout Saint James Street, they hauled their whole lives around in plastic bags, their heads fixed to the ground, looking for loose change. Their clothes were often tattered, and they were usually talking with themselves. Sometimes, they would stand at the entrances of stores, their hands outstretched, begging for their next meal.

Would I soon join this category of outcasts?

I was already aware that Shannon's kidnapping had damaged my mind, and I had begun to lose little pieces by then. But I needed to keep my focus on finding her. I couldn't afford to worry about what others thought about me. The desperation and hopelessness put me at significant risk and opened me up to ridicule and further abuse.

I had arrived to find that after so many years had passed, Montego Bay was still littered with higglers, hustlers, and the insane. I had chopped off the long hair that usually flowed down my back, my eyes had lost their sparks, and I was ten pounds lighter, rearranging my face. I replaced my six-inch heels with strapped-up slippers and was no longer the aggressive go-getter with the four-year plan and the single-minded focus on being a professor. My long dress flowed past my ankles, and I hid the figure I had shown off to Jasmine years before.

I swung the small handbag across my shoulders, holding my belongings, and stepped like a girl without a clue where she was going.

Like my first trip to the city, Barnett Street was still the central point for travelers. I found myself close to where I spent my first date with Jonathan. I avoided it. I ignored the name-calling as I walked past men working on construction sites. They whistled and yelled vulgar names to get my attention. But they soon noticed the rapid deterioration in my appearance.

"Hey, mad gal," they hollered out to me as I crossed Bogue Road in search of Shannon. They smashed empty bottles against the asphalt near my feet when I ignored them, and with that came more verbal abuse.

I made my way downtown and sat on the concrete base of the light pole in Sam Sharpe Square. I watched pedestrians rushing past me while the thunder roared above my head and lightning crashed against the dark sky. As everyone hurried to safety, I sat still, unconcerned.

"What's your story? I know you have one. It must be difficult," a tall woman said as she walked up to me, holding an umbrella. She couldn't be less than six feet.

I'm not in the mood to pour out my heart to you. Can you please go away? Even if I tell you my story, what good will that do?

"What's your name?" she asked. "I've not seen you here before. Have you eaten today?" My eyes said no. "Here, take this," she offered me ten dollars. I ignored her outstretched hand.

"Go ahead, take it," she insisted. "Well, at least take my card. If you want to talk, call me. I want to help you." She turned her head toward the sky. "I hope you have somewhere inside to be in the next few minutes, or you'll get wet."

I took the card out of her hand and hurried down St. James Street, then onto Barnett Street, heading toward Puerto Bello. Five minutes later, the clouds opened.

"Get out a di road!" The driver of the blue Lada Car honked, peered out his window, and yelled at me. "Are you trying to kill yourself?" He swerved to avoid hitting me.

I quivered, soaking wet as I wiped the water from my face. I jumped out of the way of the car that whisked by. I had no idea why I had chosen Puerto Bello to look for Shannon. I could have been listening to the voices in my head for directions. Puerto Bello turned out to be yet another waste of time.

I opened my palm. *Bay West Regional Hospital, Dr. Arlene Spencer.*

Lord, have mercy on me. Does she think I'm crazy? Everyone knows Bay West Regional is for mental patients. That's the last place I want to go.

The potholes proved hazardous. Drivers had little time to swerve to avoid them. The water splashed onto me as cars sank into potholes. I might be losing my mind, but that didn't stop me from lamenting over what I had become.

***

Weeks later, as my search for Shannon continued, I was frantic. My feet burned against the scorching hot asphalt. I was coming up on another anniversary of my flight from Montego Bay. Being away from my parents for such a long time also took its toll. The voices in my head sometimes talked in chorus, and there was no way of tuning them out. I fumbled into my pocket and pulled Dr. Arlene Spencer's business card. The voices seemed to be winning the fight, and I needed help quickly.

I nervously dialed the number from the phone booth at the corner of Church Street, next to the blue and white police station. I had one eye out in case an officer spotted me. They had started their campaign to clear the streets of the insane. "I need your help, Dr. Spencer," I said after she came on the phone. "I know you may not remember me, but we met in Sam Sharpe Square some time ago. It was raining the day you handed me your business card."

"Of course. How are you doing, my dear?" Her high-pitched voice echoed in my ear.

"Not good," I said. "When can you see me? I need to talk to you."

"Let me check my calendar." I constantly propped my head outside the phone booth to see if there were any police officers nearby. "It so happens that I have an opening this evening," she said a minute later. "Are you able to come to see me today? If you'd like, I'll come to you."

I sighed. "I'd rather come to you this afternoon, even though I'm a mess."

"That's not a problem at all. I have an opening at three o'clock."

"I'll be there." I quickly hung up the phone and hurried down the street.

At three-fifteen, I sat across from Dr. Spencer, unsure whether I wanted to tell her my whole story or just the part where someone kidnapped Shannon. I needed to talk about my spiraling condition but didn't know where to begin or whether Dr. Spencer was the right person to help me. I leaned forward, opened my mouth, and then as if to catch myself, I leaned back into my chair, nervously tapped my fingers against the wooden desk, and sighed.

"My name is Vivienne. I'm here because you are the only person who might be able to help me. And as you can see, I need help. It's been a long time since I had any real conversation with anyone. Most of the time, I'd rather talk back to the voices that refused to keep quiet. Today is one of my better days. I've had a few, but sometimes I'd go for days without a bath or a meal."

"If it's any comfort, Vivienne. I was once in your shoes. How do you think it was easy for me to recognize your predicament? I was right where you are now. Young, confused, and 'crazy.'

At least, that's what they used to call me. Until one day, someone reached out to me, just like I did to you. The good thing is that you are young, and there is still time to get to a better place. I don't know your story, but you have one. I once had that same look on my face, like a dear in a headlight, and I know you'd rather be anywhere but here."

Dr. Spencer got up, walked over to the small kitchen counter in her office, reached for the brown paper bag on top of the mini fridge, and handed it to me with a water bottle.

"I'm sorry, but I can't take that," I said.

"Yes, you can. If you are hungry, you cannot tell your story the way I need to hear it." Your pride cannot help you. You must know when to accept help like the kind I am offering."

"But what if I can't get better? What if I'm beyond recovery?" I took the food out of her hand and let out a soft sob.

Doctor Spencer looked at me. The straps on my leather slippers had begun to unravel. My tangled hair needed a good shampoo, and my nails were desperate for a trim.

"I'd like to help you, Vivienne. That's if you'll let me. I gave you my card because I know I can help you. You have made the first step, and after you have eaten, I'd like you to tell me why you are homeless," she said.

She returned to her chair and peered through the window as the car sped by five stories below. Any other time, I'd be looking for a way to throw myself out of the window to my death. But now I had another life to think about.

"I am not homeless. At least not yet," I said before taking a bite. "Someone took my daughter. I need you to help me get her back."

"What's your daughter's name?" Dr. Spencer asked. She was more attentive after I said that.

"Shannon." I looked away. "Shannon Jane Pearson," I said.

"Do you know who took your daughter?"

"No." I nibbled on the coco bread, picking it apart. "I've been hearing about the Black Heart Man. I'm not sure if he took her."

Dr. Spencer stared at me, then smiled. Her teeth were sparkling white. "I hate to tell you, Vivienne, but the Black Heart Man is a myth. I had been told the same story when I was a child. So, let's keep him out of the equation. If you don't know who took your daughter, I'm not sure if I can help you to find her. But I can make sure you get well enough so that you can start taking care of yourself. You need to be well again. Otherwise, no one will return her to you when they find her. Don't spend your time focusing on a bogeyman. That won't help you, but I can."

"What do I need to do, Doctor Spencer? I'll do anything you ask." I perked up, desperate for any help she could give me.

"I can set you up in a treatment facility, which will allow you to clear your head of the chatter."

"You mean a nut house?" My eyes widened, and my teeth were stuck on the coco bread in my hand.

"We don't call it that. It worked for many of us and can work for you, too. You're not the first to suffer a mental breakdown. But it will help if you allow yourself to accept the treatment." Doctor Spencer rested her arms on her desk and leaned into me. "Before I get you into the program, I'd like to visit you at home. If that doesn't work, that's when I'll recommend a more permanent arrangement. But Vivienne, you must want the treatment. Otherwise, you will not get better."

"I'm not sure about that." My eyes wandered to the other side of the room to the long rows of filing cabinets.

"Did something else happen that drove you to the streets?"

"I'd rather not talk about it, Doctor." I fumbled with the empty paper bag in my hand.

"I'm here to help you, remember? Don't hold out on me now, Vivienne."

But I needed more time before talking about the real reason for my mental breakdown. "Maybe next time. I don't want to overwhelm you," I said. "Today is a better day than yesterday, but there are days I don't even know where I am, and if you don't help me to get to where I need to be, I'll continue to wander about the streets for the next twenty years. I need to get back home to my parents, and I hope you can help me to do that."

"I want you to do something for me, Vivienne," she said, her eyes hadn't left me since her questioning began. "I want you to write a letter to someone you love, it could be your parents, or just anyone. Do that every day for a month." She pulled out a black notebook and handed it to me. "Tell them how you feel. It will help you not to talk back to the voices so much. Can you do that for me?"

"It will be hard. It's not easy to ignore these chatterboxes," I said.

"Would you like me to contact your parents?"

"Not now!" I said immediately. It was the last thing I wanted her to do. "I can't let them see me like this. It will break them."

"Don't you think not knowing where you are, has already broken them?"

"At some point when I'm better, you can tell them, but not now."

She held my hands in hers, and tears fell out of my eyes.

My long journey back to reality had begun. I needed to mend the relationship with my parents, and there was no way I'd allow them to see me in the terrible shape I was in. My brain was locked in a permanent state of derangement and grief, with voices in my head all the time, and I realized only the universe could save me at this point.

***

I wandered throughout the city day after day, and when I was alone at home, I paced back and forth in my confined space. The battle for my sanity had heated up. It was a war I couldn't win. So, I did what Doctor Spencer ordered. I grabbed a pen and paper and started writing.

My chest rose and fell with each stroke of my pen. I was afraid I couldn't stop quarreling with the voices that took up residence in my head. My life was unraveling fast. I was hanging on by a thread, and I couldn't do anything to get the loudmouths out of my head. I didn't know how to mend my broken heart and mind. It was way beyond my ability, and I was up against the clock in my desperate search to find my daughter. Each morning when the sun rose, I started my routine of ransacking Montego Bay. It was the crossroad where my life took a detour. A sense of déjà vu engulfed me, and I had to do whatever it took to ensure my daughter did not suffer the same fate as me.

Chapter 38

Out of My Mind

May 20, 1991.

Dear Universe,

It's three a.m., and today is Shannon's sixth birthday. I woke to the sound of someone knocking on my neighbor's door. I wonder if today my baby will finally come home. A year has gone by, and I cannot find her anywhere. There's no place else to look, I've traveled everywhere. People keep telling me it's way past time for me to move on, but now I'm out of my mind and running out of time.

They tell me that I'm crazy when I talk to myself. But why is it so terrible for me to talk back to the voices in my head? I scream and holler. I cannot bear this much trauma, one after the other. I hear the dogs howling outside, and I cannot sleep, it's as if I can hear Shannon's tiny feet.

I'm all alone, and I don't know how much longer I can go on. Very soon, I may have to make my bed on Barnett Street under the big tent because I cannot pay my rent. Or Dr. Spencer will have no choice but to lock me away to save me from myself. I wrap my head to keep it from exploding. Sometimes, it feels like it will pop open. The voices are getting louder, and the throbbing inside is unbearable sometimes. I don't know how to get past this internal battle that consumes me. Something in me is taking over my will to survive. I need to end this misery inside.

I keep seeing the blood splatters on the sheet and feel a knot on my head. I hear my screams for mercy bounce off the bedroom walls. It's like my life is over, and I'm already dead.

And that's not even the worst part, losing my daughter was how my madness started. I am in for a long fight to find Shannon. I've walked almost every corner of Montego Bay. Strand Street is off-limits, though. I cannot bring myself to get close. It reminds me too much of Jonathan. The voices in my head grow louder whenever I get close, and my heart beats faster as if it's coming out of my chest.

My meals are exceedingly rare, though I don't have the time to sleep, much less to eat, and I haven't taken a shower since last week. If I stay awake, Shannon might walk through my gate. Tell me, Dear Universe, am I getting better? Or have I gone completely insane?

A piece of my shoe fell off yesterday. My feet are sore, and I'm tired to my core. I don't know how much more of this heartache I can endure. I won't be able to sleep tonight. That's when I am most afraid. I must keep my eyes open in case the ruffian attacks me again.

Until next time,

-Vivienne

December 24, 1991

Dear Universe,

It's been seven months since our last conversation. I'm no closer to finding Shannon, and the terrible feelings are not going anywhere. I hear the airplanes over my head. Maybe they took her to America. Christmas is tomorrow when I'll be at my lowest, and my heart sinks deepest. My medication is running low, and if I don't get a refill soon, I'll begin talking to the moon.

The headaches have not disappeared. I can still hear the voices. They are talking so loudly today. You may not hear from me tomorrow, but if you see Shannon, make sure she knows I refuse to stop searching. I will not get out of bed today. It's as if I can still feel the pain in my pelvis and my head, but I'll try to hang on for her sake. She must know my decision to have her was not a mistake. She just happened to be the result of a brutal rape.

The doctor dropped by my house yesterday. She wanted to take me up the hill to Bay West Regional Hospital. She said she'd come for me tomorrow and that I need a more permanent arrangement for my treatment if I'm to be around when Shannon comes home. I'll try not to fight her again. Last time, the struggle caused too much pain.

I'll write again soon to let you know what happened.

Until next time,

-Vivienne

January 1, 1992

Dear Universe,

The doctor did not come to take me to the hospital like she said she would, so I went to look for Shannon in West Gate Hills, Porto Bello, and Norwood, to see if the kidnapper had taken her there. I am exhausted and down to my last pill. To search for her tomorrow, I may not have the will.

I tore my dress today, and that's the only one I have left. I will have to find another from somebody's wastebasket.

On my way to Porto Bello, little boys on the street attacked me. They threw rocks and empty bottles at my head and called me ugly names. On top of that, I was cold and battered by the rain. But I don't mind it. Searching for my baby will never be in vain. Tomorrow may be better than today. The sun is out now, so perhaps this will be the day. The voices are getting louder, sometimes, they make me turn around, and one time, I swear one of the voices sounded just like Shannon.

Today is New Year's Day, a new year to start over, and another opportunity for this pain in my head to go away. But, until I find Shannon, my feet will keep on trotting. I cannot afford to stop looking.

I'll write again soon when it's time for the next update.

Until next time,

-Vivienne

January 2, 1992

Dear Universe,

I may have spoken too soon. The doctors are here to take me to Bay West Regional Hospital. There, I get to see a doctor every day. From now on, I'll be living on the 10th floor, in room 44. They are hurrying me to come along, so I'll have to keep this letter short. When I get back, I'll let you know what happened.

Until next time,

-Vivienne

July 25, 1992

Dear Universe,

It's been a while since our last conversation. My life is more manageable now, and I don't hear the rumblings in my head anymore. The doctors successfully untangled the cobwebs in my brain.

The headaches are also gone, but it's been a challenging time. The guards didn't allow me to leave the building, I was always locked inside. Now that I'm out in the open, I'm getting a lot of fresh air and sunshine.

I'm sleeping much better now, too, and I don't feel as sad and blue. The Post Traumatic Stress Disorder the doctors diagnosed me with traced back to that awful August night on Valence Avenue, compounded by the kidnapping of my daughter, which tipped me over. They said I'm to remember the positive memories, not the negative ones. So, I'm choosing to forget the cruel attack orchestrated against me.

While I was in the hospital, the nurses gave me books to read and games to play, and on Sundays, we would sing songs of a better day.

I stood up to the guards each time they told me to go to sleep. I wouldn't let them touch me. I kept reliving the night Shannon was conceived. The doctors should check on me next week to see how well I'm adjusting, but for the time being, I'm looking out the window to find a new beginning.

The place they gave me feels empty, but I won't be here for long. I'll be traveling to America, Dallas, Texas, to be exact.

I finally got to see my mother. She visited the hospital. She's living in America again and is taking me there. I'm starting to feel a little guilty that I will not get to write as often while I'm there, but then again, you are everywhere. I'm getting nervous about traveling thirteen hundred miles in the air.

Wish me luck! I'm not sure what to expect. But I'll keep you updated as often as I get.

Until next time,

-Vivienne

Chapter 39

Working My Way Back

Jonathan

I had been working on a multiyear project for my parents in Scottsdale, Arizona. My mother threatened to disinherit me if I didn't leave Jamaica after years of searching for V and not finding her. I would have gladly given up everything I owned if it meant getting V back. But with each passing year, the hope of finding her grew dimmer, and I began to feel less hopeful as the pain of her disappearance cut deeper with each day.

For the next three years, I lived in absolute torment, and with everyone telling me to move on, I still couldn't. I traveled between Scottsdale and Montego Bay each chance I got, returning to the city with the hope that a miracle might happen for me.

"Dammit, Blaise, where are you?" I glanced at my watch and then surveyed the airport parking lot. He should have picked me up fifteen minutes ago.

I hope Jasmine reminded him I'm coming in today.

Yeah. Jasmine and Blaise hit it off after I introduced them four years ago. It only took them six months to tie the knot, and now they were on to their second child.

Blaise pulled up exactly thirty minutes late. He jumped out of his car, quickly grabbed my luggage, and flung it into the back seat.

"Welcome home, Bro. Terrible traffic on the way. There was an accident on the road," he said, hugging me. "Where should I take you, Round Hill?" he asked after letting go of me.

"Valence Avenue," I said reluctantly. "It's time I face my fear."

"Are you sure? You haven't been there since Vivienne left."

"I will have to go back at some point. It might as well be now."

As much as the years had been tremendously painful, had Blaise not been there for me, I could have easily not been alive. Believe it or not, I was not the only one in our group devastated by V's disappearance, although none of the guys knew the real reason why she left me.

Blaise pulled out of the airport parking lot like a bullet train. His driving skills were why I let him drive when we were together. Before long, he turned onto Valence Avenue. I looked out the window and realized Sean's house was no longer Sean's house. It looked desolate, as if no one lived there, a stark difference from what it once was. I remembered my quarrel with him like it had happened yesterday, and the images of me pulling V out of the ocean emerged. I closed my eyes and took a deep breath.

I tried everything to fill the void V's disappearance left in my life. I even took karate lessons from Blaise to work out the anger he said was destroying me. Surprisingly, I was better at it than I thought I would.

"How is Jas?" I asked. I didn't need him to see me fighting back tears. Somehow, he convinced himself that grown men don't cry. "Did you take the interior decorator to see her like I asked?"

"Yes. They have done a ridiculously wonderful job with the construction. Everything will be completed in time for the upcoming winter season."

"It's going to be bittersweet when we open. I already have bookings for full occupancy at the launch. Who knows, maybe V will come back by then."

"She would have been proud of what you've done with Greenspring. When you decided to build the retreat, I couldn't see your vision. I'm proud of you, man. Not everyone cares about the countryside. But what you've done to that place is mind-blowing."

"I built it so I would never forget her."

Blaise's car came to a stop. I rubbed my hand over my face, pulled on my goatee, took a deep breath, and then buried my face in my hands. It felt like I was ready to move on, but I didn't want to.

"I wish I could get Jas to stop crying whenever someone mentions Vivienne's name," Blaise said. "She is no better than you. You are like weeping willows. I can't get her to stop crying. I haven't seen you in six months, but here you are. It's like nothing's changed. You're stuck. I hate to tell you, but you must get over her and find a wife. No one will blame you if you do."

"Did you tell Jas what happened to V?" I asked, ignoring his comments.

"Heck, I don't even know what happened to Vivienne," he said flatly. "You refused to tell me why a perfectly normal human being would just run away from her perfectly normal family."

I looked away from him, avoiding his stare.

"I can't talk about it, Blaise," I said, my voice breaking.

I unbuckled my seat belt and shuffled into my seat. "I can't get the words out of my mouth to tell you what some freak did to her. All I could tell Jas was that she just left me. But she didn't just leave me. She left her entire world behind. I came back to search for her, and this time I'm not going back to Arizona until I find her."

"So, let me get this straight." It was as if I could feel Blaise's eyes burrowing a hole into me. He had been begging me for years to tell him what made V leave, and I couldn't. "You're telling me now, after so many years, someone hurt her? Is that what you're telling me?" I looked at him, and my lips began to tremble. "Did someone rape her?"

I shrugged. "Yes," I said eventually. "That's why she left."

We sat in the car, neither of us wanted to leave. The stare Blaise gave me felt like an arrow piercing through my soul. It was as if he wanted to kick my ass to Timbuktu or back to Arizona.

"Your girlfriend went missing seven years ago." He narrowed his eyes on me, his brows touching. "Your girlfriend is fucking missing for seven years all because someone raped her, and you never said a damn word to any of your friends?" He opened the car door and then slammed it. He kicked the tires and punched the air.

"We're going to find her this time." I exited the car, followed him up the steps, then opened the veranda gate.

"You're damn right. We are going to find her." He had never been this angry at me before.

"I told her she was safe with you. I hope Sean kicked your ass for letting that happen."

"I haven't seen him since he quit Hideaway. Maybe he went back to America with his parents. They were getting ready to return the last time I visited them."

"I loved Vivienne like she was my sister. We hung out every other weekend in this very house. She was not just your girlfriend. She was my wife's best friend. Jasmine deserves to know what happened to her. She needs closure. God dammit, Jonathan, her disappearance destroyed her family."

"We'll come up with a strategy to find her. This time we won't stop until we do."

I stepped into the living room, but Blaise refused to follow me. He gave me a shitty look, disappointment plastered all over his face.

I thought about selling the house a few times, but there were too many memories of V. I didn't want to let go of them.

Blaise didn't speak to me for the next five minutes. Tension was building between us, and each second ticked by. He paced up and down the veranda, threatening me to himself.

"Stop threatening me!" I yelled.

My mail was neatly placed on the kitchen counter, and the house was clean like Patrica always kept it. I kept her on to ensure the house did not deteriorate, and I couldn't let her become a casualty of what happened to V.

I scanned the mail. The large air-mail envelope at the bottom of the pile stood out. Oddly, all correspondence was to be forwarded to my office address at the hotel. I pulled out the letter, flipped it, and the familiar handwriting jumped at me.

Immediately, I remembered the letter that ripped my life apart.

"Yo!" I yelled out for Blaise. As resentful as I was at him for being pissed off at me, I couldn't hide my shock. "Blaise!" I yelled louder when he didn't answer. He couldn't ignore me this time. I sounded like I'd seen a ghost. "Look! This is from V," I shoved the letter in his chest.

He grabbed it, turned it over, and looked up at me. "It doesn't have a return address. How do you know it's from her?" he asked.

"I know her handwriting. I'm sure it's from her."

I quickly opened the envelope and pulled out a legal-size yellow two-page letter. My hands trembled, and Blaise placed his arm around my shoulder to calm me.

July 30, 1992

Dear Jonathan,

I'm sorry. That's the least I can say. I shouldn't have blamed my assault on you. I was immature and stubborn. I know that now. I had no reason to make you feel you had done something wrong, and I regret not allowing you to grieve with me. It would have made the hurt less painful for you and me. I am sorry I caused you so much heartache. God knows you didn't deserve the way I shut you out.

But today is a new day, which compelled me to tell you what's happening to me. I don't know if you'll get this letter, but my therapists said I should try and make amends to the people I hurt the most.

So, here I am, Jonathan. I would never have been able to move forward without including you and telling you how sorry I am for the clumsy way I left you. These days, I am smiling again. It's not the same, though. It was so much better when you'd smile back at me.

So much time has passed, and I'm sure another woman must have captured your heart. Guys like you are so hard to come by. If it's any consolation, I think about you every day. It's hard to forget someone as beautiful as you.

Do you still think about me, Jonathan?

I took my mother down to where you rescued me. I just had to tell her you did everything to save me. She's not crying anymore. If I hadn't told her what happened, I could not have gotten to where I am now. As for Daddy, he's happier than the last time you saw him. He's thankful I've come out alive, and that's in part because of you.

It makes me sad that I don't have a future with you. But if I never get to see you again, I hope you know I wouldn't have changed a thing about you and me. You are perfect, just as you are. It's such a pity I got knocked off my path.

As hard as I tried, I could never fall out of love with you. A miracle may happen to us. We deserve another chance, but you never know. The Universe may have its plan.

My new journey begins now. I'm on my way to getting that degree I wanted, and if, by chance, we meet again, I'll be Professor Pearson, just like you predicted.

And so, my love, if I keep dreaming, you and I together again are a real possibility.

Your love,

Vivienne.

Blaise hugged me for two minutes. He wouldn't let go. "She's alive, man. She's fucking alive!" He gripped me tighter and then screamed as loudly as he could.

That was the first time I saw him cry.

Chapter 40

Finding My Way Back

Vivienne

August 2000

It had been eight years since my mother brought me back to Dallas. I had finally gotten past the worst of my trauma. The relationship with my parents had mended. Sean and I were okay with each other again, although sometimes I was sure he had one eye trained on me just in case I became light-footed.

I had completed my education and was now a productive member of society. I committed my time to the local community center, dedicating my life to ensuring no one else experienced what I had been through. But my heart felt bruised, my mind was still fragile, and I had no hope of finding Shannon.

Dr. Walsh had warned me that stress could trigger another nervous breakdown and advised me to occupy my time with school and work. She had been working with me since I returned to Dallas. I had a gnawing, gut-wrenching, stomach-churning premonition that something was about to disrupt the normal flow of my life again. I couldn't shake the dread that consumed me for two days.

I called my therapist in a panic, thinking I was having another nervous breakdown. Understanding the root of my anxiety, Dr. Walsh assured me that it was because I was coming up on another anniversary of my assault, and it might have triggered a temporary reaction that would eventually pass. She told me I had to get past what Damien did to me and stay away from any revenge-seeking venture. She said it would eat me alive if I didn't.

I had successfully masked the pain of losing Shannon and Jonathan, although they never left my mind. There was no active search to find my daughter. She was not a hot or cold case, there was no case at all. I wasn't expecting a detective to call me in the middle of the night to tell me they had found her. There was just no hope of finding her.

The telephone rang at the worst time, as I was already late for work. The phone call came from the most unlikely person. It was short, and the message was simple, *"2522 Farragut Street, room 303, Scottsdale, Arizona."* I opened my mouth to let the caller know she had the wrong number. Instead, she had the answer I sought, which cost me my mind. It was by sheer grace that I survived. Nothing I did. God knows I tried to end my misery.

"Damien Hastings has your daughter. Get here now!" the caller said before the phone went silent.

I didn't recognize the woman's voice. She was American. Her thick Southern accent was hard to miss.

I couldn't bring myself to tell anyone except my parents that Damien was my rapist, even after so many years had passed.

The feeling that came over me was indescribable. I dragged the closest chair and collapsed onto it. I just had to sit. I could not process what I had heard. It didn't make sense. Damien, having my daughter was never a possibility I had considered. He didn't know I was pregnant, much less think my daughter belonged to him. But then again, anything was possible with all his money and family connections.

I recovered from the shock of the news, scrambled closer to where my mother could hear me, and screamed as loudly as possible. I may have rattled the picture frames on the living room wall. Either that or my body went into a convulsion.

"Mom! Mom!" I screamed at the top of my lungs. "She is alive! Shannon is alive!" I dashed across the room to find my mother. I lamented daily how much my disappearance caused her to suffer. She was delighted when I decided to move back in with her and my father after college. I wanted to make up for the lost time from my long absence. "I must leave tonight," I said.

Finally, I would get my daughter after such a long struggle. "Tell Daddy I'll be back in a few days."

When I told her where Shannon was, my mother said, "Go get her, Honey. Call us the minute you get there. "

Five hours later, I arrived in Scottsdale. I pulled into the almost empty parking lot of the motel on Farragut Street and sat in my car. The building has seen better days. Advertisements with a decent management team could turn it around, especially since two newer hotels were across the street, with excess parking and more unique amenities. The flashing lighted sign said they offer free cable. But the complimentary breakfast they advertised would sell it for me. That's the one I'd book if I were making the reservation.

As I sat there, still firmly holding the keys securely inside the ignition cylinder, contemplating whether to go up or drive off, Damien's assault on me suddenly became fresh in my mind. The urge to get away from there became intense, too. The thought of another trap was beginning to seep into me, but the fact that the caller knew I had a daughter meant there might have been some truth to her claim. Running away from the possibility of finding Shannon seemed unwise.

You've come this far, Vivienne, don't turn back now, the small voice in me said.

I prayed, exhaled, wrenched the keys out of the ignition, shuffled out of my car, and headed toward the elevator. It must have been the longest three-floor elevator ride in history. The tiny elevator rumbled up, and I was relieved when I stepped out of the shaky, deteriorated enclosure.

I searched for the room number, and what should have been a minute-long walk to 303 from the elevator took me ten minutes. Sensations ran through me as I struggled to move forward. When I finally arrived, I lifted my hand to knock, but before I could, the door opened, and a hand grabbed me, quickly pulling me inside, causing me to trip. Luckily, I prevented myself from falling onto one of the double beds before me.

"No one can know you're here," a woman said after I regained my balance. "This meeting did not happen, do you understand? No one knows we spoke, and I'm risking everything by meeting with you."

"I understand," I assured her. "But why such a crappy motel? There are newer ones across the street. I'm sure you can afford a better room than this. Why the cloak and dagger?" I asked.

She matched my image of the caller—a long-haired, blue-eyed blonde in her mid-late thirties. She smiled at me, which made me feel at ease.

"No one expects me to be here, my husband especially. He'd never think to look for me here," she said. "I'm JoAnn Hastings. It's nice to meet you finally, Vivienne." She stretched out her hand and then pulled me in for a hug. "You are a hard woman to find. What took you so long to come up? I saw when you pulled up."

"I was gathering my nerves," I told her. "It was not easy for me to come here. Where's Shannon?" I asked, scanning the room as if to find my daughter.

"Vivienne, what I'm about to tell you cannot go beyond these walls, do you understand?"

"Don't play with me, JoAnn! I've been through too much to be playing games. I can't go through another trauma. I've come too far."

"I'm a mother of two girls, and if one of my daughters went missing, I wouldn't want to live. So, as one mother to another, I must apologize for what my husband put you through." She pulled me down onto one of the beds inside the room that smelled like a cigarette dispenser. "I was sworn to secrecy about how Shannon ended up with Damien, and I'm sorry it took this long for me to find you."

"You're married to Damien Hastings?" I asked, dragging my hand away.

JoAnn seemed surprised that I was a bit hostile. "Vivienne, I'm not your enemy. Otherwise, I wouldn't be sneaking around my husband's back like this." Her eyes seemed genuine. "I raised Shannon as my own."

She whipped out an envelope from the black bag on the small table beside the bed and handed it to me. I nervously rummaged through the package, unsure what I'd find inside. And one by one, I flipped through the stack of letter-sized photographs after tossing the manila envelope aside. A smile crept up on me, then a sniffle. I rubbed my left hand under my nose. I looked at my daughter and realized she was no longer the little girl I remembered. Her resemblance to Damien was all the memories I had of her. The pictures were of her time in high school. I could no longer hold my emotions. I burst into tears.

"Wow! My sweet baby!" I cried.

The Hastings DNA was still dominant in her, and slowly, I moved my eyes toward JoAnn, hoping to hear more information about Shannon. "When I met Damien, he did not tell me the truth about Shannon's mother. All he told me was that she died in childbirth. I took him at his word. I had no reason to question whether it was true. It wasn't until a year and a half ago, when I traveled with him to Jamaica, his friend, Alvin Clarke, inadvertently told me that Shannon's mother was not dead, so I forced more information out of him."

"You're not making sense, JoAnn. Who's Alvin?" My fingers were still flipping through the pictures.

"Alvin was the one who told Damien where to find you. I spent months searching for you. Alvin's stories seemed too much like a plot."

I looked up at her and smiled, hoping she would see through my desperation when I said his name. "Jonathan?" It had been a long time since I spoke his name to anyone. "What about Jonathan? Did you ask him who Shannon's mother was?" I asked, afraid of what her answer might be.

"No. I couldn't let anyone know I had suspicions." JoAnn got up and walked across the room. Suddenly, her countenance changed. She was beautiful and seemed well-educated, roughly five feet, ten inches. Approximately one hundred and fifty pounds. She was nothing like Damien's type. He was used to his women lacking self-esteem with daddy issues. Those were the girls he usually deceived because he was a Hastings. He was a sloppy dresser with too much money who drank like a fish. I couldn't see the attraction for JoAnn.

Maybe he cleaned up his act.

"I don't get it. How did you find me?" My eyes followed her every move from when she moved away. I could see the difficulty in her eyes as she searched for the words to explain how my daughter ended up in her custody. Then I realized JoAnn did not know half of my story.

"I found you because I knew exactly where to look. It took a while, but I have my way. All I needed was your name, and Alvin provided me with that. He told me they orchestrated a plan to find you after you disappeared, and when they did, you had a little girl. Their initial plan was not to take the girl, but after they saw her, they changed their strategy. When he told me, I was convinced I had to put my detective skills to work. I had to find you," she said, returning to where I sat.

"Are you sure you've never mentioned my name in Jonathan's presence?" I needed to know more about him. Whether she'd heard him mention my name, I wanted her to tell me he talked about me constantly. I needed to know Jonathan did not forget me.

"Jonathan and I weren't as close as we should have been. He and his brother weren't the closest, and because of that, we were just cordial with each other. Sometimes, I wished I had married him instead. He is so different from Damien."

"You deserve better than Damien; there's no doubt about that."

She sat beside me again, held onto my hands, and stared at me for over thirty seconds. Her firm grip scared me. Her stare seemed apologetic, and I was beginning to shake by this time. I locked my hands so she wouldn't feel them trembling. I should have been more cautious than to meet a stranger alone in a motel room. The last time someone lured me, it cost me everything. I should have learned my lesson not to be so trusting. But I heard my daughter's name and forgot everything that had happened to me. I was willing to risk everything to find her.

"Shannon died two weeks ago. Her funeral is in two days. "I'm so sorry. I know that's not what you want to hear," JoAnn said.

I spent what seemed like an eternity mourning Shannon. I didn't know that I still had any grief left in me. "No. No. No. Oh God, no!" I sobbed, falling off the bed. JoAnn grabbed me and pulled me back up right before I hit the floor. She held on to me. Her grasp was the strength of someone twice her size. She kept me from falling.

Fifteen minutes later, after I had stopped screaming, I pulled out a black and white picture of Shannon and handed it to JoAnn. "I took this about a month after she was born. I carried it everywhere. It was the only one I had of her. That made it difficult to find her during the brief search. There was not much the Police could do with the description of a missing black-haired five-year-old girl," I said.

"I cannot imagine what you've been through."

"How did Shannon die?" I asked, barely able to speak.

"She had a severe asthma attack at school. She had left her inhaler at home, and we couldn't get it to her on time," JoAnn said, her voice breaking, her eyes filled with tears.

"You'd tell me if Damien abused her, wouldn't you?" I asked, my voice trembling with fear and uncertainty. My mind was topsy-turvy, a whirlwind of suspicion. It was hard for me to see him treating my daughter like a real father. He reserved a special kind of hate for me. Assuming he'd vent his anger on Shannon wouldn't be a stretch.

"What are you asking me, Vivienne?"

"I'm asking if Damien sexually abused Shannon."

She squinted as if surprised I'd be so bold as to ask such a question. But beneath the façade, I could tell the question made her uncomfortable.

"Damien may be many things, but molesting his daughter?"

"Are you sure about that, JoAnn? Really sure about that. I'm not sure you know him like you do." Her face turned red after I said that. "Tell me more about my daughter. I'm sorry I made you feel like you must defend your husband. But there are things you don't know about him. Or maybe you do. What was my baby like?" I asked, changing the intensity of the moment. The pictures I held didn't tell me much, and I couldn't stop thinking about how JoAnn ended up with such a monster for a husband.

"Shannon needed help developing trust. Looking back, she must have been dealing with the internal struggle of being taken. I could not get her to talk to me or her father. But she was protective of her sisters. They were the only ones she was comfortable around. When she was younger, about ten years old, she'd talk about her mama. That she would take her to school with her when she was little, and I'd brush it aside, thinking it must have been something she saw on television. But when Alvin told me you were not dead, I realized there might be something to her story."

"I taught at the school she attended. It's amazing the things children sometimes remember. It could be that she remembered her kidnapping, too," I said. "That is why she wasn't comfortable around Damien. A father is so much more than a sperm donor. Damien was a jealous brother who thought he must have me by any means, and he planted his seed that I couldn't get rid of. I loved my daughter with my whole heart, but she constantly reminds me of the brutal way in which I conceived her."

I wept on and off inside that motel room as I listened to JoAnn relate the whole story of what had happened to Shannon. And when darkness fell, she handed me the room key, then soothed me to sleep. When I woke six hours later, I found the note she left on the nightstand. My heart sank as I read the time and address of Shannon's funeral, a fresh wave of grief washing over me. At that moment, as I stared at the note, a plan for retribution had begun to form in my mind—a chance to make Damien pay for what he had done to Shannon and me.

***

My fingers trembled against the telephone as I dialed my mother's number. It took a while to compose myself, my tears refusing to stop. Giving her the news of Shannon's death was just as devastating as the day Damien stole her from me.

"Oh, Sweetie, I'm so sorry. Your dad and I can be there first thing in the morning. I don't think you should be going through such a loss alone," she said.

"The funeral is tomorrow, Mom. I don't think it's necessary to come. I'll be on the first flight after it's over. I'll get out of here as soon as possible," I said.

"How's Jonathan? Have you seen him yet?"

"I don't think I want to, Mom. There's only one heartache I can bear at a time. I don't think I can handle seeing him now."

"What happened was not only to you, Dear. Don't forget that. I knew how much he suffered when he couldn't find you. You might want to reconsider giving him closure."

I had been dreading the possibility of running into Jonathan at the funeral. Just thinking about him increased my heart rate tenfold. It was unlikely he'd miss his niece's funeral. After all, they were a very tight-knit family. I was beginning to feel the butterflies in my stomach as I thought about how I'd explain my presence at the funeral.

Tears streamed down my face as I remembered the night Jonathan brought me back to life on the dark seashore. It was as if I could feel his hands on me as he grazed them over my face, begging me not to die and leave him.

There was no way I could forget the letter I was forced to leave for him as I ran away from him like a battered wife as I escaped from Montego Bay. I grieved the loss of Jonathan while I was hiding. I remembered how I cried myself to sleep every night and the courage it took not to run back to him.

My body shook, and my palms became sweaty as my mother, the eternal optimist, brought up memories I had tucked away for over a decade.

"Mom, it's been a long time since I've seen him. I'm sure Jonathan has moved on and has forgotten about me. What if he's married with kids?" My chest discomfort was a sign I was having trouble processing the possibility of running into him with his big, happy family.

"I'm not asking you to marry him. I'm just suggesting you get closure for both of you. You will never be healed unless you close that chapter of your life."

"I know you, Mom, with you, it's never as simple as that," I murmured.

I never understood how my mother was able to separate Jonathan from what his brother did to me. She loved Jonathan like a son.

I wish it were easier to get a clean break and not have to face my tortured past again. It was impossible to see Jonathan without having a full-blown meltdown.

"You lost your daughter a long time ago, Honey. It didn't just happen. I wish you had gotten a better outcome."

"I have to shop for clothes to wear tomorrow. I didn't come prepared for a funeral. I'm going to stay in the background at the church and not draw attention to myself. I want to see my daughter one last time."

When I hung up the phone, I realized I had lied to my mother and myself.

Chapter 41

Tulips and Daffodils for Shannon

Vivienne

Damien Hastings raped me at eighteen. Ran away with my daughter at twenty-three. At thirty-three, the son-of-a-bitch was about to bury the evidence of his crime, and I was supposed to grin and bear him? I didn't think so.

Time and distance did not soften the impact of the trauma I suffered. No matter where I went, everything around me was a cruel reminder of the shame of it all. But sitting at the back of the church, contemplating murder and reigniting the anger I was sure was gone, I was determined to get my revenge.

In the next pew, an elderly gentleman glanced over at me repeatedly and might have concluded I was re-living terror. The sounds and struggles coming from the bench as I rubbed against the pinewood had alerted me to him. But he did not know that a mental breakdown had compounded my calamity. He had no idea the woman behind him, struggling to remain composed, walked an entire city to find a daughter that resulted from that terror. He could not have imagined that all my meandering was an effort not to remember the minute-by-minute brutality I had endured.

It was a warm Sunday morning, I sat at the back of the church in Scottsdale, Arizona. Sorrow overcame me when the hearse pulled up outside. Six young men, all in their thirties, wheeled the white casket into the church. The top was laden with Tulips and Daffodils, and a familiar face appeared out of the sunlight that struck the coffin. He tapped a white handkerchief against his eye as tears ran down his face. Instantly, my mind returned to the August 24 evening that forever changed my life.

The cries that haunted and drove me to madness had suddenly resurfaced. They crashed into the wall I built around me like a thunderbolt.

As the lifeless body approached the foot of the altar, it dragged me back to my past. I didn't build a thick enough wall to block memories forever. My eyes welled with tears, and my body stiffened against the hard bench, twisting and shuffling as I let out a soft whimper. The black veil that hid my face shifted to the side of my head, and the struggle caused me to kick off my shoes without realizing it. It appeared as if I was having a seizure. I had begun reliving my youth's trauma as if I were in that moment. My mind had left the funeral service and traveled home to Montego Bay.

Mourners strolled into the church, and the audience swelled to capacity.

The familiar face behind the casket belonged to Damien Hastings. "It is Well with My Soul" opened the service. I listened to the song's first two lines before my thoughts trailed off again. I could not focus on the bereavement service of that day, a day to which I hoped I would not have to bear witness. I remembered the tiny face that pressed up against the window of the black car that sped off, leaving me wallowing on the ground. I could not forget the frantic search and the mental breakdown that followed when I could not find her.

Losing my daughter was the fuse that lit the time bomb that had been ticking since the summer night in 1985 on Valence Avenue, and my daughter's kidnapping had set off the chain reaction that eventually confined me to an asylum.

Seeing Damien again awakened everything God, therapy, and medication put to sleep. The anger and the need for revenge were building within me with every step he took behind the casket. The memories were overwhelming, pulling me away from the funeral service and back to Montego Bay.

Shannon's birth jolted me and brought me back to the funeral service. I had bottled the trauma, the loneliness, the shame, the loss of Jonathan, all of it for fifteen years.

The memories catapulted me off the bench and bolted me toward the altar during the eulogy. I didn't care about the tumult my interruption would cause, nor did I pay attention to the groans and stares from the congregation either. It's as if something supernatural pulled me out of my seat, casting a spell on me, and thrust me toward the podium.

I had lost a decade of my daughter's life, for which Damien robbed me of being a mother to the only child I birthed, and no one would take away my chance to say goodbye to her.

"Ma'am, please sit down." An usher rushed over as I made my way toward the podium. The pin on his lapel noted his name was Joseph.

I scanned his name tag. "Joseph, that's my daughter lying in that casket," I said. "I searched an entire city and could not find her, and when I did, she was dead. I will not let you or anybody stop me from saying goodbye to her." I pushed him out of my way, staggered forward, focused my attention on the young man giving the eulogy, and watched as he lowered the microphone from his lips, unsure whether to continue.

I leaned over the open casket and let out a scream like the one I made when the black car drove off with Shannon. Seeing my daughter for the first time after so long overwhelmed me, and my outbursts sounded like something that had built up that I could no longer hold.

I lifted my veil, then faced the packed church. "Vivienne? What the f...?" Damien screamed as he tripped over the bench when he saw me, trying to prevent me from grieving the daughter he stole from me.

But he could not stop me now, not this time. There were too many witnesses, and there was nothing he could do to me. "You can't be here!" he yelled.

The congregation went silent. I was face-to-face with Damien at last. I had nothing to lose and was willing to risk my life, if necessary, for payback.

I silently prayed, focused my attention on the people sitting in the pews to my right.

"I would like to talk about my daughter."

"Vivienne!" Damien snapped at me again. He grabbed my arm. "Now is not the time, you can't be here, you need to leave," he said.

Damien's was the leading voice I could not get out of my head, and to be confronted by the person who had extinguished the light I had in my eyes at eighteen, made me want to punch his lights out.

"Now is not a good time to touch me, Damien." I stared at the arm where he grabbed me, my eyes slowly moving upwards until I'm staring into the dead eyes the bore into my brain as he held me down.

His grasp was firm and reminded me how vicious he could become. "You raped me, then kidnapped my daughter, and you think you could just get away with it? Everyone will know the real Damien Hastings today. I am your worst nightmare."

"I'm not asking you again to leave." His tone was hushed, as he tried to hide his anger.

"Make me. I dare you to drag me out of here. You took my daughter from me, and this is where it got her, in a casket thousands of miles away from home. You don't get to tell me to leave. Take your hand off me, or I'll scratch your eyes out. Consider today your payback." I yanked my arm away and grabbed the microphone off the podium.

"My name is Vivienne Pearson," I said, eager to tell my story, even if it meant delaying my daughter's funeral service. "To the people who know me best, I am Viv. I had the most beautiful childhood of any girl I knew, and I was hoping I'd give my daughter something similar. I was very young when my dad packed up his family, moved to Jamaica to raise me and my older brother. In a brief time, I spoke patois like everyone else and served as an amateur interpreter for my mother. It took her a bit longer, but eventually, she adapted to the Jamaican way of life.

"Fifty miles south of Montego Bay was where I grew up, submerged in my father's culture, and I loved it. Those were simple times. There, everyone protected me and treated me like royalty. It's as if they locked me in a cocoon, safe and secure from outside influences. The villagers called me "The Little American Girl" until I was fourteen before they settled on Viv. But since then, a lot has happened. I am a long, long way from the days I felt protected."

The packed church quieted, and everyone seemed intrigued.

"It was hard to see me as a victim. I was not a poor thing, and it was not easy for anyone to seduce or deceive me.

I always exuded confidence and was undoubtedly not naïve about how men think. But, one Saturday night, I made an ill-fated journey to Valence Avenue in Ironshore, Jamaica.

"I had ambitions that my best friend used to tell me were more than most girls our age. I was off to change the world when I packed my suitcase and ventured to Montego Bay. My dad had warned me that the city could swallow me. But I had convinced him not to worry. That I was smart enough to avoid this pitfall. It wasn't the pollution that got me, a slash from a machete, the political upheaval, or the Black Heart Man from the '80s.

Damien Hastings raped, tortured, and mutilated me. An encounter that was brutal and colossal in the extent of its damage was undoubtedly why I considered it worse than death.

"'Don't waste your time hating me, Vivienne,' Damien told me after I hung my head and limped out of his brother's house. But I was too exhausted to answer him, I stumbled through the iron burglar bars in shame, tears, and blood stains. I set off down the hill with the night sky hovering over me, forcing me on my face as I struggled to keep my feet on the wet grass. I tried to run, but I couldn't lift my feet. I had no energy to get them off the ground. Between fighting him off and him slamming me against the bedroom walls, there was hardly any energy left for me to walk.

"But I did spend time hating him, not all my time, but much of it. How could I not? His grimacing face had been frozen in my consciousness since he waged war on me, though I had reserved most of the anger for myself.

I floated away, desperately trying to die among the coral reefs. When that failed, I stepped in front of a moving car that almost gave the poor driver a heart attack. And when I failed at taking my life, I walked away from my entire family. But that was only the beginning of my suffering, compared to what would eventually follow.

"It was as if I was falling in slow motion into a bottomless pit of nothingness, and Montego Bay was where my unsound mind and unhealed body returned after I ran away and had resisted going back for more than five years. It was then that the torrents of emotions erupted.

"I was out of my mind and running out of time, searching for my daughter.

"There were no television alerts, radio announcements, or a swat team helping me to find her, just my weary feet trotting along the roadways and on every corner. People often dismissed me as crazy and called me a mad gal, but they could never have survived my trauma."

Tears streamed down the faces of some in the congregation. No one moved from their seats. My story had a more significant impact than I could have imagined.

I continued telling my story without interruption.

"I lost my virtue, all hope, mind, and daughter, so please bear with me a little longer.

"Speaking of my daughter, let's talk a little bit about her. After all, very soon we'll be putting her into the ground." A soft sob escaped me. "Here in this coffin," I paused and rubbed my hand across it. "Here, lies my daughter, whom I have not seen since the day Damien kidnapped her. Besides Damien Hastings, I don't think any of you know I am her mother. But, today, I want to say a few words about her before he sticks her under the earth forever, and if he ever tries to interrupt me again, please tell him to stop, or else I won't be responsible for my actions."

I took another deep breath. "There is absolutely nothing worse he can do to me than what he already did.

"When my daughter was born, I had only one estranged family member and God." Another sob escaped.

Damien stormed out of the church. All eyes centered on him as he fled. "Let him run away. It's his turn to run. I ran up and down, and throughout an entire city because of the misery he caused me. From the first day Jonathan introduced me to him, we didn't get along. But little did I know that he was an entitled slob, jealous of his brother. He is a predator, and he saw me as his prey, and like the beast he was, he devoured me, and from then on, my life became a living hell. I was afraid of my shadow because of the voices in my head. For the time that I lived at the asylum, my parents, Shannon Pearson, and Jonathan Hastings, were the people I thought about constantly. Not even sedatives were strong enough to make me forget them.

"But long before I was institutionalized, I walked the streets of Montego Bay until my clothes and shoes fell off, trying to find the daughter I recently learned Damien Hastings stole from me. At one point, I had convinced myself I didn't have a daughter, that I only imagined I did, all due to the voices in my head, stemming from the trauma I had suffered.

"I've been spat on, kicked, and called ugly names because I refused to stop searching for Shannon. But if you ask Damien about my suffering, he'll tell you he doesn't know anything about it. But he should have known that he left me broken after kidnapping my daughter and leaving the island. To this day, I'm still not sure how he found us."

The Hastings' clan sat still in the first two rows to my right. Rachel Hastings gripped her husband's hand as her eyes widened with disbelief, as if trying to make sense of what I was saying. Her husband contorted his mouth, his lips pursed together as if he was about to cry. Both their eyes fixed on me.

You could hear a pin drop as I focused my attention on the Hastings.

"The man you saw, pretending to grieve, telling me to leave, is a horrible human being who preyed on his younger brother's girlfriend. Then he kidnapped the child that resulted from that perverse attack because he thought I was a stupid country girl, and he was an heir.

"I didn't know my daughter because he never allowed me to be her mother long enough. Losing her when she was so young was not enough time for lasting memories, so I'm sure Shannon went to sleep believing I was dead.

"The crimes Damien committed against me will be why decent people like you give him a taste of his own medicine. Damien Hastings should know what it feels like to be scorned and shunned by society.

"I fled my home because an oversized, sex-crazed, ganja-smoking alcoholic with a ferocious appetite for vengeance against his brother, raped me.

"Until now, the only people who knew what he did to me are my parents and brother. I've been unable to tell anyone else. Even when Jonathan was running through the emergency room carrying my half-dead body, screaming for a doctor, I couldn't tell him I was dying because of Damien. I couldn't tell him that his brother was responsible for the bruises on my face as he stroked the bandages while I was in the hospital or that his brother caused me to lose consciousness twice during the assault.

"I repeatedly opened my mouth to tell him, but the words couldn't come out. I kept thinking that our relationship could never survive my scandalous reality. I didn't know him long enough to think he'd take my side over his brother's, so I hid from him to save him the shame and the pain, as well as for me to escape the terrifying ordeal inflicted on me. I wanted to get away from it all. Get away from the city, Jonathan, my parents, and life. But I didn't run far enough away from Damien. I couldn't. With all the money he had, there was nowhere far enough I could have gone. He hunted me like I was an escaped criminal that he must apprehend. And eventually, after he found me, Shannon was gone, and I went back to where it all began without my daughter, and the consequences of my unaddressed trauma manifested.

"But nothing prepared me for losing my baby to the same son-of-a-bitch who brutalized me.

"If anyone should eulogize my daughter, it's me. Fifteen years, four months, and three days have been the length of my suffering. From the day I left my brother's house to visit Jonathan because Damien told me he was in an accident, only to realize that it was a trap. Five hours, thirty minutes, and twenty-five seconds was how long he held me captive and forcibly penetrated me. Seventeen hours, forty-five minutes, and twenty seconds, I was in labor to deliver my daughter. That is more than enough time and gives me the right to be here to talk about what he put me through.

"After Jonathan pulled me from the bottom of the ocean, I decided I couldn't keep putting him through yet another distress of trying to save my life. I had caused enough heartache to him, and I didn't want him to save me. Damien had damaged me beyond Jonathan's ability to appeal to what sense of reasoning I had left at that point.

"The devastation that followed my disappearance was more than I had bargained. My parents barely recovered, and I'm not sure about Jonathan. I hope he moved on from what he went through and found happiness.

"I gave birth to Shannon Jayne Pearson in an estranged aunt's house after she took me in. She'd given me a chance to escape the city's constant reminder that I didn't belong there. All I felt was emptiness, self-pity, and pain, physical and mental.

"Mandeville had become my refuge. Even for a few minutes a day, I could think of something besides what I endured in the city, and I got to refocus my energy on my daughter instead of worrying about the story surrounding her birth, the nightmare from which I could not wake. When Shannon was born, I knew hiding her from Damien forever was impossible. Every feature she had was from him. I had begun to feel that was either my punishment or the irrefutable proof that Damien raped me. I had concluded that was my punishment.

"For years, I held out hope of finding Shannon alive. But I never did, and here we are, a tragic ending to a horrific beginning. A life cut short and dressed up with tulips and daffodils."

Chapter 42

All Shook Up

Jonathan

It felt like I had been holding my breath for the last decade and a half. I breathed through my mouth, exhaling years of built-up hurt.

I listened to V tell her story—the one I pleaded with her to tell me, and a tear rolled down my cheek. The details of her assault were brutal and more graphic than I could ever have imagined.

I stood when Damien yelled at her but was quickly pulled back to my seat by my friend, Luther. I watched Shannon grow up for years and did not connect her to V.

I had taken Damien's word that Shannon's mother had died. If I had paid closer attention, I could have saved her from the years she spent searching for her daughter.

I pulled myself off the bench and shuffled through the row, brushing up against curious onlookers as I moved toward V. I hustled through the pew into the aisle, stood, and faced her. Heads turned to follow my every move. The congregation had figured something dramatic was about to happen. My eyes locked with V's, and after a minute or so, my jaw nervously widened into a smile.

I stood motionless after she lowered the microphone from her lips, and her voice trailed off. The mic had slowly left her right hand and landed on the carpeted floor with a thud, her left hand covering her mouth. With one foot in front of the other, she moved toward me. She shuffled closer as if an invisible hand was guiding her with precision. Her eyes were still fixed on me as she walked down the aisle. The closer she got, the weaker I became. The slow tingling of my skin felt like a burn, but I was eager and determined to make contact. I just had to feel Vivienne Pearson's touch. If she were before me, nothing would stop me, not this time.

Standing in front of me was the one girl I could not stop thinking about, and from a distance, the same smile pulled me into her like a magnet in the late spring of 1985. I was unsure if what was happening was real. I didn't think I'd ever see her again. But the force that often overwhelmed me was pulling me toward her. Only one person had that effect on me.

She didn't look a day older than eighteen, as if she had stopped aging. Her face no longer had the scars that seared in my brain. She looked youthful and vibrant, with no trace of the brutal assault that almost killed her.

I reached forward. It was no longer a fantasy. It was a dream come true.

My touch was more difficult than she could withstand. She could no longer keep her footing on the ground; she collapsed.

I broke her fall. Joseph, the usher who tried to prevent her from approaching the altar, rushed to her aide. "Vivienne! Vivienne! Get up, please, V." I shook her.

The funeral, at this point, was in turmoil as I lifted her off the floor and dashed out the door. Old memories resurfaced, like the time I stormed through the hospital lobby in Ironshore, carrying her, not knowing whether she would survive. Here I was, again, her limp body hung from my arms and whisked away to yet another hospital, leaving Damien to deal with the fallout of what she had revealed.

"Come on, V. You have come too far to give up now. Stay with me, please!"

I braced against Luther's car's soft interior as he hit the accelerator to a heart-stopping ninety miles per hour. My heart raced. I had begun to feel like being around me was not good for V's health.

I wasn't guessing when I told V she was my soulmate. Right from the start, I realized our connection was freakishly amazing, and I'd be lying if I said her disappearance hadn't ruined another love for me. I was stuck on Vivienne. Stuck in 1985 after she disappeared with my heart. Vivienne Pearson was the only love I ever wanted. Whatever happened to her happened to me. I agonized over her until it had become detrimental to my health. If I hadn't left Jamaica, I would not have survived, and whatever it was that made her collapse into my arms again was proof that our souls were inextricably linked.

I ran my hand across her forehead, trying to gauge her temperature. I caressed her cheeks while I cradled her head with my right hand. It had suddenly dawned on me that it had to be divine intervention that brought her back to me from out of nowhere. She fell right into my lap, literally.

For fifteen years, I walked around like a zombie with half of my heart missing, never thinking I would get it back. How, after all these years, have we found each other? And what a sick joke to know that I practically helped raise her daughter and never thought for a second Shannon was the product of such an evil act.

Fifteen frigging years and my brother never once expressed remorse, felt guilt, or regretted what he had done. What nerve it must take for him to be so heartless. He had to be a different breed, a bad seed. For my brother to feel nothing after watching her daughter, day after day, knowing what he did to her mother, was pure, unadulterated evil. How could I be related to such a soulless, emotionless jerk?

I could never forget V's near drowning. I would have died that night if I hadn't found her, and a week later, I watched her brother weep until he almost collapsed. On each journey I took to Greenspring, I wondered whether her parents would survive the next day. Damien wrecked so many lives, someone who shared my DNA. Someone I grew up loving, living in the same house, attending the same activities, and being influenced by the same people.

What does that say about me? Could I have possessed the same evil traits waiting to be triggered?

The day I found V lying on her bedroom floor seemed like yesterday. A piece of me died that day. The same fear engulfed me as I held her. And here we were again, speeding and praying that she'd survive yet another trip to the hospital.

Minutes into our drive, V grabbed my shirt and pulled me forward.

"Pull over, Luther, pull over!" I yelled.

He gripped the padded steering wheel of his SUV and swerved to his right. Dust and gravel clouded our view as the car screeched to a halt.

"Vivienne?" I held on to her tight, terrified yet relieved she was conscious.

"Did you know Shannon was my daughter?" That was her first question.

She held the back of her head, slowly lifted herself out of my lap, and shuffled to the empty seat. "Oh, V, no! I had no idea Damien was your rapist. Now I understand why you refused to tell me who raped you. No matter how much I begged."

"I wanted to tell you, especially after I realized how badly you were hurting. But I thought it would hurt you more if you knew."

She shuffled closer and held my face as if studying it to ensure it was me.

"Hey, Jonathan, it is you." The glee in her eyes made me smile, the first in many years. I almost broke down in the church, but at that moment, I had to be strong; breaking down would have to wait.

"How did you find out Damien had your daughter?" I shook my head, trying to understand how she found me.

"I got an anonymous tip," she said softly.

"I'm so sorry. I wish I had figured out earlier that Shannon was your daughter. I couldn't have imagined that my brother would be responsible for almost killing you."

I hugged her, buried my head in her neck, and squeezed her as tight as my strength let me. My heart broke all over again.

"Hmm." The deep groan she let out alarmed me. "I'm still not feeling well, Jonathan. I need to see a doctor to make sure I am okay."

"Luther, you heard her. Let's go!"

***

Thirty minutes later, I dashed towards the parking garage to find Luther after the doctor took V in for evaluation.

I pressed my trembling fingers on P2, and as the elevator descended, I staggered against the door and stumbled out. I slipped against the black SUV, plopped onto the ground, pulled my legs forward, and rested my head between my knees, wrestling with the revelation that confronted me.

I pulled out the letter I had tucked in my wallet for fifteen years and read the faded ink. The paper had turned light brown from aging.

"Dear Jonathan." So many emotions ripped through me as I read the old letter. *"I will be long gone when you receive this letter..."* My heart broke into a million pieces, remembering when it froze to lock in V's memory and shut off access to everyone else.

As I struggled to read the letter, Luther sat beside me and squeezed my shoulder to ease the broken man before him. There was nothing he could say to take away my pain, but it seemed he couldn't stand by and watch me fall apart and do nothing.

After sitting silently for over ten minutes, he helped me off the ground and led me back inside the hospital waiting room. I folded the letter and tucked the wrinkled paper inside my wallet. "What if she still blames me, Luther? All this time, I still can't get the image of what happened to her. Her battered and swollen face tortured me, still tormenting me. In an instant, Damien turned our world upside down.

"From our first kiss in Ironshore, our wild summer romance in 1985, which ended abruptly, to now, there has never been a day I don't think about her. I remember our conversation in the hospital in Ironshore as if it had happened yesterday. I pleaded with her to tell me who raped her; I just couldn't break through. Over fifteen years, Luther, fifteen frigging years, I never once thought that my brother was responsible for nearly killing my girlfriend. I knew he didn't like her, but it never occurred to me that he would hurt her, and I should have known that if a stranger had raped her, she would have told me. I introduced her to a monster, and he broke her. I will never forgive myself for that."

I ran my fingers through my hair, my mind traveling a million miles a minute. "If I weren't at the hospital, Damien would be a dead man," I said.

***

"Get me out of here, Jonathan. The doctors gave me the all-clear. I have a daughter to bury," V said as she sat beside me. But my mind was far away, reflecting on how it took us this long to find each other. She rubbed the back of her hand against my cheek and looked up at Luther with imploring eyes.

"He's devastated," he told her.

"I looked everywhere for you, V," I said. "When I couldn't find you, I figured you were dead. I went through a series of internal wars, a battle I couldn't win. The beach where we were the last time had become my refuge. I'd sit by the water and scream in the darkness at night. It was pure torture. But nothing that I've been through comes close to what you've endured because of what Damien did to you. I should have broadened the possibility that he might be responsible, and I blame myself for not realizing he was capable of such brutality."

"We're here now, Jonathan." She rubbed the middle of my back with the palm of her hand to comfort me, then smiled.

"I lost it after you left me that goodbye letter. It tore me, and I became someone you wouldn't recognize."

Our eyes locked as she slowly pulled me into her. "Hi, my name is Vivienne. What's your name?" she smiled, and my world of gray burst into vivid colors and possibilities again, and all the sorrows drained out of me.

Chapter 43

Mommy Dearest

Vivienne

Rachel Hastings stumbled through the emergency room door. Her steps were hesitant, eyes red and mascara ruined.

I was not expecting to see her at all.

She tapped her handkerchief under her eyelids repeatedly, slowly making her way toward me. I hadn't thought much about our interaction if I saw any of the Hastings. I was aware they might be at the funeral, but I was more focused on my daughter. It had been years since I saw Jonathan's mother, and I held residual resentment for everyone connected to the man who raped me, except Jonathan. He had suffered enough.

Mrs. Hastings should have known what her son was capable of. She deserved blame, so did her husband. If she was here for absolution, there was no way I would pretend I had fully healed. What would I even say to her after so many years. Less than an hour ago, I had ruined her son's reputation and probably the entire Hastings brand.

Jonathan looked at me, then at his mother, his eyes pleading with her to tread lightly.

Without a word, Mrs. Hastings gripped my chin, rubbed her hand against my jaw, and let out a soft cry. I must say, that was unexpected. She pulled me in for a hug. I was not expecting that kind of reaction either.

"How are you doing, Vivienne?" she asked. Her voice filled with desperation and sadness. She kept up nicely for a seventy-something-year-old, although she was used to fine things. She hardly looked a day older than the last time I saw her. She no longer sported the Afro, but the perm made her look gorgeous and elegant, especially with the strands of gray hair highlighting the shoulder-length hairdo.

There were no signs of any illness. Even my mother showed signs of aging, but then again, there was the period I was missing that added at least ten years of aches and pain to her life. Rachel Hastings didn't seem to have any stress at all. She was still as fit as the woman who took me on an hour-long tour of her property. As a matter of fact, all the Hastings seemed to be just fine, as if their entire lives were nothing but joy. I wished I could say the same about mine or my parents'.

"I'm doing fine, Mrs. Hastings."

I welcomed her hug, glanced over her shoulder at Jonathan, wide-eyed. I was too surprised to show resentment, especially when the person that mattered most looked so adoringly at me. "The doctors said I was dehydrated. They think that was why I fainted. It's been a while since I ate," I said, surprised that she came to the hospital, even after everything I said at Shannon's funeral. I expected her to be angry, or at least resentful. Instead, she seemed more concerned about my health than the hourlong sermon I preached about her son's brutal assault on me.

My speech had multiple targets. I wanted the world, and especially the Hastings, to know what I've endured at the hands of their son. They had a right to know there was evil among them. My revelation could do damage to their business, but I was way past sparing their feelings or reputations. I had suffered more than any of them knew, and there was no way I could hurt them more than how Damien destroyed me.

I tried to be polite to Jonathan's mother, though. Rachel Hastings had developed an affection for me, and I for her the day Jonathan took me to meet her. I felt her attempt to reach out to me was genuine.

"I'm glad you're okay, Sweetheart. Where have you been all these years?"

"Mom, not now. Not here, please," Jonathan said.

I released myself from her embrace and moved toward Jonathan. I placed my hand on his chest. "May I speak with your mother alone?" I brushed my left thumb against his cheek before rubbing the back of my hand against his chin. "I'll be okay, I promise, I'm all fainted out," I said, then tipped forward and kissed him.

I smiled at Mrs. Hastings, tucked my arm under hers, and led her through the glass door as it slid open. "We really need to talk," I said.

We sat on the long bench in front of the hospital driveway to the emergency room entrance, looking out at the Imax theatre across the street.

It had taken a decade to recover from all my self-hurt. But I still nursed an unhealthy feeling toward Damien. Since I had ruined his reputation earlier that day, the least I could do was listen to what his mother had to say. I wasn't obligated to answer her questions, but I'd do my best not to let her feel responsible for the monster she unleashed upon the world. I owed her that much, and it was long overdue.

She held my face in her hands, and it disarmed me. "Had I known Shannon was your daughter I would have hunted for you myself. I believe every word of what you said at the church today. You didn't have to convince me my son is a monster. I've been dealing with his viciousness since he was a teenager.

"Damien just showed up with a little girl, saying her mother had died, and I didn't question it. For years, he had us convinced Shannon's mother died in childbirth. I should have recognized you in her. She had your smile, but Damien's genes were so dominant no one could see you in her unless they looked closely. I should have seen you in her.

"I'm sure Jonathan doesn't want me to tell you this, but I had to send him away after you left. He was dying before me, and I couldn't help him. I couldn't just sit by while he dies of a broken heart. I'm sorry about that too. If he had stayed, he might have found you sooner.

"He's a good man, it was hard to watch him go crazy over you and not help him, so I sent him here to start a new franchise of Hideaway. I thought it would have been easier for him to deal with what happened. But even that did little to heal him."

What could I have said after hearing that? I was in love with one of her sons while the other brutally raped me. I wished I didn't have to confront my past in such intimate details in front of an audience at my daughter's funeral. But somehow, with all that, I empathized with her, knowing her child turned out to be such a disappointment.

Jonathan and Luther burst through the door with concerns in their eyes.

"I hope I get to see you again, soon, Vivienne. We have more to talk about, but I'll let you get some rest," Rachel Hastings said. We got up off the bench, my hands in hers. "Please get something to eat. JoAnn postponed the funeral, so tomorrow we'll decide what to do next. Call me." She handed me her business card, kissed me on both cheeks, then tapped Jonathan's and Luther's shoulders, and walked to a waiting limousine.

The full-blown Post Traumatic Stress Disorder I had gone through, was constantly triggered by the slightest memory of my assault. If not for my desire to find my daughter, I would have succumbed to the stranglehold it had on me.

But now, the resolute woman I had become would ensure Damien Hastings didn't breathe the same air as me.

Chapter 44

At Last!

Vivienne

They said if you love someone, you let them go. Bad advice. Whoever came up with that had yet to learn what it took to let go of someone like Jonathan Hastings. I had been trying to let go of him for fifteen years. My heart just wouldn't let me.

Jonathan held my face in his hands. His eyes filled with a mixture of longing and regret. "You haven't aged, V. You still look like the girl I met before you ran away with my heart." He leaned in for a kiss. His sorrowful eyes still held the youthful exuberance that held my heart hostage.

I smiled at him. "You're still using those cheesy lines, Jonathan?"

"I've never said anything to you I didn't mean. There has never been anyone else that comes close to making me feel the way you do."

"I don't want to hurt you again. But I can't just forget about what Damien did to me. He took everything from me. I can't forgive him or forget it as if nothing happened. Damien is your brother. I can't ask you to choose me over him."

"I chose you the first day I saw you," he said immediately, his voice breaking. He wrapped his arms around me, and my body trembled beneath his fingers. "Come home with me tonight." He chuckled nervously, and my heart overflowed.

Jonathan lifted me off the ground and pressed his lips against mine. They were soft and warm, his heartbeat sounding like a horserace. Every organ in my body responded to his kiss like a symphony, giving me little chance to deny his request.

We headed to Jonathan's house after he checked me out of the motel. Two brown and black Doberman Pinschers jumped on him when we got there. They slobbered all over him, standing on their hind legs and wagging their tails. The younger of the two dogs had a dark patch over his eyes, making him look like Zorro. I was surprised they completely ignored me, but I was not scared of them. They seemed well-trained, and I posed no threat to them or their owner.

At ten o'clock, darkness blanketed the sky, and after the dogs finally ran to their corners, Jonathan took my suitcase and placed it inside one of the massive guest bedrooms. Everything looked brand new. The walk-in closet was enormous, spanning over twenty feet.

There was no female apparel in any of the closets. Only rows of work suits and formal wear. Another closet across the other side of the room was designated for shoes. The orchid plants in the corners on top of the bedside tables accentuated the color-coordinated thick drapes and area rug in the middle of the floor.

I was lost in the comfort and coziness of Jonathan's home when he hugged me from behind. His right hand enveloped my waist, and his left hand hung over my heart. I leaned my head against his arm and wove my fingers through his fingers. I closed my eyes and was immediately transported back to our first date. I reflected on when we stood outside his house on Valence Avenue, listening to the roaring waves as they crashed against the seashore.

"Penny for your thoughts."

I turned and faced him. Jonathan pushed my hair away from my eyes and gently rubbed his thumb against my cheek.

Fighting my love for Jonathan would be a losing battle. My heart had lost that a long time ago. There were still shrapnel wounds from the last one. Whatever the undeniable connection between us, the magnetic force that snapped us back so smoothly was impossible to ignore. Our hearts beat with a familiar rhythm as if dancing to a melody only we could hear. It had been silent for far too long.

"V, I'm alive," Jonathan whispered.

"Me too," I said, hardly able to bear the emotions ripping through me.

"The letter you sent me in '92 breathed life into me. Before that, I was like a zombie, in search of my heart. Knowing you were alive was the medicine I needed to keep me until I find it."

Like a gentle breeze, Jonathan's lips caressed my face. The familiar glow of his eyes had returned. The last time I saw the light leaving his eyes was the day he fell apart in my hospital room in Ironshore.

Jonathan was the missing puzzle piece of my life. His love had the power to transform me, bring back the butterflies, and set my heart ablaze—a connection that transcended time and distance.

He led me outside to the back of his mansion. There was an Olympic-sized lighted swimming pool to my left and a hammock tucked in the corner to my right with a barbecue grill nearby. I had a spectacular view from the hilltop. The estate was breathtaking. But it didn't surprise me Jonathan had built such an elaborate home. He had spent his entire time in Jamaica wrapped up in the glamour of his family's resorts. But I also saw how he treasured the outdoors in Greenspring. He loved nature. The same tranquility and peace, surrounded by the beautiful red mountains and rock formations in the desert. The ruggedness was a clear reminder of our time together, like a spiritual retreat.

As I surveyed Jonathan's mansion, I realized he brought a piece of Jamaica. A fold-out domino table was tucked aside near the barbeque grill. It reminded me of the bubble we floated in before Damien popped it.

He tucked his hand inside his pocket and pulled out an old, dingy sheet of paper. "I promised myself I'd carry this letter everywhere until I find you," he said.

My eyes widened with disbelief. "I almost didn't write that letter, but I didn't want to leave with you thinking I eventually succeeded at taking my life. I must have rewritten it ten times before settling on the final draft. Leaving you tortured me."

"Now that you're here with me, I'm afraid this will be its final day in my wallet." He looked at me, ripped up the paper, and blew the pieces out of his hand. The wind carried them away and scattered them like ashes across the valley. A warm flush came over me after he pulled me into him. His touch against my skin, his sweet breath wafting against my face, made my knees buckle. He lifted me off the ground. I wrapped my hands around his neck, his, wrapping around my waist. I rubbed my lips against his lips and gently pulled onto his bottom lip. The scruffy beard suited him and enhanced his handsome face.

His bright eyes were still as prominent as I remembered them. His hands around me activated every nerve cell in my body at the tip of his touch as if to sing hallelujah.

Jonathan rubbed his nose against mine, gently moved his lips across the edges of my lips, and rested, and our bodies vibrated.

I was amazed at how little had changed between us. The butterflies that crawled beneath my skin came alive again.

"In a weird way, your letter became a lifeline for me," he said.

"How?" I asked, feeling guilty that I had caused him so much hurt.

"Each time I'd feel punctured, I would read it to find peace, but I didn't think it would take me this long to find it," he said.

"I'm no better than you. I wrote dozens of letters to you. That's how I survived. If you're ever in Dallas, I just might let you read them," I laughed.

I rested my head on his chest, and my world slowly came together like a slow-motion reversal of a 7.7 earthquake.

Jonathan scooped me off the ground and carried me toward the pool. We sat for another hour with our feet submerged in the shallow end.

"I did everything to find you before I left Jamaica. When I couldn't, the only thing to do was get as far away as possible. If I hadn't left, I would have gone completely insane."

We had not discussed the despair into which I had fallen. I wanted to delay telling Jonathan I cried under the midnight sky because I thought my daughter was calling me from above. Or the times two boys sat their dogs on me, almost mauling me to death when I stopped to pick mangoes from their tree. Or how, after my doctor confined me to Bay West Regional Hospital, I constantly fought with other patients to prevent them from assaulting me. Every man I encountered was a threat, and I would erupt at them.

"Sean knew where I was while I was in the hospital. Why didn't you ask him?" I rubbed my hand up and down his arm.

"Sean, oh man." He threw his head back and sighed. "He was so mad with me that he quit Hideaway one week after you left and didn't speak to me for years. He hated me. He blamed me for everything. Who could blame him? I blamed myself, too."

"That seemed like a lifetime ago, Jonathan," I said as I waded my feet on top of the water. "What have you been up to lately? Why aren't you married? Or are you?" I asked, dreading his answer.

"I couldn't stay married to anyone who wasn't you. I'd see you in every woman I met. I expected them to be you. Everything reminded me of you. It was impossible to love someone else. It felt like I betrayed you. It made me miserable. You were all I wanted then, as I do now. I'm hoping you'll have me again."

"Are you sure? I've been through quite a lot, and I'm not eighteen years old anymore."

A light flickered in his eyes. "More than you can imagine," he said immediately. "Until death us part, V. I spent too much time living recklessly, trying to numb myself because I couldn't protect you. I used alcohol to numb me, but instead, it only made me miss you more. It was not easy for me to walk down the aisle when I married.

"Then why did you?"

"To get over you." His voice softened. He tugged me closer. "But I still couldn't. With each vow I took, the more the memory of your battered face kept flooding my mind. My wedding day was the most painful reminder of losing you. I was supposed to be making those vows to you."

"Jonathan, I meant what I said about you and Shannon at the funeral. That's why I survived. Shannon, because I just had to get her back, and you, because our love was so powerful, even when I was medicated, your love still broke through, and I'd smile."

He rubbed his thumb over my lips, then kissed me. "I was thousands of miles away, and I still couldn't get over you," he said.

"Did you tell your wife about me?" I wasn't sure what he'd say, and I didn't want an answer.

"Why did you think we broke up? Every damn day I'd talk about you. At the end of our very short marriage, she wished me well and told me not to stop searching for you."

"How long ago did you break up, and where is she now?"

"We were married for less than two years, and she remarried a year ago," he said.

"Did you love her?" I locked his fingers through mine and braced for his answer.

"I tried. But I didn't have all my love to give to her, I already pledged it to you."

"I did finish college," I chuckled nervously, changing the subject.

He squeezed me tight and let out a calming breath. "Of course, you did, Babe. I know you would. Come with me. Let's go somewhere more comfortable."

We moved to the giant hammock, laid together, and talked about his life since he left Jamaica until we eventually rocked each other to sleep.

Jonathan seemed peaceful when I woke up at midnight in his arms. I stared at him as if I couldn't take my eyes off him. I just had to pinch him to make sure he was real. Then I gently snuggled up to him again.

He woke me up two hours later and led me inside the house.

"You don't lock your doors at night?" I asked.

"It's pretty safe here," he said. "You've seen my dogs. No one dares to intrude."

Jonathan led me into his massive bedroom. It could comfortably hold four of mine with extra room to spare. We were still exhausted, so falling asleep in each other's arms again didn't take long.

Chapter 45

Bad Blood

Vivienne

I woke to Jonathan's lips pressing against my ear.

"Wake up, Honey," he whispered, rubbing his cheek against mine. His voice was unique and kind. It carried the same melody that stuck with me through my insanity. I hung on to every sound as if my life depended on it.

My love for Jonathan was not a temporary, casual, or a *feel-good* emotion that would eventually fade so I could move on to the next suitor. It was an all-consuming force that kept me from declaring all-out war against his family.

Getting justice for what Damien did to me had been my number one goal since August 24, 1985. The urge to hurt him as much as he hurt me had only gotten stronger since I saw him at Shannon's funeral.

But my reunion with Jonathan began complicating my vow to get revenge. I didn't spend the last fifteen years preparing for payback only to blow it up because of my love for Jonathan.

Damien still lived in my head. Unless he's no longer able to hurt anyone like he hurt me, I would never be at peace. I wanted him to lose more than just his freedom. Men like Damien didn't change. I made the mistake of not telling the police he was my rapist. I wouldn't make another mistake like that again. He shouldn't be able to continue to live his golden lifestyle.

He shouldn't have the last laugh.

"What time is it?" I asked as I snuggled under the soft comforter.

"Seven o'clock," he said, cuddling me.

"It's too early," I murmured, clutching the comforter like I was using it as a barrier between us. "I need a couple of hours more, please," I said. "You kept me up all night." My voice was hoarse from sleeping under the open sky.

Then, Jonathan rolled on top of me, and I panicked.

"Jonathan. No." I pushed him off me, jumped out of the bed, and bolted to the other side of the room. I had begun to re-live the night Damien swallowed me with his body.

"V, you don't have to be afraid of me." He rushed over to where I stood, trembling.

I buried my head into his open red and black checkered pajamas, my tear-stained face pressing against his chest. For the next two minutes, I clung to Jonathan as tightly as I could, my fingers sinking into his flesh until my heart slowly returned to its normal rhythm. Damien had damaged me, inflicting pain that rendered me incapable of forming any meaningful romantic relationship.

I raised my head off Jonathan's chest, stared at the wall-to-wall mirror, and caught the reflection of a man standing in the doorway. I blinked to make sure what I saw was real or that I wasn't dreaming. The man in the mirror looked incensed. I froze when a wave of cold air washed over me.

I couldn't speak when he stepped into the bedroom. My heart felt like it had collapsed. The scratch under his left eye seemed fresh, like he had fought with someone before barging in. He narrowed his eyes to me and pointed a gun directly at my head. Suddenly, it felt like my organs had failed me.

"Step aside, Jonathan!" Damien commanded. His voice was filled with rage. "You brought this fucking bitch into our family to destroy me," he said.

Jonathan spun around when Damien cocked the gun. He pushed me out of Damien's line of sight, shoving me behind him.

He stepped towards Damien. "I'd like to see you fire that gun. Go ahead, since you're such a badass. Give me a reason to put you down like the diseased dog you are," Jonathan said.

"Move, Jonathan! I swear I'll shoot you too."

"You barged into my house, pointing a gun at me? You must be out of your damn mind," he said, inching closer. "You want her? This time, you must come through me to get to her."

Damien gritted his teeth. "She ruined me!" His voice shook me, bringing me back to the night he raped me. "No one wants anything to do with me! She told the world I raped her. JoAnn wants nothing to do with me. I lost everything. Everything!" he screamed.

He stabilized the gun in his trembling right hand with his left.

"Good for her," I said. "I knew she was too smart for you. Way to go, JoAnn!" I cheered. "You were a pathetic loser who no one wanted, so you forced yourself on me. You were a loser then and an even bigger loser now." Bravery suddenly came over me. "Go ahead, shoot me. You don't have the balls."

"Yeah, Damien, go ahead. Shoot her," Jonathan said. "I dare you to pull the trigger. Give me a reason to end you."

Jonathan might have learned a thing or two from Blaise after I left. Or maybe my rape changed him so much that he was willing to put his life on the line for me again.

"Did you or did you not rape her?" Jonathan clenched his fist and inched closer to Damien. "Answer me!" His voice roared throughout the room, and Damien tightened his grip on the gun. "You coward, answer me. You like raping girls?"

"I didn't rape—"

"Shut up!" Jonathan cut him off before he could finish. "Shannon was V's daughter that you kidnapped. I saw what you did to her face, you freak. If JoAnn took everything, it's because you are a rapist who deserved everything you got. Keep pointing that gun at me, and I will take the only thing you have left. Put the fucking gun down!" Jonathan shouted.

Before Damien could respond, Jonathan elbowed the gun out of Damien's hand and kicked him across the room. The kick was too precise for someone who was not trained. It was apparent Blaise had taught him well.

They scrambled to get control, and I ran into the adjoining room and locked the door behind me. I snatched the telephone off the small table and quickly dialed 911, my fingers knocking against the phone.

A few minutes later, a loud bang erupted from Jonathan's bedroom and reverberated through the walls. The sound of a single gunshot jolted my hand away from the telephone. My heart raced at the sound of a woman shouting. But all I could think of was Jonathan. If Damien got the upper hand, I might as well be dead. The likelihood of me surviving another brutal assault at the hands of Damien was zero percent. He wasn't going to let me leave to talk about it.

But what if it was Jonathan who fired the gun? He'll never be the same for taking the life of his brother. Whether Damien or Jonathan pulled the trigger, my future looked bleak.

"There's an intruder in the house!" My voice broke, and the telephone rattled. "Please, send help now!" I screamed. It was then I realized I didn't know the address to where I was. I rushed back to Jonathan's bedroom. My heart pounded in my ears, and my legs lost their strength.

I pushed the door. Something or someone blocked it. I braced against it with all the strength I could muster.

Standing in front of me was the last person I expected to see. Her eyes were black and blue and bloodshot, almost shut. Her blouse was ripped, an obvious sign of a struggle. She stood over the body sprawled out on the floor in front of her with a hole in the head as blood oozed onto the lush carpet. I covered my mouth and braced against the wall, screaming in my hands as I slid down to the floor.

It wouldn't have mattered if I wanted to perform CPR on the blood-stained body. The woman with the gun wasn't going to let me save him. From the rage in her eyes, I dared not even try.

But I pushed myself forward, shuffled on my elbows toward the body, and screamed at the top of my lungs.

"Jonathan!"

Chapter 46

From This Day Forward

Jonathan

Say what you want about JoAnn's willingness to stick it out with Damien for as long as she did. She was at her breaking point.

It had been three months since she blew Damien's brains out on my bedroom floor, and no one blamed anyone except Damien for wrecking his own life. Damien had to have known justice was coming for him. I doubted he saw it coming from his wife, though.

He could not have inflicted so much devastation on another human without expecting karma to get him. It was unsurprising to learn that he had been beating JoAnn for years.

But on this special day, the woman my heart bled for was letting me love her again.

It was a challenging three months, getting beyond all that had happened, both in my home and to Vivienne. Although V had done much therapy to help repair the damage done to her, it was her incredible strength of character and resilience to get past it all that got us to this point.

Our parents had front-row seats, witnessing the start of the second half of our lives.

I wished Jasmine and my friends were here. It would have been the perfect gift to V.

In the elaborate star-studded wedding, there were frantic camera clicks and roars from the crowd that packed the large, elegant ballroom, but only one girl stood out above everyone else, and she wasn't even loud.

A soft cloud appeared as my love glided down the aisle into my arms, enveloping us in a cocoon of emotional bliss. It was a manifestation of fate, as if it were just us in our private universe, with blessings from the heavens.

I kissed her softly, and our hearts harmonized.

"I must have played this moment over in my head a thousand times, V," I said, her hand in mine, her head tilted, looking up at me with her unforgettable smile. I wrapped my hands around her. A bolt of electricity shot through me. "I used to hear the

Electric Slide playing at other people's weddings, and I would fall to pieces. But now it's our time, and we can dance to it all night."

"I promise you, Jonathan, I'll let this night last a hundred years, and whenever I am scared, I'll use it to drive out all my fears. But I have one last request to close our wedding day."

"Anything for you, my love." I smiled as I waltzed with my new bride.

"Take me home, Mr. Hastings, take me home."

***

I took a sip off my wine glass, then placed it on the table next to V's. I lifted her off the ground and carried her into the bedroom.

Playing softly in the background were romantic melodies from the eighties.

To say V was a stunning bride would be an understatement. My eyes hadn't left her all night. I swallowed hard, thinking how far we had come to get here. How lucky I was that she chose me to love. It was nothing short of miraculous we found each other again. V looked up at me, and the light in her eyes filled me with awe. I had been dreaming of this moment from the first day I saw her. I could never fully explain why I loved her this much until now.

"Unequivocally, I believe God created you for me. That was why my heart was stuck on you."

She pressed her lips against my bare chest, then dragged her fingers against my ribs, running her hands all over me and electricity from her touch sparked a fire within me.

I placed her on the bed and lowered myself beside her.

"Why did it take this long to get here?" she whispered.

I brushed the hair away from her face and kissed her softly, slowly peeling off her gown one layer at a time.

"I can't believe you love me this much to give me another chance. I will spend the rest of my life to deserve you, V," I said.

I rubbed my palm over her stomach, applying light pressure, slowly, deliberately making my way upward. I paused when my eyes caught the faded scars. I ran my thumb over the burn marks where Damien used her chest as an ashtray. I traced the circular outline with my lips, and my heart broke again.

I had to keep it together, though. I couldn't afford to ruin this moment. But as my lips lingered on her breast, her body relaxed.

"Don't think about it, Jonathan," V said, as if she read my mind. "He can't hurt me anymore. It's just you and me from this day forward. The demon is gone."

It was as if every part of me had a pulse, and my heart felt like it was about to escape from my chest. "There's no going back, V," I said.

She laughed. "You're mine now, Jonathan, and I did promise to deflower you."

"Go easy on me, Babe," I said.

V's touch felt like it had struck a match under my skin. I closed the space between us with my body. She brushed her lips against my ear and moaned.

I liked how she allowed me to explore her and love her without reservations while her hungry mouth craved me. Her legs wrapped tightly around me. "You feel so damn good, V," I whispered, my lips tracing the curves of her body.

She whispered back softly, "Jonathan."

The sound of my name sent another ripple of electricity traveling down the length of my body. I didn't know anything could feel this amazing.

It felt like I was floating.

"Take me now, or I'll dissolve," she said. Her voice filled me with anticipation, and her sweet breath was intoxicating, rendering me incapable of logical thought.

I groaned. "Come with me to the stars, V," I muttered. "We'll surf them for the rest of our lives." I inhaled her deeply, resealing the space between us as we climbed to heights none of us had ever gone.

"We're on top of the world now. We finally made it," V said.

At *last!* Vivienne Hastings and I took one giant leap as we surfed the stars, and our bodies shuddered as one.

***

Being the husband of the woman I had agonized over for so long was the perfect ending to our shared trauma and the most satisfying feeling to a new beginning.

Mr. and Mrs. Hastings felt surreal, as if V and I were picking up right where we had left off. There was nothing about our wedding I didn't plan, down to every detail of our honeymoon, with the help of Jasmine, who had been my right hand when I thought I had lost V.

I waited ten minutes to get a word in after I said hello. Jasmine could not stop crying.

"Is everything all set, Jas?" I finally asked after she had dried her tears.

I could not have survived V's disappearance without creating a lasting memory. Every year she was missing, we held a memorial. But discussing my honeymoon plans without her knowledge felt sneaky, and Jasmine warned against unintended consequences. She had been reluctant to leave V in the dark, but it would not have the same impact if I had told V what I had planned, and I wanted our honeymoon to be as memorable as possible.

"Just waiting for the honeymooners," she chuckled. "What time is your flight?"

"Ten o'clock," I replied.

"I've arranged for the Limo to pick you up from the airport. Blaise is running around getting last-minute things together with the other guys, and everything else is all set. Except for the fact that I may have to take sedatives. I don't know what I'll do when I finally get to see Viv. Tell me she's the same, Jonathan. Tell me my best friend did not forget me. I've been moving like a robot all day, trying not to think about the years between us. I want to remember her the way I saw her last, and that's the way I want it to feel when I get to hug her."

"She's more beautiful than you can imagine," I said.

"Are you sure you don't want to tell her what we've done? Viv does not like secrets, and if I were you, I wouldn't keep it from her," she said.

"If there's one thing I know about her, she's forgiving. We both know that what we did got us through the heartache of losing her. The emptiness is gone, and I can breathe again. I'm alive, Jas." I exhaled through my mouth.

"I can't wait to see her. Give her a special hug for me."

"I'm bringing her home to you, Jas."

I hung up the telephone and turned to find V leaning against the door frame, holding two wine glasses. She handed one to me and walked onto the patio overlooking the roadway. I followed behind her, sat my glass on the small table in the corner, placed her glass beside it, and pulled her into me for a long, take-my-breath-away kiss.

"I heard you on the phone. I know there is something you're not telling me. Now spill," she said after I let go of her lips.

"Depends. How much did you hear?"

Chapter 47

Vivienne's Hideaway

Vivienne

We boarded Jamaica Airline flight 797 two days later, returning to the city where we first met. Jonathan was taking me home to start over, but I was less sure I could go back and not have a full-blown relapse. His reassuring arms relaxed me as I snuggled in my seat and wrapped my arms around him.

"Buckle up, Mrs. Hastings!" He smiled at me, then snapped the seatbelt in seat 4A as we ascended ten thousand feet. He had made all the arrangements for our honeymoon, a destination outside of Montego Bay.

As the jumbo jet closed in on Sangster International Airport, my heart pounded as it descended and inched closer to land, and the shoreline over the water where I tried to end my life came into focus. I tried not to think about that night, and as the buildings came into view, I snuggled next to Jonathan to forget. But he was remembering, too.

We were back where our love had begun. Back to the place I lost my mind. Back to the place I walked about like a Nomad and the place that tore my world apart.

Jonathan smiled at me. "Our first stop will be Greenspring. We have a date with destiny," he said.

"Greenspring?" I asked, surprised he'd even remembered the name, let alone how to get there.

I had not seen Jasmine since 1985 and became anxious about seeing her again. The letter in my bag didn't come close to explaining my disappearance, and I wasn't prepared to open Pandora's box. But Jonathan knew I had one last apology to make. "I doubt I'll remember anyone there, Jonathan. Since my parents no longer live there, there's no reason to return. I am not sure if taking me there is a good idea. By now, everyone knew what happened to me."

"Trust me. You'll love it. Wait, you'll see," Jonathan assured me.

"What am I walking into, Jonathan? Are you sure I can withstand the surprise you planned for me?"

"This is our honeymoon, V."

Jonathan's eyes never lie, and if he said not to worry, his eyes would put my mind at ease.

The voice over the intercom announced our arrival at Montego Bay, and the passengers cheered after the wheels touched the runway. I held on to Jonathan, not wanting to get up out of my seat. I was not ready to leave the plane, so I waited for everyone to deplane. Finally, when no one was left, I crawled toward the front, clutching Jonathan's hand, as we descended the airplane's steps toward customs.

He lifted me off the ground and carried me to the open door while our luggage lay unattended. An older woman at the entrance cheered as he swirled me around.

"I'm taking you over the threshold, Vivienne Hastings," he said, smiling.

It was then that I freed myself from the lingering burdens of my past. I was happy again and starting to feel like I deserved to be, just like before I met Damien. Jonathan and I were back in our bubble, and he was taking me back to where I felt safe.

I was not about to complain about him lavishing affection on me. I had been starving for his love. I stretched out my left hand to flaunt the huge diamond on my finger and pinched myself to make sure it was real. But little did I know that the country road of Greenspring would do more than take me home.

We pulled off the main road, heading to a place I had not been in fifteen years. We drove for five miles off the coast into the hills.

It has been a while since I've been here. Have I forgotten the way?

"I think we're lost, Jonathan," I said, thinking the young driver had taken the wrong route.

"We're fine, Miss Vivienne. I know where I'm going," he said, quickly turning his head to reassure me. "I've been coming here weekly for the past two years." After all, he was an employee of Hideaway Resorts.

Vivienne's Hideaway, this way, the massive lighted sign at the entrance read as we turned into Greenspring, and that's when I screamed. "Jonathan! What did you do?" He could only have been responsible for the facelift to the rugged countryside, home to me, for ten years.

"I would have died if I hadn't done something to honor your memory, V," he said.

Happy tears streamed down my face. The love and pride I had for my husband overwhelmed me. I didn't know I could ever be this happy again. "Jonathan, you transformed Greenspring into a tourist attraction? It is so beautiful. It resembles a cross between a safari and a resort. You even made a hiking trail."

"I wanted this to be a romantic getaway for love-struck couples to experience the same as what this place did for me when you took me here. It would have been selfish not to share such an adventure. So, I built this retreat in your honor. It had become more than a honeymoon getaway. It is the source behind Greenspring's rejuvenation. All the staff are residents."

"Wow! My small hometown is alive and thriving. You did what I couldn't. You put Greenspring on the map."

After running away from the rocky country road of the rugged Hanover community into the claws of a monster, I was once again standing in the place I roamed throughout my young life. It looked like nothing I remembered.

Everything seemed modernized. Even the homes had significant improvements. The narrow tracks I walked to school had widened to accommodate the steady stream of tour buses filled with honeymooners.

Residents lined the street. They had choreographed that, too. They waved little handheld flags and signs imprinted, *Welcome Home, Viv.*

A mob of jubilant little boys greeted Jonathan like he was a rock star. After we exited the car, they gleefully snatched our luggage and led the way to rows of bungalows on the mountain overlooking the valley. It was the perfect spot to watch the sunset.

But I was afraid to ask about my best friend. I didn't know if she'd shun me or if she even still lived there. We were barely adults the last time we spoke, and I didn't know if Jasmine would blame me for the state of our friendship.

"Does Jasmine still live here, Jonathan?" I asked, tapping his shoulder. "If she moved away, it would be a pity for her to miss all this upgrade," I said.

"Who do you think helped me with all the changes?"

"Jasmine? How is that possible?"

"Be patient, my love, and enjoy your return. This night is the reunion to rival all reunions. It's all about you," he said, lifting me off the ground and kissing me.

***

At nightfall, couples sat on the edge of the rocks. The night was set to music, from the soft sounds of R&B to hardcore dance hall. Everyone had a taste of something satisfying.

Jonathan wrapped his arms around me and led me to where we sat when I took him to Greenspring. The area had changed to accommodate the upgrade, but I found the spot near the river where we watched the sunset. Jonathan had left that area intact. It was where we lay in each other's arms when he told me I'd be the mother of his seven to ten kids.

We moved farther down the river to the small group of about twenty men and women, chatting and laughing under the moonlight. I was afraid to greet them. I didn't want to say the wrong names. None of their faces looked familiar. But the closer I got, the more they came back to me. They were staring at me, forcing me to remember them.

"This long-time gal mi neva see yuh, come mek mi hold your hand." They sang as they surrounded me, forming a ring with their locked arms, singing and dancing.

Jonathan walked out of the ring, allowing them to welcome me home. I was sure they thought I was dead.

They were still serenading me when a woman appeared out of the darkness, wiping tears as she entered the ring. She wore braids, looked my age, and had two young boys by her side. Their faces looked familiar, too. They were the ones who scooped up our luggage after they greeted Jonathan.

As the woman approached me, the singing stopped, and everyone watched in anticipation to see what we would do next. As she got a little bit closer to where I was, I realized I'd seen a younger version of her before, and without a word, I walked timidly over to her. I waited for her to stop crying, but she couldn't, so I got closer, and with my handkerchief, I dried her tears. It was Jasmine. She still had a particular drama about her whenever she was emotional. She had a family. The diamond ring indicated she might have found her soulmate.

I held on to Jasmine, releasing over a decade and a half of hurt. Jonathan walked over and hugged us, and I let go of the final piece of my pain. Jasmine was the last piece to my painful past, to whom I had to make amends.

She held me tight and wept openly, and my heart swelled. "I thought you had left me for good, Viv," she chuckled nervously.

"Not a chance," I told her. "I'm sorry for what I put everyone through, but if it's any comfort, I think about our time together all the time. There's so much to tell you, Jas. But that'll have to wait." I wiped away her tears again.

She pulled me away from the excitement after the concert had begun, and we sat under one of the freshly painted pavilions, decorated with confetti. My name in bold print was hanging all around it.

"So, Operations Manager, ah? I see you went to college."

"I did it because of you, Viv. Plus, Jonathan insisted, and if you were in Heaven, you'd be proud of me. I didn't even have to worry about the school fees. You have the most generous man I've ever met. He is the best, even though I gave him a tough time after you disappeared. I needed someone to blame."

"So, whose idea was Vivienne's Hideaway?"

"As if you must ask. I told Jonathan I'd manage it only if he named it after you. I didn't have to do much convincing." She wiped her eyes and smiled.

"You run the place like a five-star attraction. Greenspring is no longer the God-forsaken place I escaped."

"I had to, Viv. Your name is on it. I couldn't afford to let your memory be attached to failure now, could I?"

"You did well, my friend," I said, looking around as I tried to capture everything simultaneously.

There were certain things I had come to appreciate—my family's abiding love for me, my best friend, and Jonathan. But as I looked around, I was captivated by his commitment to Greenspring. There were waterfalls, hiking trails, canoeing, kayaking on the river, and bungalows with fabulous views of the magnificent sunset, while preserving the lush greenery of the rainforest. Jonathan had developed the vast landscape into a scenic attraction. Cattle and horses roamed and grazed and provided another form of entertainment, and my once poverty-stricken village and its residents thrived.

Jonathan was a rare gem that almost got away, and while it may no longer be possible for me to be the mother of his seven to ten kids, I am honored that he chose me to love. Having experienced his love and generosity, no matter how life dragged me through the mud and tore me to shreds like a body tied to a railroad track, his love was the most significant force that picked me back up—a man who was one of a kind.

Was Jonathan Hastings the match God created for me? Absolutely. There was no other way to describe him.

I have long believed that I had a guardian angel protecting me. I was now more convinced that the master of the universe was looking out for me in the darkest moments of my life. Otherwise, I would not be alive to experience genuine happiness after such unimaginable trauma. Life gave me another chance to celebrate with my husband and my best friend in the place I was happiest. If I could come back from such unbearable pain, there would be nothing I could not overcome.

***

The celebration went on for two days and nights. It was good to see Jonathan's friends again. They were all living remarkably successful lives. Seeing them as committed to each other as they were in their younger days overwhelmed me.

"Oh, my God, Vivienne! I didn't think you could look more beautiful." Blaise snuck away to talk with me.

I welcomed his broad smile and bear hug.

"So, you and Jas, ah. How did that happen?"

"Because of you. Plus, Jas is an amazing woman," Blaise said. "Without you and Jonathan, I wouldn't know what it feels like to love someone."

"I always thought about you guys when I was in hiding. I had hoped Jonathan could rely on you. I knew he would be broken after I left, but I had no doubt you'd be there for him. Thank you for looking after him."

"I prayed for you every day. We had a vigil every year when you were away. That's how *Vivienne's Hideaway* was founded. It was never the same after you left, however. Even Fredrick, who had the emotions of a hyena, broke down several times."

I didn't think Jonathan would survive. I've never seen a grown man grieve like that. It scared me. I don't know if I should tell you this, but one night, I followed him to the beach in Ironshore. I was afraid he would swim out and not come back. I sat with him for hours until he calmed down."

"I'm sorry you all had to go through that. I shouldn't have left. That was selfish of me, but it was just an overwhelming situation. I did not know how to cope."

Blaise beckoned for the other guys to come over.

"So, which one of you named your kid after me?" I smiled.

Blaise, Fredrick, Jude, Noah, and Pierre wrapped themselves around me and we exhaled.

From across the wide-open space, Jonathan raised his beer bottle and blew a kiss. I tried to convince him that although my traumatic memories would never leave me, I was now a productive member of society, determined to move forward without another mental breakdown. But I'm talking about Jonathan Hastings here. The guy who stood outside my job in the late spring of 1985 for weeks until I said yes. That delightful twenty-two-year-old man loved me unconditionally and took me on a whirlwind romance. An incomparable guy who couldn't stop mourning when I was hurting.

Some love refused to die, and Jonathan Hastings' love was one of them.

After everything quieted down and I was alone with him, I slid my hands underneath his pajama shirt. His skin was warm and soothing. I wrapped my arms around him, snuggled up, then exhaled.

I looked up at him and smiled. "Thank you for taking me home, Jonathan."

THE END

Epilogue

Vivienne

Jonathan and I had no grand plans, just a simple stroll from Greenspring to Chapel Hill. The early morning dew was balm for my skin, and the gentle wind at six a.m. felt like I had been given a facial.

There was something magical about waking up in the countryside, feeling the cool Jamaica breeze. They said it's the secret to wrinkle-free skin, and perhaps they were right because my skin had always been smooth, even in my teenage years.

But let's put that aside for a minute.

I didn't think the short walk would change our lives completely. I only wanted the wind on my face with Jonathan by my side. When I moved back home, it wasn't a hard choice to help Jonathan and Jasmine run the lucrative business of *Vivienne's Hideaway*, a popular getaway that had become a tourist magnet. I could be active or uninvolved. But becoming part of the day-to-day operation wasn't a hard decision.

If you had told me that I would be embracing motherhood after what had happened, I would have thought you were living in a different reality. Yet, here I was, experiencing joy I never thought possible. And despite the occasional flashback to my past, I couldn't help but feel a giddiness and a sense of gratitude for my new life.

The seven to ten kids Jonathan had promised me were never supposed to happen, nor were we supposed to have a happy ending to our shared trauma. But since Jonathan had done a marvelous job keeping the memories of my trauma at bay, I refused to dredge them up.

The spring morning began like always, with the sun peeping through the sky. We walked up to the tiny house on top of a hill in less than ten minutes. The doors were already wide open, as everyone did in the country. But to my surprise, it wasn't just one of our usual early morning strolls. It was a day that would be the beginning of the newest chapter of our lives.

As Jonathan and the occupant of the tiny run-down shack with boarded-up windows and screaky board floors exchanged greetings, it became clear that this was not a casual encounter. Their conversation had a weight, a sense of history, and shared secrets.

It was as if they had been having prior discussions, with a deal or promise hanging in the air. The one thing I yearned to give Jonathan was beyond my reach. I longed for my husband to experience the profound joy of fatherhood, but it was the one gift I could not bestow upon him.

The tiny bundle cradled in the woman's arms, and her conversation with Jonathan revealed that we were there to take her home, along with an older brother. She looked barely a week old.

The void in my heart that had always haunted me suddenly burst with emotions, as if I had been saving all my love, especially for them.

Judging from the conversation, the boy asleep in the corner of the bed, with his back against the wall and legs curled up to his chest, was her three-year-old brother. It was as if they had always been mine. The pulsating rhythm in the pit of my stomach was almost too much to bear. I clutched Jonathan's arm to steady myself, overwhelmed by the unexpected happiness.

Having children was not supposed to happen. Damien had ruined any chance of it happening, and I never thought I would heal from the trauma he unleashed on me. But this burning unconditional love for these two innocent lives said that more than just my health was restored. It also meant my mind, body, and soul were mended.

I furrowed my eyebrows at Jonathan, my voice trembling with uncertainty. "Is this for real?" I asked, my feet unsteady on the ground, my legs threatening to buckle. They had been knocking against each other for the last minute and a half, a physical manifestation of my inner turmoil.

I scrambled closer to the woman. Judging from her conversation with Jonathan, she was the great-grandmother to both children, but she was no longer capable of caring for them. The tiny hand wrapped around the wrinkled pinky, eyes shut as she pulled onto the bottle, occasionally kicking her feet. I was scared to touch her. I moved closer to her older brother and stood over him while he slept. I wasn't sure how much a three-year-old's mind could comprehend the loss of a mother and the stranger who would replace her.

He rubbed his eyes, waking from sleep, and looked up at me, then at the tall man he was told would be his father. The smile on his face said he had gotten acquainted with his new dad, who would forever change his life.

"My name is Jake," his soft voice tugged on my heartstrings.

"Hello, Jake," I whispered, my voice barely audible. I didn't want to disturb his sister. "It's... it's a pleasure to meet you." My words were a feeble attempt to quell the butterflies in my stomach, to mask the joy that threatened to overwhelm me.

Jonathan lifted Jake off the bed. "Hey, sport. Are you ready to go home? Your mom and I can't wait to show you your room. I'm sure you'll love it," he said with his winning smile. "We're here to take you and your sister to your new home, and Granny can visit you as often as she likes."

Jake wrapped his arms tightly around Johnathan's neck.

Jonathan had not lost his magic.

The following years saw one child after another fill up the space in our hearts. Mothers voluntarily gave up their babies when life became overwhelming.

With six children becoming one big happy family, there was still enough room for baby Natalie.

Baby Natalie was two days old when Miss Mabel called the police about a crying infant from the basket left on her grocery store steps.

I was delighted to take temporary guardianship of her until the courts made a final decision. My heart almost jumped from my chest after the judge ruled that we could take her home for good. I lunged for her the minute the ruling came down. I burst into tears knowing she was now legally ours.

Jonathan and I rushed down the courthouse steps with little Natalie to the waiting car. He buckled her into her seat, and we sped home to a house full of rambunctious children.

After all the tragedy and trauma, my life turned out better than I could have imagined. I had the love of my life and the family I thought I would never have.

Author's Note

Getting this book published was an emotional roller coaster ride, and I sometimes doubted whether I wanted to tell this story. However, I realized the crucial role of staying vigilant in my children's lives. This responsibility must not be compromised. Telling this story, albeit harrowing, can help others understand the gravity of the risks to our children as they grow up in a society that places little value on women and girls. I cannot stress enough how important it is to recognize and stave off the threats they face every day.

Be a "helicopter mom" or "helicopter dad" if it means your children will be safe. You must agree that protecting our children from predators should be paramount to all parents.

Acknowledgment

I want to express my deepest gratitude to my family, whose unwavering support and understanding have encouraged me on my writing journey. Your belief in me has been a constant source of inspiration, and I am truly grateful for your role in bringing this book to print.

I would also like to extend my heartfelt thanks to my dear friend Lorna, whose belief in me is the guiding light through this writing process. She has been instrumental in making this book a reality, and I am deeply grateful for your significant role in its completion.

I want to thank Alicia and Althea for their decades of friendship. Your impact on me is immeasurable.

I want to express my profound appreciation to Michele Miller from the Olney Writer's Group for her comprehensive review of my book. I couldn't have asked for a better review. Your feedback, insights, and selfless dedication have been invaluable.

About the Author

Cherry's path to becoming a writer is unconventional. She often refers to herself as the accidental writer. As a young adult, she had the incredible opportunity of working with a renowned published author, where she developed a love for writing. This allowed her to improve her skills and learn from a professional. During this time, it ignited her passion for storytelling, and she honed her ability to write compelling and engaging narratives.

Cherry quickly realized that her passion for writing needed nurturing. Although it was a gift that came naturally to her, she didn't rely solely on her innate talent. Instead, she took proactive steps to develop her skills. She enrolled in writing classes and attended seminars to improve the skills she had nurtured through years of dedication and hard work.

Her first novel, *Bad Seed: The Midnight Cries of an Island Girl,* is a testament to her resilience, years of hard work, dedication, and faith in her abilities.

Her early life in Jamaica, which empowered her with the resilience she needed to persist, is a significant part of her journey.

www.ingramcontent.com/pod-product-compliance
Lightning Source LLC
Chambersburg PA
CBHW061238120726
48001CB00001B/21